THE SAGA OF ASBJORN THORLEIKSON

THE SAGA OF ASBJORN THORLEIKSON

A Novel of Vikings in Scotland

By
WILLIAM SPEIR

RISING PHOENIX PRESS

All rights reserved.
Published 2015 by Progressive Rising Phoenix Press, LLC
www.progressiverisingphoenix.com

ISBN: 978-1-940834-71-9

*

Printed in the U.S.A.

Cover Artwork: "The Iron Fleet" by René Aigner, Munich, Germany (http://www.rene-aigner.de). Used by permission of the artist, © Copyright 2013 René Aigner.

Map of The Saga of Asbjorn Thorleikson Illustration by: Mag. Robert Altbauer, Cartographer and Illustrator, Salzburg, Austria (http://www.fantasy-map.net).

Book and Cover design by William Speir
Visit: http://www.williamspeir.com

Acknowledgments:

I want to thank all of my loyal readers, without whom I would not enjoy the creative process of writing.

Thanks to Amanda Thrasher and Jannifer Powelson at Progressive Rising Phoenix Press for giving my books a new home. I am honored to be one of your authors.

Special thanks goes to Celia Eidex Ciemnoczolowski, Jennifer Cook, Ray Flynt, Jim Newman, Zame Kahn, and Linda Speir, for their valuable edits.

Deepest gratitude goes to my wife Lee Anne for putting up with me. Every day I love her more than I ever thought possible. I am also grateful for my family, without whom there would be no words worth writing.

And finally, I want to thank to the judges of the 2015 Royal Palm Literary Awards, who made *The Saga of Asbjorn Thorleikson* a semi-finalist in the Pre-Published Historical Fiction category.

To Dr. Stephen O. Glosecki, professor of Arthurian Legends and Norse/Icelandic Sagas at UAB. Though you are no longer with us, I hope you will be pleased with this Viking story, which you asked me to write thirty years ago. I'm sorry it's so late.

Author's Note

This is my second work of historical fiction. While much of the story is fictionalized, I have tried to keep it within in the historical context of real events taking place during the 870's AD in southwestern Alba (modern-day Scotland). Most of the story takes place in the area around Áth Cliath (modern-day Dublin, Ireland) and Airer Goídel (formerly Dalriada in modern-day Argyll, Scotland) on the banks of the Abhainn Fìne River (Loch Fyne) during the reign of Causantín mac Cináeda (Constantine I of Alba).

Few records have survived that age, so there is much speculation and disagreement as to dates, names, and places of certain events. I have tried to rationalize these disagreements as much as possible, but there will be readers who will point to elements that disagree with their own viewpoints and attempt to discredit what I have written. To those readers, I can only state again that this is a work of fiction, and I have attempted to be as accurate as possible under the circumstances.

This story is inspired by a family legend told to me by my father when I was young. It was a story about how a Viking raider became Scottish when his longship was destroyed during a raid. I have researched Scottish history and the Viking raids in Scotland as well as I am able, and I now feel I can share the story with others.

I hope you will enjoy this story of my family, and I hope that, while reading it, you can get a sense of what life was like during the 9th Century AD in the kingdom of Alba. *Tapadh leat!* (Thank you)

It is to all of the descendants and kin of Alexander Speir and Mary Campbell of Kilmarnock, Scotland that this book is respectfully dedicated.

William Speir
June 2013

ALBA

THE VILLAGE

STONE
DOLAIR

DUNADD

DUMBARTON

ÁTH CLIATH

IRELAND

BRITAIN

N
W E
S

THE SAGA OF ASBJORN THORLEIKSON

CHAPTER 1

The ravens always knew when the fleet was about to get underway. Their black wings and mournful calls seemed to beckon the Norsemen to the sea, as if true Norsemen ever needed encouragement to sail their longships in search of tribute, conquest, and glory.

A young man anxiously watched the harbor from the platform along the top of the longphort's walls. He had just turned fifteen, and the mid-autumn winds blew his cloak and his blonde hair straight back, revealing his lean build and the family features that marked him as a son of Thorleik.

Asbjorn Thorleikson surveyed the activity going on around Áth Cliath's harbor with a sense of growing excitement. The ships not beached on the shore of the harbor rocked and swayed in the afternoon winds. Several new ships were nearing completion to replace the ones that had left earlier in the summer with settlers heading for new lands in the west. He watched as the masts and rigging were put into place, which were the finishing touches needed for the longships to be ready to sail.

A raven landed on the wall of the enclosure next to Asbjorn. The raven stared at him, tilting its head back and forth in the manner of birds.

"Are you one of Odin's ravens?" Asbjorn finally asked the raven, knowing that ravens were associated with one of the two greatest gods of the Norse people. "Are you here to watch me, or are you here to give me a message?"

The raven continued to stare at Asbjorn and then flew off. Asbjorn watched as the bird soared over the fleet and then flew straight at a man approaching the enclosure from the harbor. The raven circled the man three times and flew off into the distance.

Asbjorn recognized the man immediately. It was his father, Thorleik.

Here to give me a message.

Asbjorn had been watching for his father all day. Thorleik was overseeing the men fitting the mast onto his new longship. Because Thorleik was heading back to the enclosure, Asbjorn knew the work was finished.

Asbjorn climbed down and made his way through the crowd to the gates of the enclosure, hoping to get there before his father walked through and disappeared into the sea of people. There was a conversation that the two needed to have, and Asbjorn didn't want to delay it any longer.

Asbjorn was the son of Thorleik Meginbjornson and his wife, Bergdís. Thorleik was a member of King Amlaíb's council and a praiseworthy warrior who had participated in dozens of successful expeditions and gained great glory for himself and his family. His sandy blonde hair was greying, and his great beard was braided on the sides to keep it out of the way since it seemed to want to spread out like an apron. Bergdís was half-Scot and looked more like one of the Scots than she did a Norse woman. Her mother had been a Dalriadan Scot from Ireland who married Asbjorn's grandfather, Sólmundr "The Ironfist." She understood and spoke the language of the Scots, and she had taught this to Asbjorn over the objections of her husband, who didn't see any need to communicate with his prey.

Asbjorn's older brother, Bjornkarl, was also a mighty warrior and had recently been accepted into the ranks of the berserkers, who were the lead warriors in battle and fought with a wildness that terrified all who opposed them. He was tall and broad, but his hair was darker than the rest of his family. There were blonde streaks running through his hair and beard, but it was mostly brown in color, giving him a cold look when he stared with his deep blue eyes. His lips were usually twisted into a wicked sneer, and when he smiled, he looked like a bear about to attack.

Berserkers were both revered and reviled in the Norse longphort of Áth Cliath, which was common throughout the Norse kingdoms. As fighters, they were unequalled in their skill and their thirst for blood. They wore the head and pelts of either bears or wolves into battle, giving them the reputation of being shape-shifters who actually transformed into animals. They consumed an elixir before and during battle, made of a strong liquor infused with wild mushrooms, which put them into a frenzy where they didn't know friend from foe. They were able to fight for hours without feeling wounds, pain, or fatigue. They always went into battle first, and while many were killed, they easily killed many more of the enemy.

The berserkers were well treated and rewarded for their service. They lived better than anyone apart from their king and his council members, they were granted the larger shares of the tribute taken on each expedition, and their indulgences and transgressions were forgiven without question. But what made them great as warriors made them a terror to their neighbors.

One of the side effects of the elixir was that it gave the berserkers an insatiable sexual appetite. They raped women during battle, they raped the wives and daughters of their closest friends and neighbors, and they'd even rape brides on their wedding night. It was no secret that berserkers consumed the elixir on a daily basis, even though it was only supposed to be used just before and during battle. In the resulting frenzy, berserkers would kill their friends and even their kinsmen, and they'd never realize that they had done the deed themselves.

Bjornkarl had always been a great warrior, but Asbjorn knew him as a great bully. Even though he was older and received the newest and best of everything, Bjornkarl still coveted everything Asbjorn had and took what he wanted whenever he pleased. When Asbjorn resisted or protested, Bjornkarl beat his brother and then took more as tribute. Now that Bjornkarl was a berserker, Asbjorn stayed as far away from his brother as possible and hid everything of value. When Bjornkarl was given his own place to live, Asbjorn felt liberated for the first time in his life.

As Asbjorn climbed down the walls to find his father, he thought about his last encounter with his brother and gripped the hilt of his dagger so tightly that his knuckles turned white. The dagger was a birthday gift from his father. Bjornkarl had stopped by the next day and saw the knife. Wanting it, he took the knife and started to leave. Asbjorn launched himself at his brother and grabbed him around the neck from behind to keep him from leaving. Bjornkarl lurched forward, sending Asbjorn over his brother's shoulder onto the floor. Bjornkarl, with a look of rage in his eyes, unsheathed the knife and raised it over his head.

"Stop!" Thorleik thundered when he saw what his firstborn was about to do. He grabbed his son's wrist and shook the knife loose, which landed on the floor a couple of feet from Asbjorn.

"Thor's Hammer!" Thorleik swore loudly. "Would you kill your own brother for a knife, Bjornkarl? Haven't you taken enough from him? Do you need his life as well?"

Bjornkarl laughed, and Asbjorn felt a chill run up his spine. "It was all in fun, Father," he said smoothly as he tossed the knife's sheath to his brother. Looking down at Asbjorn he added, "The boy needs to learn his place. He attacked me, and I have the right to his blood."

"Not when you started it by taking the knife that I had just given him yesterday," his father countered. "It's you who owes the blood debt, not Asbjorn."

Looking at his father and then his brother, who had retrieved his knife and was sitting up with his back to the wall, Bjornkarl smiled. "Let him take my blood if he can."

Asbjorn didn't move. Then he slowly put the knife back in its sheath. "I don't want his blood," he said to his father. Looking at his brother, he added, "But someday I'll face you and repay you for your years of *kindness* towards me."

Bjornkarl roared with laughter and left the house. Asbjorn heard his brother laughing until his voice faded into the distance. Looking up, Asbjorn saw his father extend his hand. He took it, and his father helped him to his feet.

"Are you all right, son?" Thorleik asked.

"Yes, thank you, Father," Asbjorn replied.

"Best you stay clear of your brother, son. You're not ready to take him on yet."

Asbjorn nodded and tucked the dagger into his belt. He knew that there was no way to win a fair fight against his brother, but he also knew there'd come a day when he'd no longer allow Bjornkarl to bully him.

Asbjorn reached the gates and saw his father talking to a kinsman who had just arrived. Asbjorn recognized the man's face, but couldn't remember his name. Thorleik had many kinsmen, and Asbjorn didn't see them often enough to remember who all of them were.

As he walked toward his father, Thorleik turned and saw Asbjorn approach.

"What are you doing here, son?" Thorleik asked pleasantly as the kinsman he had been speaking to walked through the gates and disappeared in the crowd.

"I was looking for you, Father. Do you have time to talk?"

"Certainly," he replied. Looking around at the crowd, he added, "Why don't we take a walk by the river?"

Asbjorn nodded and followed his father away from the enclosure.

Áth Cliath was built on the island's northeastern coast. It sat on the southern side of a river flowing from the center of the island. The Norse settlement and its harbor were protected by the largest longphort in the west – a triangular earthwork enclosure supported by a timber structure. A wooden platform ran along the top of the structure, coming to a stop at the massive gates overlooking the harbor.

Thousands lived inside the walls of the enclosure, and many more lived in the settlements and villages surrounding the longphort or along the river. There were markets just outside the walls where people from the settlements sold their wares and where freshly caught fish from the eastern channel were brought daily. Farmers from the surrounding settlements also sold their grains, ales, and smoked and salted meats at the markets, which often gave the market side of the enclosure walls a pungent odor.

Many great trees had been cut down to build the longphort and the longhouses and smaller buildings lining the streets inside, leaving the south bank of the river completely bare except for the sacred groves where the gods were still worshipped. Many more trees were cut down to build the fleet of longships, cargo ships, and longboats that filled the harbor. There were almost one hundred and fifty longships, in addition to cargo ships and longboats, protected by the longphort's ever-watchful guards.

Every day for the past fortnight, heavily armed men and wagons filled with supplies had poured into the enclosure, which was already overcrowded from those answering the call of Amlaíb Conung. Amlaíb, the self-styled Norse King of Áth Cliath, was the kinsman of Ívarr who claimed the title of King of all Norsemen in the Western Islands. Amlaíb was making final preparations for his next great expedition to the island of Britain.

The arriving men were welcomed to the longphort by the members of Amlaíb's council. At night, banquets were held where the warriors would swear their loyalty to Amlaíb and be accepted into his service.

Asbjorn knew that only warriors who had proven themselves in several battles were allowed to swear an oath of loyalty, and he hoped this expedition would give him the opportunity to taste battle for the first time.

As Asbjorn and Thorleik walked toward the river, supplies for the expedition filled the staging area near the harbor. Given the amount of supplies there already, Asbjorn knew this would be the largest expedition he'd ever seen sail from Áth Cliath.

The noise of the harbor and the enclosure faded in the distance as Asbjorn and Thorleik walked toward the settlements built further inland. They had just passed the longhouse of the first settlement when Thorleik asked, "What's on your mind, son?"

"I want to go with the fleet when it sails, Father," Asbjorn replied quickly.

"You're not a warrior yet, Asbjorn," Thorleik point out.

"And I'll never become one if I don't go on an expedition. There has to be a first time, and I want this expedition to be it. I haven't done anything praiseworthy in my life, Father, and if I'm going to carry your name, I want people to speak it with pride for your entire family, not just for you and Bjornkarl."

"But you *have* lived a praiseworthy life, son," Thorleik stated, referring to the Norse virtues governing their society. "You're generous, brave, courteous, and tolerant. You're not lazy. You're constantly learning new things and seeking out those who can teach you. You honor your elders. You're loyal to your friends and your kin. You're not arrogant or mocking. You keep yourself clean. You put the needs of our people before your own needs. And you honor your elders and the dead. Your entire life is praiseworthy!"

"But you know that victory in battle and bringing home tribute and prisoners to sell is also praiseworthy and what our people seem to value most," Asbjorn said.

Thorleik looked at his son intently for a minute. "Can you handle a longship on the open sea?" he asked. "Can you fight with a sword and a spear?"

"I've taken longboats out into the channel before," Asbjorn answered, referring to the smaller boats used for fishing and for training the younger Norsemen how to sail. "And you taught me the spear and sword. Besides," he added, "I'd never be in the middle of the main battles on my first expedition. I'd be guarding supplies, the longships, and prisoners well away from the fighting. So you tell me, Father. Am I ready for an expedition?"

"Does it mean that much to you?" Thorleik asked.

Asbjorn nodded. "Yes, Father. I'm the same age that you were when you went on your first expedition. My friends are all going. How can I face them when they return if I stay behind? What honor and glory would that bring to our family?"

Thorleik looked appreciatively at his son. Asbjorn had made a good case for going. Finally, he said, "All right, son. I'll mention it to Amlaíb tonight, and if he has no objections, you have my blessing. But I'll let you tell your mother. I can't face a woman whose son is about to leave home for the first time."

"Thank you, Father!" Asbjorn grasped his father by the forearm. Then he asked, "Mother won't be happy for me?" It never occurred to Asbjorn that a Norse woman would be sad about such a thing.

"Happy *for* you, yes," Thorleik replied. "Happy at the thought of not having you around for months at a time, or losing you at sea or in battle, no. No mother is ever happy about that."

"She always seems happy when you and Bjornkarl go on expeditions," Asbjorn commented, still thinking that it was odd for a Norse woman to feel that way.

"She puts on a good act when I'm going away, but she's sad at the thought that I might not come home," his father said. "As for Bjornkarl, well, that's a different matter altogether..."

Asbjorn understood what his father was saying. Bergdís loved her family, but Bjornkarl made it difficult for anyone to love him. Asbjorn believed Bjornkarl had raised his hand to their mother once, but the incident was never discussed.

As the two turned to walk back to the enclosure, Asbjorn asked, "Father, if I fall in my first battle, is there any chance of the Valkyries taking me to Valhalla?"

Asbjorn was raised believing that divine beings called "Valkyries" were drawn to battlefields where they'd choose the greatest of the fallen warriors to go to Valhalla. There the fallen would become part of the army that would defend the gods during Ragnarök, when a battle would take place between the gods and their enemies. It was the goal of every Norse warrior to earn his place in Valhalla. It signified that the gods considered him one of the most worthy warriors in the world.

"I don't know, son," Thorleik answered. "The Valkyries choose who they will for reasons that only they truly know. All you can do is fight to the best of your abilities, and if it's your time to die, die with honor."

"Do you think the Valkyries would choose Bjornkarl?"

"I think they probably would. He's a great warrior, in spite of his other... issues. As long as it's his skills as a warrior they need and the rest doesn't matter, he'd be a fine addition to the army of the gods."

The two walked back to the enclosure in silence. Asbjorn was pleased with how well the conversation had gone, and he was confident that Amlaíb wouldn't object to Asbjorn joining the expedition. Amlaíb held Thorleik in high regard and wouldn't normally refuse one of his requests.

As they approached the gates to the enclosure, Asbjorn thanked his father again.

"I'm proud of you, son," Thorleik said, facing Asbjorn. "I never asked my father if I could go on my first expedition. You honor me by coming to me first, and I know you'll bring honor to our family."

"I'll do my best, Father," Asbjorn said, smiling.

"I know you will, son."

CHAPTER 2

Asbjorn was still awake later that night, waiting for Thorleik to return home from the banquet. Asbjorn tried to sleep, but he was too anxious to know if Amlaíb had approved his request to join the expedition. Finally, he got up and sat on the bench closest to the door. He wanted to be able to hear the sounds of his father approaching the house.

After what seemed like hours, he finally heard his father's voice. Thorleik was talking with another man whose voice Asbjorn didn't recognize. The voices grew louder, but Asbjorn stayed on the bench out of respect for his father. Asbjorn had to fight the urge to run to the door and interrupt his father so he could hear what Amlaíb's decision was.

He heard the two voices talking outside for several more minutes, although he still couldn't hear what they were saying. Then he heard the voices go silent, and a moment later, his father came through the door.

"Good evening, Father," Asbjorn said softly as his father passed him in the low light of the dying fire.

Thorleik reached for his dagger and turned quickly at the sound of his son's voice. When he saw Asbjorn sitting on the bench, he relaxed.

"Why are you still awake?"

Asbjorn looked at his father with surprise. "I was waiting to hear what Amlaíb thought of my request to join the next expedition."

"Oh, that," Thorleik said, waving his hand dismissively. "Of course he gave his consent for you to go."

Asbjorn jumped to his feet and grabbed his father by the forearm. "Thank you, Father!" he said excitedly. "When do we leave?"

"The first of next week. I'll give you all the details in the morning, and then you're going to be spending most of your time helping to load the supplies onto the ships and training with the sword and spear until we leave. Right now, though, I need sleep, and so do you. You can tell your mother the news in the morning."

"Yes, Father," Asbjorn said, knowing he'd be getting little sleep.

Several hours later, Asbjorn heard his mother making the morning meal and got out of bed. He dressed quickly and went to tell her his news.

His mother appeared to be happy when he told her that he was joining the expedition, but he saw in her eyes that she wasn't as happy as she pretended to be.

"Why are you sad, Mother?" he asked.

"Because I'll miss you when you're gone," she said, turning to finish making the morning meal. "Everything around here is so quiet when the men are off seeking tribute, and this time I won't have you to keep me company. Don't get me wrong, I think it's wonderful that you're going, and I'm happy you're ready to take part in an important tradition of our people. It's just that I'll be lonely until you and your father return."

She turned and flashed a smile at her son. "Don't worry about me, Asbjorn. I'll be fine. You just make sure that you bring honor to your family. And make sure you come home. And bring your father home with you. If you do all of that, how could I be anything but proud of you?"

"I will, Mother. I promise."

Don't make promises you can't keep, son, Bergdís thought as she worked to finish the morning meal. Then she closed her eyes and prayed. *Oh great Odin, wisest of the gods, send your ravens to protect my son, and give him wisdom and cunning so he may return home with honor. Almighty Thor, warrior of warriors, give my son the strength to smite all those who would keep him from returning to me safe and whole.*

10

Asbjorn had no trouble sleeping for the rest of the week. By the time he got home for the evening meal, he was completely exhausted.

On the first morning, after he found out that he was going on the expedition, his father took him outside and drew in the dirt a map of the expected route that the expedition would take.

"We're sailing almost two hundred longships and cargo ships north to the Briton kingdom of Alt Clut," he said, pointing to the coastline he had drawn. "With favorable winds, it should take about two days to get there. If we have to row, it will take a little longer. The Britons have a fort there called 'Dumbarton Rock' that we need to capture and destroy. It's their capital, and once it's gone, they'll have no defenses left against us. It'll make our work much easier."

"Ívarr and his forces are already across the channel to the south of Alt Clut," he continued, pointing to an area on the dirt map southeast of Dumbarton Rock. "We'll meet up with them when we land and surround the fort. It won't be easy to take the fort, so we're preparing for a siege that could last several weeks."

"So this expedition is for the conquest of Alt Clut?" Asbjorn asked, referring to when the Norsemen attacked an area where they planned to stay and control.

"No, our part of the expedition is for tribute only," Thorleik replied.

Asbjorn knew that when Norsemen started moving into new territory, they gave the inhabitants a taste of what would happen if they resisted. If the inhabitants agreed to surrender tribute and keep sending tribute year after year, the Norsemen would usually leave them alone. If they didn't keep sending tribute, the Norsemen would come back and take the tribute from the inhabitants, as well as their lands, their women and children, their animals, and everything else they owned. Asbjorn never questioned this – it was simply the way of the Norsemen.

"Ívarr wants all of Britain for himself," Thorleik continued, "so he may stay and treat this as part of his overall campaign of conquest, but Amlaíb is only looking for tribute in return for helping Ívarr."

"What's this land up here?" Asbjorn asked, pointing to the coastline north of Alt Clut.

"That's the kingdom of the Picts and Scots. Some call it 'Pictland' but we call it 'Alba'." Adding some detail to the map he had drawn, he continued. "Our kinsmen control the northern and western islands around Alba, which makes their raids easier because they're closer. We normally raid to the south of the outer islands, which is where Alt Clut and the old kingdom of Dalriada are located. Sometimes we go further south than that, but not this season."

"Will the Albans try to help the Alt Cluts?" Asbjorn asked.

"Possibly," Thorleik answered thoughtfully. "The sister of the King of Alba is married to the son of the King of Alt Clut, so they might answer the call of a kinsman to help resist us. It means we'll have to take Dumbarton Rock that much sooner."

"What tribute are we seeking?" Asbjorn asked.

"Prisoners bring the highest price at market, so all of the cargo ships we take with us will be filled with prisoners on the way back. But if the King of Alt Clut wants to buy the freedom of some of his people, we'll take his gold and silver in exchange. We might even take bronze, but only if we need it to make up any losses for the expedition."

"So I'll be guarding the cargo ships, the supplies, and the prisoners?"

Thorleik nodded. "You and the other lads who haven't been on an expedition before. You'll be training with them daily starting today. You'll learn to fight in the mornings, and load the ships after midday."

Looking up at the position of the sun, Thorleik added, "You'd better get ready to start your training. You're to meet Djúrgeirr Eldgrímsson near the staging area for the supplies. He'll be handling your training and overseeing the loading."

Thorleik stood up suddenly and went inside the house. "Wait here for a moment," he said as he disappeared inside.

When he came out a few minutes later, he was carrying a spear and a sword. He handed the weapons to Asbjorn.

"I've carried this spear for years, and it's never broken. And this was my first sword. I took it from a cousin who was wounded on my first expedition, and I used it to kill the man who caused the wound. It needed revenge, and it continued to serve me

12

well until Amlaíb gave me my current sword. It's yours now. Treat it well, and it'll never fail you."

Asbjorn accepted the weapons with gratitude. "Thank you, Father!" he said, looking at the spear and sword in his hands.

"You'll get your shield as part of your training," Thorleik added with a note of pride in his voice. "Now get going. You don't want to be late on your first day!"

For the rest of the week, Asbjorn and the other young men who were going on their first expedition – many of whom were his friends – practiced fighting all morning and then loaded supplies into the cargo ships until nightfall.

This was the way young Norsemen prepared to be part of an expedition. Asbjorn learned a great deal about what it took to send a fleet across the channel to Britain. It wasn't just a matter of sailing ships across and attacking the local inhabitants. Norsemen had to eat at sea, and if they had to lay siege to a city or fortress, they had to have enough supplies to keep strong until they could forage for more. They also had to have enough supplies for the voyage home.

By the end of the week, tons of water, bread, smoked and salted meats, and vegetables had been loaded onboard the longships and the cargo ships. Each longship had to carry the fighting men, their weapons, and the supplies they'd need for the crossing. The cargo ships would carry the supplies needed once they had landed across the channel, and the cargo ship sailors would be used as reserve fighters in case they were needed.

As the supplies were used, it would free up the cargo ships to carry home prisoners and other tribute secured on the expedition. Asbjorn and his companions would sail across on the cargo ships and be responsible for the supplies. They'd also be responsible for the prisoners and tribute that would be taken back to Áth Cliath once Dumbarton Rock had fallen. The fleet would easily be able to carry over a thousand prisoners back to Áth Cliath, and they'd bring great wealth to the Norsemen once they were sold.

It took six days to load the ships, and by the evening of the last day, Asbjorn felt that he was just getting used to the routine.

He went to bed early, knowing that the fleet would sail with the tide before sunrise the next morning.

It was still dark when he felt someone shaking his shoulder. Turning over, he looked up and saw his father. "Time to get ready, Asbjorn," Thorleik said quietly. "Your things are laid out."

Asbjorn looked where his father was gesturing. His spear and sword were there with his clothes, as was the shield he received during his training. He had decorated it with the symbol of three bears intertwined as one. At the bottom of the shield was a hammer, which Asbjorn had added to honor his father. Thor was the Norse god who carried a hammer as a weapon, and since his father's name began with "Thor," Asbjorn thought it was appropriate. The name Bjorn meant "Bear" in the Norse tongue, which is why he had put the bear symbols on the shield.

As he got up to get dressed, Asbjorn noticed a leather jerkin and a metal helmet sitting next to the dagger Thorleik gave him for his birthday. The jerkin was a protective garment covering the chest, arms, and upper legs of the wearer, and protecting the wearer against almost anything except a direct blow from a sharpened blade or arrowhead. Since Asbjorn would be guarding the cargo ships, and not participating in the battles, it would be enough protection for him.

The helmet was a round, conical helmet with an extra piece of metal attached to the front to protect the nose. It was lined with wool and leather to help it fit properly and to absorb any impacts.

Once Asbjorn had gotten dressed, put on his jerkin and sword, and stuck the dagger's sheath in his sword belt, he donned the helmet. Then he grabbed the shield and spear and turned around to face his father.

Thorleik and Bergdís both stood there looking proudly at their son. Thorleik was wearing the traditional clothing of the Norsemen – a woolen shirt, woolen breeches covering the legs, and fur lined leather boots. He was also wearing a jerkin made of leather with overlapping metal leaves to protect his upper body. He wore a similar helmet, and his shield was decorated with a variety of symbols representing his family and his allegiance to Amlaíb. Instead of a spear, though, he carried a large axe, which Asbjorn knew his father wielded with deadly skill.

"Let's get going, son," Thorleik said.

Asbjorn gave his mother a kiss on the cheek, and then ran after his father, who had already stepped outside into the pre-dawn darkness. They both strode quickly through the enclosure, out the main gates, and down the hill toward to the harbor.

The harbor was lit by torchlight, and there were so many torches there that it looked almost like daylight. There were hundreds of Norsemen already on the boats and thousands more approaching the harbor from inside and around the enclosure.

Thorleik stayed with Asbjorn most of the way to the longships, but when they reached the place where Djúrgeirr Eldgrímsson was waiting with the other young men, Thorleik took his son by the forearm.

"I'll see you in Alt Clut, son," he said, gripping his son's forearm tightly. Then he let go and turned to make his way to his own ship.

Djúrgeirr quickly took the young men to the cargo ships and assigned two of them to each ship. Asbjorn and his friend, Hundulfr Játmundsson, took their places as the rest of the rowers came onboard. Cargo ships, like longships and longboats, were powered by both sails and rowers, but were normally rowed out of the harbor.

Asbjorn looked over the side of the cargo ship and spotted his father's longship making its way out of the harbor. Amlaíb's longship had already entered the channel and turned northeast, and the members of the council were taking out their ships next. The cargo ships would bring up the rear of the fleet since they moved slower than the longships.

On shore, the women, children, and those too old or infirm to fight, watched as the rest of the ships in the fleet rowed toward the channel. Asbjorn couldn't see Bergdís, and once the captain gave the order to start rowing, he didn't have time to look anymore.

The torchlight allowed the ships to navigate the harbor in the darkness. People from the longphort and surrounding settlements lined the waterway from the harbor to the channel, holding their torches high in silent salute to the brave Norsemen who wouldn't be returning from this expedition. Death was part of the Norse way of life, and Asbjorn remembered standing on the shore with his own torch held high for his father and brother.

Asbjorn pulled on the ship's oar to the rhythm set by the lead rower. Once the ship cleared the inlet, it entered the channel and turned northeast. The single large sail was unfurled and angled to catch the southwest wind, and then the captain shouted for the oars to be stowed as the first rays of the morning sun became visible in the east. The ship picked up speed and was soon sailing just behind the main part of the fleet on a northeasterly course toward Alt Clut.

Asbjorn hadn't seen Bjornkarl that morning, but he knew that the berserkers would be in the lead ships since they typically landed first to secure the beachhead in case the Britons attacked while the ships were unloading. *If I'm lucky, I won't see him at all on this expedition.*

CHAPTER 3

By the time the sun rose in the east, the Norse fleet was already several leagues to the north of Áth Cliath. Asbjorn looked around at the rest of the fleet with a sense of pride. Norsemen were among the finest shipbuilders in the world, and Asbjorn was excited to see the fleet in action for the first time.

There were one hundred and forty seven longships in the fleet, not counting the cargo ships. Amlaíb's longship was in the front, with Thorleik's ship just behind. Asbjorn was onboard one of the cargo ships sailing toward the rear. From his position, Asbjorn had an amazing view of the rest of the fleet in the morning sunlight.

Asbjorn saw Amlaíb's longship in the distance. He knew that only the greatest warriors sailed on the lead longship. *I hope I someday earn the right to sail with the king.*

Asbjorn and the other young men learned about the building and handling of longships from Djúrgeirr during the days before the fleet sailed.

The primary purpose of longships was to transport fighters for land battles. All of the longships in the fleet were the same shape on both ends, allowing the ships to reverse direction quickly when needed. Spare rudders kept near the front of each longship could be mounted quickly when the ships reversed direction.

Longships had a shallow draft in the water, making it possible to sail them up rivers and streams that were at least four feet deep. The ships were beached when they reached land, allowing the crew to get to shore or get back onboard quickly.

The expert way the ships were built made them sturdy and fast on the sea. Just as the wooden slats used for making barrels had to fit together just right so the barrels wouldn't leak, the oak timbers used for ships in the fleet had to fit together perfectly so the ship wouldn't sink in rough seas. The oak timbers were nailed into place, and pitch and animal skins were used to seal the seams and cracks so the ships would be watertight.

There was a single mast in the center of each ship with a large sail used when the wind was favorable. The sails were made of diamond-shaped wool pieces that were trimmed with leather to help the sail keep its shape when wet. These pieces were sewn together, which gave the sail a crosshatched pattern. Asbjorn remembered watching Bergdís and the other women of the enclosure making the sail for Thorleik's new ship, and he was amazed at how heavy it was.

Many longships had ornately carved prow ornaments, but the crews removed them while at sea. There was too great a chance of the prow ornament falling off into the water if the seas were rough, which Asbjorn knew was considered bad luck for the ship and crew. The crews put the prow ornaments back in place just before beaching the longships.

Amlaíb's longship was the largest, measuring just under two hundred feet long, as was proper for his rank. Fifty rowers sat along both sides of the ship. Shields could be mounted along the outside to provide protection for the sailors, but this was rarely done because the shields frequently came loose and were lost at sea. In addition to the rowers, there was one sailor at the front of the ship who watched for the rocks and reefs that might damage the ship, two helmsmen on the great rudder at the rear of the ship, and an additional fifty warriors onboard ready to fight for their leader in battle.

Amlaíb's ship had a dragonhead as the prow ornament, and he had his sail dyed blood red to make his enemies afraid. Some of the other ships in the fleet had colored sails, but most kept the natural color of the wool because of the expense of the dyes. Sails were very expensive and difficult to make, and many of the ship owners couldn't afford extra adornments.

Thorleik's longship was one hundred and twenty feet long, and the prow ornament was the head of a bear. The ship used thirty-four rowers altogether and carried an additional forty warriors onboard. His ship was the largest of the council members' ships. Most of the council members' ships were at least one hundred feet long with no fewer than thirty rowers and an additional thirty warriors onboard. The rest of the longships in the fleet were between thirty and seventy feet long, depending on how rich and powerful the owners were.

Asbjorn's cargo ship was the same size as the other forty-three cargo ships in the fleet. It was sixty feet long, but twice as wide as a normal longship. It took forty rowers, two helmsmen, and one spotter to sail the ship, but it didn't carry any additional warriors onboard.

Asbjorn soon discovered that there wasn't much to do onboard a longship when it was using its sail. Most of the men sharpened their weapons or played games. Feeling hungry, he pulled out some dried meat and fruit from the pouch he carried at his waist and began to eat.

He was grateful the voyage wouldn't last for more than two days since the ships weren't comfortable. He knew the settlers who had left earlier in the summer would be sailing for several weeks to reach the new lands in the west, and he couldn't imagine how difficult that would be – especially if they had to row most of the way. He shook his head and finished eating. Then he went to find his friend Hundulfr.

Several times during the voyage, the captain of the ship had the rowers take to their oars so the slow-moving cargo ship wouldn't fall too far behind the rest of the fleet. As the sun set in the west, Asbjorn was surprised to see their sail lowered for the night. The other ships in the fleet did the same thing, and as night fell, the ships moved only with the current in the channel.

An hour before dawn, the captain woke the crew and raised the sail again. In the low light, Asbjorn saw the rest of the fleet moving forward, and he thought that he saw land in the distance. He knew the plan was to land near Dumbarton Rock no later than an hour after sunrise, and the excitement of what was to come surged through him.

Rhun mac Arthgal, son of King Arthgal of Alt Clut and brother-in-law to Causantín mac Cináeda, the King of Alba, rose early and made his daily rounds, inspecting the defenses and checking in with the guards and lookouts to see if there were any enemy sightings. Dumbarton had been destroyed before by Lochlannach raiders from Ireland and the Islands around Alba, and Rhun knew that the guards in the fortress needed to remain vigilant to prevent the Lochlannach from successfully invading the kingdom again.

Reports had been coming in from the kingdoms to the south. A large Lochlannach invasion force was wreaking havoc all along the old Roman walls and the western coast. Rhun was concerned that these invaders might turn their eyes toward Alt Clut to take control of the river and split Alba from the rest of the island, effectively surrounding Alba on all sides. He was determined to prevent this from happening. His marriage bound him to Alba, and his fate might well be Alba's if he allowed the Lochlannach to land on the north bank of the river.

The fortress on top of Dumbarton Rock had a commanding view of the river and the surrounding countryside below. It sat on the north bank of the river, approximately twenty miles inland from the sea. The city of Dumbarton, the capital of Alt Clut, was on the other side of the fortress from the river, just below Dumbarton Rock and next to a branch of the main river that flowed from the north. In an emergency, most of the townspeople of Dumbarton would take refuge in the fortress, which was well provisioned and could withstand almost any attack. The fortress contained a well connected to the river by way of a narrow underground tunnel. The well had supplied water to the fortress for many years and had never failed.

The people of Alt Clut were Britons who had fled from central Britain when the Saxons invaded the island after the Roman army left to return east. It was only the Lochlannach raids that had prevented the Saxons from conquering the few remaining Briton kingdoms, but the Lochlannach raiders seemed intent on conquering all of Britain and Alba, bringing the entire island under a single ruler for the first time.

Rhun's biggest concern was that the Lochlannach might attempt to land their ships at night and seize the town before the alarm could be raised. Fortunately, Lochlannach rarely did this, preferring to strike fear into the hearts of the townspeople and defenders by allowing their approach to be seen. This gave the defenders and the townspeople time to seek safety in the fortress, but it left the countryside undefended until help arrived from one of the neighboring kingdoms. If the reports were accurate, only Alba remained free of the Lochlannach invaders, so Rhun knew that he'd need to alert his brother-in-law as soon as any longships were sighted.

Rhun stood on the south wall of the fortress in the morning sunlight, looking toward the river. The usual morning mist was thicker to the west, but it was beginning to dissipate. There was a westerly breeze blowing and a slight chill in the autumn air.

Rhun knew that most enemies would never attack so late in the year, but the Lochlannach were used to cold weather and attacked whenever it suited their purpose, slaughtering all who resisted and carrying off anyone they captured that might fetch a good price at the slave markets. He remembered seeing the piles of heads that the raiders had left on the banks of the river after the raid they made a few years earlier, and he wondered how he could prevent the same from happening again.

He stood in silence, watching the sun climbing higher in the east. But an all too familiar sound broke the silence. It was coming from behind him. Turning to the west, he saw shapes on the river through the mist. They were getting closer and louder by the minute. Then he heard a bell ringing out the alarm from the northwestern bank of the river.

Without hesitating, he called to one the messengers who followed him on his daily inspections. "Ride to Alba and tell King Causantín to bring his army as quickly as he can. Lochlannach are on the river with an invasion force."

"Yes, my Prince," the messenger said with a salute. Then he turned, ran to his horse, and rode out of the fortress and to the north with his message.

Rhun called to another messenger. "Ride down to the city and tell the townspeople to take refuge immediately in the fortress and bring as much food as they can carry. Then ride throughout the countryside and tell anyone you can find to hide themselves and their valuables."

"Yes, my Prince," the second messenger responded and he turned to get his own horse.

Alarm bells were sounding all around as Rhun gave orders for several other messengers to ride out and alert the countryside of the invasion force. He then ordered one of the guards to alert the rest of the fortress' garrison to prepare to meet the invaders where they landed and to send word to the king about what was happening.

Rhun turned back to the west. As the mist continued to dissipate, the longships became plainly visible on the river. He was shocked at the number of ships rowing toward him, and estimated that there must be almost two hundred ships in the invasion fleet.

Thousands of warriors!

Looking around, he saw the garrison soldiers preparing the defenses. From the sounds behind him, he knew that the first of the townspeople had started arriving. Even the bells of the monastery were now ringing, alerting the countryside of the danger approaching from the river.

Archers lined the western walls to attack the longships as the Lochlannach turned north to attack the city. Rhun saw shields being mounted on the sides of the longships as they approached, but a wooden shield wouldn't do much to protect against an arrow with a flaming rag attached to it. The archers would rain fire down on the longships while the soldiers deployed along the riverbanks to attack any Lochlannach who made it ashore.

King Arthgal joined his son on the west wall and watched the longships approaching. As the largest longship they had ever seen turned north, father and son knew this must be the ship of one of the Lochlannach Kings because of its size.

"Let's go down and meet them," King Arthgal said as more longships reached where the river branched and turned north.

"Yes, Father," Rhun replied as he followed his father to the stairs leading down to the courtyard below.

Soldiers hurried down the causeway to meet the Lochlannach as the townspeople were making their way up to the protection of the fortress. The soldiers stationed in the city were already deploying along the riverbank. King Arthgal and Prince Rhun rode their horses quickly to the base of the hill, followed by their personal guards and the rest of the garrison.

Looking up, Rhun saw the archers unleash a hail of arrows in the early morning light. Most had pitch-soaked rags tied to the ends that were set on fire. The pitch would splash when the arrows hit, spreading the fire across a wide area and making the fire harder to contain. He saw fires breaking out on several of the ships and knew that the archers would continue firing at the ships for as long as they could.

Rhun watched as one of the ships sailing just behind the lead ship burned out of control, but it was still heading for the riverbank. Rhun speculated that the longship would probably reach the shore before the fire killed most of the raiders onboard.

"Do you think they'll land the berserkers first?" Rhun asked his father.

"That's what they normally do," King Arthgal replied, watching several of the smaller longships heading for the riverbank closest to where the soldiers were deploying.

The King and his son joined the soldiers waiting where the first longships landed. As the longships beached, men wearing the pelts and heads of bears and wolves leapt from the ships and spread out in front of the soldiers. Several drank from leather bags around their necks while others drew their swords and axes.

At first, the Lochlannach stood facing the soldiers until the landing area filled with the fur-covered warriors. Then the warriors began to sway and shout – caught up in a frenzy that made them act more like animals than men. One of the warriors cried out in the Lochlannach tongue, and the mass of howling and growling warriors attacked.

Archers from the fortress above fired down at the berserkers as they approached the soldiers, while other archers continued firing at the beached longships and at the longships on the river. The soldiers held their ground and waited for the warriors. When the two forces finally met, the soldiers were no match for the ferocity of the warriors' attack. A fourth of the soldiers died or fell from their wounds in the first thirty minutes. The king ordered the soldiers to fall back so the archers could safely fire more arrows at the raging berserkers, and the soldiers redeployed on higher ground to prepare for the second attack.

Longships carrying the rest of the Lochlannach landed all along the river on both sides of the city. Warriors joined the berserkers in attacking the soldiers while the rest sacked the city. More longships made their way further upriver to attack the farms and settlements around the city. The monastery on the north end of the city fell first – its religious artifacts, gold and silver chalices and candlesticks, and other items of value seized and taken to the waiting longships.

The Lochlannach attacked the soldiers a second time, but the higher ground made any approach more difficult. Archers who weren't shooting at the longships took positions above the soldiers and rained arrows down into the ranks of the invaders. Many shields had dozens of arrows imbedded in them, and hundreds of dead and dying Lochlannach lay all around the field.

Throughout the day, the battle raged. The soldiers attacked and then fell back to the high ground. Berserkers attempted to get around the soldiers to the right several times, but they were beaten back each time with heavy losses on both sides. The archers had a deadly effect on the Lochlannach, helped by the fact that most of the longships moved further upriver from the fortress to prevent more ships from catching fire. This allowed the archers to concentrate on the warriors, and from their position along the ridge below the fortress, the Lochlannach had no practical defense.

The Lochlannach captured many soldiers and townspeople who were cut off from the fortress. King Arthgal saw the fires raging around the city and knew that the Lochlannach had finished looting everything of value that had been left behind.

As the sun set in the west, the king ordered his remaining soldiers to fall back into the fortress. The archers along the walls provided cover for the retreating soldiers so the Norsemen wouldn't follow them up the causeway. The gates of the fortress thudded shut once the soldiers were safely inside.

The Lochlannach ran up the causeway and looked for ways into the fortress. Archers on the walls fired wave after wave of arrows at the invaders. Soldiers poured giant cauldrons of hot pitch onto the heads of the invaders before flaming arrows ignited the pitch. Almost a hundred Lochlannach caught fire and died along the walls before the rest retreated down the hill out of the range of the archers.

As the sky darkened, the king watched as the Lochlannach deployed around Dumbarton Rock. The light from the burning city allowed the king see the Lochlannach's preparations well into the night.

When the sun rose the next morning, the city of Dumbarton lay in ashes. The Lochlannach, deployed for a siege, surrounded the fortress. Given the size of the force below, King Arthgal knew that the siege might last for quite a while. The Lochlannach had the ability to sail back to their base to resupply quickly. The townspeople of Dumbarton only had the food stores inside the fortress and the water from the well.

"I hope it will be enough to last until help can arrive," Rhun commented after the king shared the situation with his son.

The king looked down at the ruined city and the invading army below. "*If* help arrives."

CHAPTER 4

Shortly before midday on the first day of the invasion, Asbjorn's cargo ship beached just north of the city of Dumbarton. The battle was raging between the Norsemen and the soldiers defending the fortress, and much of the city was already burning as the ship ran up on the riverbank and the rowers secured the oars.

Asbjorn grabbed his spear and shield and then jumped down onto the riverbank, moving away quickly to make room for the others behind him who were waiting to jump down. The crew secured the area around the ship and started unloading supplies.

Norsemen brought the prisoners taken from the burning city and the battlefield. Asbjorn and the others quickly built a holding pen for the captives. Asbjorn knew that the prisoners would be loaded onto a cargo ship and taken back to Áth Cliath once there were enough to fill the ship. The ship would then return with any needed supplies. Some prisoners, like soldiers and prominent citizens, would remain in the holding pen for interrogation, but the women and children left for Áth Cliath as quickly as possible, along with the tribute already seized. This way, if the battle should turn against the Norsemen, forcing the longships to leave quickly, there would still be profit from the expedition.

"We have to be careful about how many prisoners we take," Djúrgeirr said to Asbjorn as the prisoners were loaded into the first cargo ship. "Take too few, and the local inhabitants might feel that they're strong enough to refuse to send their annual tribute. Take too many, and there might not be enough people left to raise the annual tribute amount."

"How do we keep track of the prisoners that are loaded onto the ships?" Asbjorn asked.

"Recording the number of prisoners each Norseman takes is the job that the captain of each cargo ship handles," Djúrgeirr replied. "Prisoners are the property of their captor, or captors, and are sold with the captors' permission. Each prisoner and captor has to be recorded to settle accounts at the end of the expedition. Once prisoners are sold, the captors are taxed so the king and the members of the council get their share of the overall tribute for the expedition."

"What happens if the captor dies before returning home?" Asbjorn asked.

"If the captor dies before the prisoners are sold, the council decides who receives ownership of the prisoners. If the prisoners have been sold already, the council decided who gets the remaining tribute."

Asbjorn nodded. It was an orderly system, and he watched it with great interest. By the end of the first day, two cargo ships had already returned to Áth Cliath with prisoners and tribute from the city. Asbjorn had little free time since the holding pen stayed full with new prisoners arriving from the surrounding countryside.

It was two days before Thorleik came to see his son. Asbjorn's father had received an injury during the fighting on the first day, but the wound was slight, and Thorleik seemed happy with the way the expedition was going.

"I captured six of their soldiers myself," he told Asbjorn happily. Pointing to where they were standing, he added, "Make sure they aren't loaded onto a ship yet. We may need to question them at some point. They've seen the inside of the fortress, and we may need to know more about the defenses before this is all over."

"Yes, Father. Have you seen Bjornkarl?"

Thorleik nodded. "He led the second charge of the Berserkers on the left side of the Britons, but he was pushed back by the archers. He was hit by three arrows, but he's all right. None of the wounds festered, so he should recover soon. We captured almost twenty prisoners that he wounded, so his share of the tribute will be substantial."

"Should I go and see him?" Asbjorn asked.

"It's up to you, son. We're going to be here for a while, so it might be good for him to see that you're here and learning to be a warrior."

Asbjorn nodded. He wondered if his brother might start to respect him knowing that he was part of the expedition, but he knew better than to get his hopes up. *I think it'll take more than one expedition to earn my brother's respect.*

It was another two days before Asbjorn's duties allowed him to go visit his brother. He found Bjornkarl outside the monastery with one of the Healers, who was changing Bjornkarl's bandages. Bjornkarl had several injuries on his left arm, but the wounds seemed clean and appeared to be closing.

"Hello, brother," Asbjorn said as the Healer finished wrapping the arm again.

Bjornkarl looked up sharply, and then gave Asbjorn a sneering smile. "What are you doing here, Asbjorn," he asked with the usual sound of contempt in his voice. "This is man's work, not a boy's outing."

"How do I become a man if I don't learn man's work?" Asbjorn answered.

Bjornkarl laughed, and for the first time, Asbjorn felt it was genuine. "That's the same thing I told father when I asked to go on my first expedition," he said, still sneering.

Pointing to Bjornkarl's arm, Asbjorn asked, "How are your injuries healing?"

"Quickly," his brother replied. "The archers did the most damage, but one soldier managed to cut me early on. I killed him, of course."

Asbjorn nodded. "Archers set our ship on fire, but we put out the flames before we beached. We lost only eight rowers coming up the river."

"Father's new longship took a lot of damage," Bjornkarl said, getting off the rock and stretching his legs. "He's overseeing the repairs like a nervous mother. The prow ornament was destroyed and the center deck is burned in a few places. At least they didn't get the sail."

Asbjorn was about to say something when several berserkers came up and started talking to Bjornkarl. Asbjorn waited for a minute, and when he realized that his brother had forgotten all about him, he left the monastery to find his father and see the damage to the longship.

A week after the siege of Dumbarton Rock started, Ívarr and the bulk of his forces arrived. His fleet of longships beached to the east of Dumbarton, and that night there was a great feast in the encampment set up near the old monastery.

Ívarr had already sent home dozens of cargo ships filled with prisoners and tribute from his campaign in the south, and he was waiting for those ships to return and take home the remainder of the prisoners that he had brought with him.

Since Asbjorn spoke the tongue of the Dalriadan Scots, which wasn't very different from the language of the Britons, he was instructed to communicate with the prisoners and make sure they understood what was expected of them.

As the days went by, he learned much about the people of Alt Clut. He saw the fear in their eyes. *They're so afraid of us. I never thought about that before. They live in fear of being attacked by a Norse fleet. We must be their worst nightmare.* He forced himself to push these thoughts out of his mind, though. Norsemen were conquerors, and someday Asbjorn would be leading expeditions like this to bring wealth and glory to his family. It was expected of him, and he never once questioned the way of life into which he had been born.

Eight days after the sighting of the longships on the river, the messenger from Alt Clut arrived in Scone, the capital city of the kingdom of Alba. He was escorted to the king immediately.

Causantín mac Cináeda, King of Alba, was meeting with his earls and discussing the Lochlannach conquest of Britain when the messenger entered the council chamber. The king looked up and recognized the uniform immediately. "What news do you have from my sister's lord?" he asked.

"Great King," the messenger began, "a fleet of two hundred longships was sighted on the river approaching Dumbarton Rock eight days ago. I fear by now the city will have fallen and the fortress will be under siege. My master commands me to beg you to remember the alliance between your two kingdoms. We need your army to help us break the siege and take back the lands that the Lochlannach have taken."

"Was this a part of Ívarr's forces that have been attacking Britain, or is this a new invasion force?" Causantín asked.

"I don't know, Great King," the messenger answered. "I was commanded to ride to you as soon as the ships were spotted. Prince Rhun was making his morning rounds when the longships were sighted shortly after sunup."

Causantín nodded. Turning to his earls, he said, "We need to go to the aid of the King of Alt Clut. If Dumbarton Rock falls, our southern border will be exposed to Lochlannach attack. Go and rally your clansmen. We'll meet in ten days with whatever force is available by then."

Looking at the map on the council table, he pointed to a spot on the border of Alba and Alt Clut directly north of Dumbarton. "We'll concentrate our forces here," he said.

Raibeart mac Stiùbhart, the Earl of the lands of Airer Goídel, which used to be the heart of the old kingdom of Dalriada, spoke up. "King Causantín, my clans are the closest to the border. I can have our horsemen ride down and see what's happening in Alt Clut. They can join us at the meeting place and let us know what we're facing."

Causantín thought about this for a moment. "Do it," he said finally. "We need to know where the Lochlannach are and if the fortress is still standing. But be careful. If your horsemen are seen, the Lochlannach will know that we're coming and be ready for us. If we're going to break a siege of several thousand Lochlannach, it'll have to be by surprise."

"Yes, My King," Raibeart replied.

Turning to the messenger, Causantín asked, "Can you go with them and show them the best way to Dumbarton?"

"Yes, Great King," the messenger replied.

Less than an hour later, the messenger was on a fresh horse and was riding with Raibeart and his escorts toward Airer Goídel. Messengers were sent ahead to alert the villages about the invasion and to spread the word that the army was gathering on the border of Alt Clut. The horsemen of Airer Goídel, however, would be told to wait for Raibeart near the old Dalriadan fortress of Dunadd.

Ívarr was fuming. It was early in the morning ten days after the beginning of the siege, and he was reviewing the progress of the siege with Amlaíb and the council in the monastery because it was the only structure left standing in Dumbarton.

"The flow of prisoners and tribute from the countryside is slowing considerably," Amlaíb reported. "I don't know how long we can afford to continue the siege without more captives and tribute to offset the expense of the expedition."

"It's not a question of conducting a prolonged siege," Ívarr said. "It's a matter of securing Alt Clut as part of My Kingdom."

"I understand that, Ívarr," Amlaíb said, trying to calm down his kinsman. "But I'm not here just to help *you* conquer new lands. I have an expedition to fund, ship owners to pay, and men to reward so they can feed their families until the next expedition. There's little tribute coming in, there are few prisoners left to take, and if the siege lasts too long, I'll never be able to recoup the expense of helping you. Your expedition of conquest has brought you thousands of prisoners and the tribute of three kingdoms in northern and western Britain. All I get out of this is what I can take from Alt Clut, and that's beginning to dry up. Besides, it's reasonable to assume that Alba will be sending its army soon. We'll have the Alt Clut soldiers in the fortress on one side and the Picts and Scots on the other side. We'll be caught in the middle."

"My forces combined with yours will keep the Alban army from doing us any harm," Ívarr stated confidently.

"I still don't like the idea of being stuck here all winter," Amlaíb said.

"What would it take for you to stay and help me?" Ívarr asked.

"We need to bring the siege to an end quickly," Amlaíb replied. "I need the tribute and prisoners hiding behind the walls of that fortress."

"So how do we do that?" Ívarr asked.

Amlaíb shook his head. "We can't storm that rock, and we can't get close enough to pull the walls down. We need to give them a reason to come out, and I just can't think of one."

"What about burning them out?" Ívarr asked.

"They have plenty of water because of the well inside the fortress. They can put out any fires we set."

31

"What if they ran out of water?"

"How?" Amlaíb asked. "According to the locals, the well has never failed."

"Why is that?" Ívarr asked.

"Because it's connected through that great rock to the river."

"Where does it connect to the river?"

Amlaíb shook his head. "I don't know,"

"Then perhaps that's what you need to be finding out, Amlaíb," Ívarr said. "If you can cut off their water supply, they'll have no choice but to come out."

"And if they see us doing that?" Amlaíb asked. "They'll start storing water all over the fortress and they'll still be able to stay behind those walls for months."

"Not if they need the water to put out fires," Ívarr pointed out. "Let them see you trying to cut off their water. Let them store the water, thinking they're still safe from us. Then, start doing to them what they tried to do to your ships. Flaming arrows in the night will use up all their water. They'll have to come out and you can take your prisoners and tribute home with you."

"I'll need someone who can speak with the prisoners to learn more about that well," Amlaíb noted.

"Forgive me, Amlaíb," Thorleik said. "My youngest son speaks their language. He's assigned to guard and load the prisoners, and he has to communicate with them. Perhaps he can help you find out more about the well."

Amlaíb nodded. "Send for him at once. We need to start finding the source of the well if we're going to end this siege soon."

Thorleik turned to one of his senior warriors and asked him to fetch Asbjorn. Thorleik didn't see the second warrior slip quietly out of the monastery a moment later.

The second warrior made his way quickly to the tents of the berserkers, which were at the far end of the tent city erected to house the Norsemen during the siege. Most were still asleep, given that their appetites for women and drink usually kept them up late into the night.

32

When the second warrior arrived at the berserker compound, he was told that Bjornkarl was asleep but wasn't alone. Nodding, the second warrior left a message for Bjornkarl and quickly returned to the monastery.

The first warrior found Asbjorn standing guard over the prisoners near his cargo ship. "Your father commands that you join him in council, Asbjorn," he said.

"Where is my father?" Asbjorn asked.

"In the monastery. Follow me, and I'll take you to him."

Asbjorn told his captain where he was going and then followed the warrior back to the monastery. He arrived as the second warrior returned from the berserker compound, and the three Norsemen entered the monastery together.

"Forgive the interruption, my lords," the first warrior said as he entered the part of the monastery where the council was meeting. "I have brought Asbjorn Thorleikson as commanded."

Asbjorn stood in shock as he realized he was in the presence of both Amlaíb and Ívarr. He waited until one of them spoke to him before saying anything.

"So this is your youngest, Thorleik?" Amlaíb asked. "A fine looking boy. I see the family resemblance… more so than in Bjornkarl."

"Thank you, Amlaíb," Thorleik said, motioning for Asbjorn to stand next to him.

"I understand that you speak the tongue of the Scots," Amlaíb said to Asbjorn. "Can you speak with the Briton prisoners from here as well?"

"Yes, My Lord," Asbjorn answered. "The languages are close to each other. I've been giving the prisoners instructions and they've understood me with no problems."

"Good. We need to begin interrogating some of the prisoners, and I'll need you to translate."

"Of course, My Lord. I'll help in any way that you need."

"Fine," Amlaíb said. "We need to end this siege quickly. There's a well in the fortress that's fed from the river. We need to find where it connects to the river so we can cut off the water supply. Can you make the prisoners understand what we want to know?"

33

Asbjorn nodded.

"And can you make sure that they understand what we'll do to them if they don't tell us what we want to know?"

Again, Asbjorn nodded.

"Good. Take some men with you and bring back the first set of prisoners. Make sure the ones we question have been inside the fortress."

"Yes, My Lord," Asbjorn said. He looked over to his father, who nodded. Asbjorn turned to leave, and a squad of ten warriors, which Amlaíb had already selected, followed him back to the prisoner holding pen.

Thorleik watched his son leave the monastery with a sense of great pride. *My son will have a chance that few his age ever get. He'll get to do a service for his king, and if he does it well, he'll be well rewarded. He'll bring glory to his family.*

Bjornkarl woke up around mid-morning and looked around his tent. Three of the women prisoners lay near him with their hands tied to stakes so they couldn't escape. Bjornkarl had been with all three during the night, but now he was done with them. He left his tent and ordered the guard waiting outside to take the women back to the holding pen.

As he walked toward the cooking fires, one of the men who guarded the compound approached him. Bjornkarl greeted him, and the guard moved closer and whispered in Bjornkarl's ear. Bjornkarl's expression went from relaxed to enraged by the time the guard had delivered his message.

"My brother was summoned to council with Ívarr and Amlaíb?" he demanded, trying to control his anger.

"Yes, Bjornkarl," the guard answered, growing frightened by Bjornkarl's expression.

"Why?"

"I don't know, Bjornkarl."

Bjornkarl had never been summoned to council with the kings of the Norsemen, and he couldn't understand how his younger brother was being afforded such an honor. His rage boiled up inside, and having no other outlet, he struck the guard, killing him instantly. Looking down at the lifeless guard lying sprawled on the ground, Bjornkarl realized that he was still enraged at his brother. He walked toward the cooking fires again, hoping to find anyone with whom to pick a fight.

CHAPTER 5

Ciaran mac Unen, the Chief of the clansmen living in the region just northwest of the fortress of Dunadd, was walking along the banks of the Abhainn Fìne River when the messenger from King Causantín mac Cináeda arrived to inform him of the Lochlannach invasion of Alt Clut.

"The foot soldiers are congregating north of Dumbarton on the border of Alt Clut, but Raibeart mac Stiùbhart wants your horsemen to meet him at Dunadd as soon as possible. The horsemen will ride down to Dumbarton and survey the situation, and then report back to the King."

"When does Raibeart want us at Dunadd?" Ciaran asked.

"As soon as you can get there," the messenger replied. "He should be there no later than tomorrow. The King needs for the foot soldiers to be at the meeting place by sunset eight days from now."

"Very well," Ciaran said. "Tell the King that we'll be there."

The messenger nodded and then turned his horse and rode back to the east.

Ciaran ran back to the village to find his sons. He found them, along with their sister Caitlin, talking with Iain mac Mànas, the village's Christian priest. Iain wasn't an ordained priest like most major cities across Europe had, but was the person selected by the Bishop at Scone to act in his place between his visits, which occurred every couple of years and lasted about a month each time. Iain was a tall, thin, and balding man in his mid-forties with a high opinion of himself and a low opinion of anyone who disagreed with him. He was tasked with defending the faith of the Church in Rome and with providing instruction to the village and the surrounding area in the ways of the Christ. Iain considered himself to be the perfect example of a pious man, and he took his responsibilities to the Bishop seriously – so much so that he proved to be a constant irritation to Ciaran, who was the chief of the clan and didn't appreciate Iain's constant interference in the way the clan was governed.

The Dalriadan Scots had first brought Christianity to the region now known as Airer Goídel. King Causantín was a Christian, as were most Albans, but the old gods and the old religions were still practiced in secret in the sacred groves and in the circles of standing stones that dotted the landscape across Alba and the Islands. There were aspects of the Christian faith that didn't sit well with many Albans, and the village priests like Iain often had a difficult time enforcing the faith. Ciaran and his family had been baptized, but he was known to show his respect to the older gods of the region. He was frequently seen at the great stone circle near the village, and while he claimed it was where he liked to go and think, no one was fooled about what he really did there. Iain had threatened to have the standing stones pulled down and the timbers burned, but Ciaran commanded that the circle remain unmolested under threat of banishment or worse.

Maol-Chaluim mac Ciaran was Ciaran's eldest son. He was twenty-three years old and was a skilled warrior. He had married three years earlier and was expecting his first child in a few months. He was a tall man with dark hair, and he wore his beard well-trimmed like his father.

Maol-Chaluim's brother was Ringean mac Ciaran, who was nineteen years old and almost as tall as his brother. He wore his dark hair longer than his brother and father, and he was a gifted horseman. He was betrothed to the daughter of one of the clan elders and looked forward to marrying to her in the new year.

Caitlin, Ciaran's youngest child, was a firebrand who was as fearless as her brothers, as accomplished a swordsman as her father, and someone who refused to wait at home while the men marched off to do battle with invaders. She was fifteen and betrothed to be married the next month to the son of one of Ciaran's closest friends. She was a stunning beauty and had light hair like her mother, who had been a Pictish woman of good family and a fearless warrior until she had been killed in a

Lochlannach raid five years earlier. Ciaran had since remarried, but hadn't produced any children with his new wife.

Maol-Chaluim looked up and saw his father running towards them. "What's wrong father?" he asked, getting to his feet and facing his father.

"Lochlannach have invaded Alt Clut," he said when he reached them. "King Causantín has ordered the armies to gather in eight days on the border north of Dumbarton. Raibeart mac Stiùbhart wants our horsemen to meet him at Dunadd by morning so we can find out what the Lochlannach are up to before the army arrives to help the Alt Cluts. I want you to raise our footmen and lead them to the gathering place."

Turning to Ringean, he said, "And I want you to gather our horsemen and get ready to ride with me to Dunadd before first light."

"I'm going with you, Father," Caitlin said, standing up.

"Blasphemy!" Iain said loudly, forgetting that Caitlin was the daughter of a chief. "Women have no place doing man's work."

"And if the Lochlannach attack here while the men are in Alt Clut, would you have the women and children just submit because the invaders are men?" Caitlin asked defiantly. "Women in this land have fought off invaders since before the Romans came to Britain. Our queens have led armies in the field, and we've defended our homes and our bodies from the godless hordes who have tried to take what's ours. Just because you think women are inferior to men doesn't make it so."

"The church in Rome says women are inferior to men and are forbidden to act in any way that implies they are equal," Iain protested.

"Rome isn't here," Caitlin pointed out. "And neither is the Bishop. But the Lochlannach are here, and I'd rather fight them before they cross the border than wait for them to reach our village and have to fight them here."

Turning to her father, she said, "If you command me to stay here, I will, but you know I can ride, and you know I can fight. I want to go with you."

Ciaran looked at his daughter and at Iain. The church's stance on women was one of the articles of the Christian faith that troubled Ciaran the most. For centuries, the Pictish women fought alongside the men. Even after the Dalriadans seized control of Pictland and renamed it Alba, the Pictish blood and customs were still evident all around. Ciaran didn't believe that women had to stop fighting and become useless servants just because the church said so. *It's not as if the women have changed. They're still as strong and fierce as ever. It's just the church that has changed.*

Turning to his daughter, he said, "All right, you can come with me."

Iain began protesting again, but Ciaran stopped him. "If it bothers you so much to see women continue in the role they've had in our society for centuries, you go with the footmen so you don't have to be surrounded by the women who will defend our lands while the men are gone," he said, barely hiding his sarcasm.

"Yes, My Chief," Iain said, knowing that he'd never win this argument with Ciaran and making a mental note to inform the Bishop of Ciaran's defiance as soon as possible.

Once his children had left, Ciaran moved close to Iain to speak without being overheard. "Iain, I respect the church, and I respect the role you play in this village at the Bishop's request. I'm a Christian, too. But I'm also the Chief of this clan, and unless you want to find yourself banished with no clan to protect you or defer to you in matters of faith, you will never accuse my daughter or anyone else in my family of blasphemy again. Do you understand me?"

"Yes, My Chief, I understand."

"Good. Now go get ready to leave with the footmen in the morning."

Maol-Chaluim left long before sunrise to meet with the footmen who'd follow him to the place where the Alban army was congregating. He'd have over five hundred men with him from the village and the surrounding countryside. Ringean had gathered almost two hundred and fifty horsemen, and they were waiting just outside the village about an hour before sunrise when Ciaran and Caitlin joined them.

They rode to Dunadd in the darkness. The leader of each company of horsemen carried a torch to light the way, and the roads to the former capitol of the kingdom of Dalriada were well maintained, so riding at night wasn't difficult. They approached the fortress as the sun was rising, and they found Raibeart mac Stiùbhart and the messenger from Alt Clut waiting for them when they reached the base of the hill where the fortress sat.

"Greetings Ciaran," Raibeart said as the clan chief rode up to him.

"Greetings, My Lord," Ciaran replied, extending his hand.

Raibeart introduced the messenger to Ciaran, and then motioned for Ciaran's horsemen to follow him. It was a fifty-mile ride to Dumbarton from Dunadd. They rode to the southeast, and crossed into the kingdom of Alt Clut early the next afternoon.

Asbjorn turned his head so he couldn't see what was being done to the prisoner. He had been translating Amlaíb's questions for two days, but so far, none of the prisoners seemed willing to talk.

Frustrated, Amlaíb decided to take an extreme approach to the interrogations. He tortured prisoners in front of each other so they'd see what was waiting for them if they refused to answer his questions. The first prisoner had been beheaded, but now Amlaíb was employing more terrible techniques in order to find where the fortress' well connected to the river.

Asbjorn was talking to a prisoner tied to four stakes in the ground. One of the other Norsemen was working on him with a long knife, inflicting as much pain as possible without killing the prisoner too quickly. Asbjorn's stomach was turning at what was being done to the helpless soldier next to him, and he saw the horror in the faces of the prisoners waiting to be questioned.

Asbjorn glanced at his father and saw Thorleik watch the prisoners and his son with a blank expression. *He understands the reasons for the torture, and he supports the King. If Father has any problems with what's being done, he knows better than to reveal anything in front of anyone else.* Asbjorn kept his face as expressionless as possible while simply translating Amlaíb's questions.

The Norseman with the knife had been working on the prisoner for almost an hour, and Asbjorn knew that the man would never be able to answer any questions again. The torture at this point was for the other prisoners to watch, rather than to induce the prisoner being tortured to answer the questions.

40

Asbjorn looked up at Amlaíb and shook his head to signal that there was nothing more to be gained from the torture of this prisoner. Amlaíb nodded grimly and made a chopping gesture. The Norsemen with the knife picked up his axe and removed the prisoner's head. The lifeless body and head were removed, and Amlaíb motioned for Asbjorn to select the next prisoner to question.

Asbjorn walked over to the remaining prisoners. "I need to select another one of you to be questioned," he said in their tongue. "It would be better if one of you were willing to tell us what we need to know."

He watched the prisoners' expressions, and saw something strange in the eyes of one of them. He thought about it for a moment and then selected that prisoner to be next. He led the prisoner to the spot where the previous prisoner had been questioned, asking the questions that he knew Amlaíb wanted answered.

The prisoner looked at the blood soaked ground, and started to tremble. His knees buckled, and he went down to the ground before Asbjorn could grab him. Crouching next to him, Asbjorn asked the questions again.

"I don't want to die," the prisoner said in a low voice so the other prisoners wouldn't hear him.

"Then tell us what we want to know," Asbjorn said. "Where does the well in the fortress connect to the river?"

"Will you let me go if I tell you?"

Asbjorn looked up at Amlaíb and repeated the prisoner's question.

"Tell him that he won't be taken as a slave and he won't rejoin the other prisoners if he tells us where the well connects to the river," Amlaíb said.

Asbjorn translated Amlaíb's reply, sensing Amlaíb's true meaning.

The prisoner looked at Amlaíb and then Asbjorn. He hung his head in shame and said, "At the point where the river forks, there's a cairn of rocks. It marks where the well connects to the river. It's deep and hard to reach, so if you're going to attempt to block the well, it'll take weeks to break through the rock."

Asbjorn translated the prisoner's answer for Amlaíb. The Norse King smiled and nodded to Thorleik to begin looking for the cairn.

"You've done well, Asbjorn Thorleikson," Amlaíb said, "and you'll be rewarded for your service."

"Thank you, My Lord," Asbjorn said, getting to his feet.

Amlaíb made a gesture to the Norseman who had tortured the previous prisoner. Knowing what was going to happen, Asbjorn stepped out of the way as the Norseman approached the prisoner kneeling on the ground. The Norseman swung his axe, and the prisoner was dead before he knew what was happening.

Amlaíb instructed Asbjorn to escort the rest of the prisoners back to the holding pen. Asbjorn left with the prisoners immediately, happy to be finished with the interrogations. He knew the information was important, but he wished he hadn't seen what torture looked like.

Prince Rhun was standing on the wall of the fortress with his father, King Arthgal, looking down at the Lochlannach who surrounded Dumbarton Rock. They watched as a group of Lochlannach walked to the cairn of rocks where the river forked. King Arthgal looked at his son with alarm.

"Do you think they know that's the source of the well?" he asked.

Rhun nodded. "One of the soldiers taken prisoner must have told them."

"We can't risk losing our water supply," the King noted.

"Perhaps we can start storing water in casks, barrels, and other containers. That way we'll still have water for several weeks if they manage to block the source of the well."

"That'll buy us some time, but not much," the King replied. "We need to protect the well!"

"Then I suggest that we start working on a plan of attack. If we can sneak out of the fortress under the cover of night, we can disrupt the siege and damage anything they're using to block the well's source. We might also be able to get some of the townspeople out of the fortress and safely away from here in the confusion. We'll need less water with them gone, which will make whatever we can store last longer."

King Arthgal nodded. "That's a good idea, son. There will be no moon in two days. Can we get something ready by then?"

"Yes, Father," Prince Rhun said. "We have no choice."

Raibeart mac Stiùbhart cautiously led the horsemen of Airer Goídel into Alt Clut. They passed several burned-out villages and frightened groups of refugees trying to get to the safety of Alba. He questioned these groups, and in each case, the story was the same. The Lochlannach had come in force and carried off anyone who was still near their villages when the attacks began. It was only the timely arrival of the messengers from the fortress that allowed anyone to escape. Most of the men in the villages had tried to fight off the invaders, but they were all either dead or taken prisoner.

Ciaran sent out several small scouting parties to try to locate any other survivors. They returned several hours later and reported what everyone already knew. The Lochlannach had destroyed most of the villages and taken tribute and prisoners to Dumbarton, where their forces were concentrated. The scouting parties were also able to confirm that there were two forces in Dumbarton. One was Ívarr's invasion force, which had been raiding the northern and western kingdoms of Britain, and the other was Amlaíb's force fresh from Ireland.

"That's a sizable number of Lochlannach," Ciaran commented.

Raibeart nodded grimly. "It might take more than the army of Alba to break the siege."

He motioned to the horsemen, and soon they were riding south again toward Dumbarton.

Bjornkarl was an angry drunk on the best of days, but on this day, he seemed particularly irate. Bjornkarl had been drinking quite a bit when he decided that he'd go find his brother. For days, he had been thinking about Asbjorn's summons to the council of the kings, and Bjornkarl was jealous of his brother.

Why should he get such glory on his first expedition?

He found his brother near the holding pens. "Hello, brother," he said with as much contempt as he could manage in his drunken state.

43

"Hello, Bjornkarl. What brings you here? Looking for more company for the night?" Asbjorn asked, referring to the women prisoners that Bjornkarl had been abusing on a regular basis.

"No, brother, I came here looking for you. I hear that you were summoned to the council of the kings."

Asbjorn nodded. "They needed someone to translate for the prisoners. Amlaíb needed to find the source of the well in the fortress."

"And they chose you for that?" Bjornkarl asked darkly.

"Father told them that I know how to speak the tongue of the Picts and Scots, which isn't too different from the Briton tongue."

Bjornkarl just stared at his brother. "I've never been summoned to the council before," he slurred, moving closer. "I've never been asked to perform a personal service for Amlaíb either."

Asbjorn didn't say a word.

"So why did you, a boy who has never tasted battle, get an honor that I've never had?" Bjornkarl asked, taking another gulp of his drink.

"I don't know," Asbjorn replied. "Why don't you ask Father."

"No, I'm asking you. I'm a berserker. I'm a member of the most honored group of warriors that our people has. You're nothing, but you've been given an honor I haven't. That's not right."

"I didn't ask for the honor, Bjornkarl."

That comment set off Bjornkarl more than anything else Asbjorn might have said. "Of course you didn't ask for it," he snarled. "You'd never ask for it. And yet you got it just the same."

"It doesn't change the honor that you receive from battle, Bjornkarl. All I did was translate a few questions and answers. You receive glory for fighting and defeating our enemies. You capture prisoners and earn a share of the tribute. When we go home, all I'll get to say is that I met the King. You'll be rich from what you earned as a berserker. You're the one with the honor, not me."

Bjornkarl looked at his brother through his blurred vision and took another drink. Asbjorn was right, but that didn't make Bjornkarl any less frustrated. Not liking where the conversation had gone, Bjornkarl suddenly lashed out and hit Asbjorn hard on the side of his face. Asbjorn fell, and Bjornkarl kicked his brother in the stomach. He smiled as Asbjorn groaned loudly. Bjornkarl took another drink and turned to stagger back to the berserker compound as Asbjorn lay in the dirt gasping for air.

Before this expedition is finished, I'm going to find something that I can take from Asbjorn.

CHAPTER 6

"Look at all those ships!" Ringean exclaimed, looking from the safety of the woods on one of the hills northeast of the city of Dumbarton.

The Alban horsemen had arrived at the base of the hills, and Raibeart mac Stiùbhart, accompanied by Ciaran mac Unen, and his children Ringean and Caitlin, were crouching just inside the tree line. The scene to the south of them was a horrifying sight.

The burnt remnants of the city were clearly visible. Only the monastery and a few stone walls remained. There were tents everywhere, and the Lochlannach had Dumbarton Rock surrounded. There were almost two hundred longships beached on the riverbank alongside Dumbarton and almost that many beached on the main river on the other side of Dumbarton Rock. Raibeart estimated there were almost ten thousand Lochlannach encamped around the fortress.

"How do we break a siege like that?" he wondered aloud.

"By trickery and guile," Ciaran answered. "We can't survive a pitched battle against so many Lochlannach, but we might be able to trick them."

"What do you mean?" Raibeart asked.

"If we let them see a small force, they might attack it. Our main forces would be hiding, waiting to attack on their flanks when they rush the smaller force we put in front of them. We'll crush the warriors they send against us."

"We'd never be able to do it more than once," Raibeart pointed out.

"True, but then we'd start attacking at night," Ciaran answered. "We can hurt them when and where they don't expect it, and if the defenders inside the fortress can attack at the same time, we might be able to break the Lochlannach siege."

"How do we coordinate the attacks with the defenders in the fortress?" Caitlin asked.

Ciaran looked at her for a moment, and then shook his head. "I have no idea."

"That's something we'll need to work out with the King," Raibeart said, motioning for them to follow him back to the horsemen waiting behind the hill.

They mounted their horses, and Raibeart gave the signal for the horsemen to follow him. They rode east to check on the settlements in that part of the kingdom of Alt Clut and soon discovered that they had all been destroyed, and their people were either taken prisoner or in hiding. For two days, they searched for any Alt Clut soldiers or settlements that had been missed by the invaders. Finding none, Raibeart turned the horsemen northward and rode for the gathering place on the border to inform the King about what he had seen.

Thick clouds covered the sky on the night of the new moon, blocking out the light of the stars and making it nearly impossible to see the outline of the fortress above. The torches along the fortress walls had been extinguished for the past several nights, so the Lochlannach below wouldn't think it strange that the fortress was dark on this particular night. The only lights for miles were the cooking fires of the encampments and the occasional torch carried by Lochlannach warriors moving from one part of the encampment to another.

King Arthgal and Prince Rhun stood with their soldiers just inside the main gates of the fortress, waiting for the signal to slip down the causeway and attack. It was just after midnight, and the sentries were watching the fires and torchlight to see when most of the Lochlannach had settled down for the night.

The plan was for King Arthgal to take two thirds of the soldiers and attack to the right at the bottom of the causeway. His soldiers would breach the Lochlannach forces and create an opening through which the villagers in the fortress would attempt to escape the siege. At the same time, Prince Rhun would take the remaining soldiers and attack to the left where the Lochlannach were working to block the source of the fortress' well.

Prince Rhun knew that there was little chance of preventing the Lochlannach from eventually blocking the well's source. However, he believed that the soldiers might hold the fortress for many weeks longer if they delayed the Lochlannach from blocking the well too soon, and if the number of people needing water was reduced by helping the townspeople escape. It meant the difference between the survival of the kingdom and the annexation of the kingdom into the Lochlannach territories in northern and western Britain.

Prince Rhun looked up at the sentries. In the distance, he thought he heard the low rumble of thunder. Rain would help create enough confusion for the townspeople of Dumbarton to escape, but it might also slow them down and make it harder for the soldiers to retreat into the fortress. He was about to mention this to his father when the sentry above the gate gave the signal to start the attack.

Too late to worry about it now.

The fortress gates opened slowly. Prince Rhun looked back one last time at the waiting villagers. He spotted his wife, who was also Causantín mac Cináeda's sister. She had argued with him for days about leaving the fortress, preferring to share in her husband's fate, but eventually she saw the wisdom in escaping and leading the survivors to her brother's kingdom.

Rhun raised his hand to catch her attention, and she did the same. *I wonder if I'll ever see her again.* He turned and prepared to lead his men out of the fortress.

The Lochlannach had no guards posted at the base of the fortress or on the causeway leading down from the top of Dumbarton Rock. The Lochlannach had grown lax in their siege, believing that no soldiers would ever attempt to attack such a superior force – especially at night.

King Arthgal led his soldiers down the causeway quickly. They formed a wedge-shaped attack formation once they reached the bottom and moved to the right. Prince Rhun led his soldiers down next, moving quickly to the left along the base of Dumbarton Rock toward the source of the well. The townspeople who were going to attempt to escape the siege came down last and formed a group to the right of the causeway, waiting for the signal telling them that it was safe to move forward. The sentries remaining inside the fortress closed the gates as soon as the last of the townspeople were on the causeway.

Prince Rhun and his men reached the far end of Dumbarton Rock quickly. He knew that there were two encampments directly in front of him. One was part of the siege, and the other was for the Lochlannach who were trying to block the source of the well. He and his soldiers would have to sneak past the siege encampment to attack the Lochlannach closer to the river. The Lochlannach trying to block the well were the primary target for the night's work, but he knew that he'd have to attack the siege encampment when he and his soldiers retreated to the fortress.

He led his soldiers forward, trying not to alert the siege encampment that there was anyone moving about in the darkness.

As Prince Rhun led his soldiers around the siege encampment, King Arthgal and his soldiers quietly moved into position between two large Lochlannach encampments. The King's soldiers separated into two ranks and prepared to attack both encampments at the same time. This would create an opening for the townspeople to use when slipping through the siege lines on their way north. The King had told his people to head toward Alba since it was the only kingdom nearby not under Lochlannach control.

The soldiers were to attack in silence and try to kill as many Lochlannach as possible before anyone raised the alarm to summon reinforcements. Once the soldiers were in position, the King gave the signal, and the soldiers attacked. At the same time, the townspeople quietly ran forward between the King's forces, and disappeared into the night. Even the small children knew that they had to be silent or risk a lifetime of slavery in a distant land.

The attack came as a complete surprise to the sleeping Lochlannach, as well as to the guards who were supposed to be watching for any activity from the fortress. The guards were quickly cut down, and hundreds of Lochlannach were killed before any warning shouts were heard.

Prince Rhun and his soldiers attacked the encampment closest to the source of the well shortly after his father's attack began. They killed all of the Lochlannach in the encampment and destroyed the engines built to move the stones protecting the well's connection to the river. They then turned to attack the siege encampment and killed many sleeping Lochlannach before the alarm was raised.

There was chaos among the ranks of the Lochlannach at the base of Dumbarton Rock. They were being attacked in total darkness and in multiple places. They couldn't see their attackers, so most of them fled back toward the ruins of the city to alert the rest of their warriors. The soldiers under both King Arthgal and Prince Rhun attacked the fleeing Lochlannach for as long as they dared, and then they broke off the attack and returned to the fortress. Both forces reached the causeway at almost the same time, and soon they were safely inside the fortress with the gates closed behind them.

King Arthgal and Prince Rhun made their way up to the walls above the gates and looked down at the scene below. Torches were lit all around as the Lochlannach searched in vain for their attackers. None of the torches seemed to be moving in the direction that the townspeople went as they fled the fortress, and Prince Rhun knew that, once the rains started, there would be no evidence that anyone had passed that way.

The raid, which lasted just under two hours, had been a complete success. All of the townspeople had escaped, and the soldiers had killed over five hundred Lochlannach. Prince Rhun lost fifteen soldiers, while King Arthgal lost seventy. The Lochlannach attempt to block the well had been set back at least a week, and with the demand on the well now significantly reduced, the defenders had the ability to withstand the siege for several months.

Lightning flashed all around as the storm Prince Rhun had heard earlier finally reached Dumbarton. He and his father watched the Lochlannach frantically search for the unseen enemy as the rains washed away the clues that would tell them what had happened.

King Causantín mac Cináeda and the bulk of the Alban army were camped at the gathering place by the time Raibeart arrived with the horsemen from Airer Goídel. Raibeart and Ciaran went directly to see the King, leaving Ringean and Caitlin to lead their tired horsemen to the encampment of their clansmen.

Causantín saw Raibeart and Ciaran riding up in the early morning light. He walked out of his tent to greet them.

"Right on time, Raibeart," he said as the earl got down from his horse. "What have you to report?"

"There are two forces of Lochlannach at Dumbarton, My King," Raibeart replied. "It looks like half are Ívarr's and half are fresh warriors from Ireland."

"Amlaíb's men?" Causantín asked.

"Possibly, My King. I'm not sure. We didn't get that close to them. I'd estimate they have about ten thousand men and four hundred longships altogether. The city is destroyed, but the monastery and the fortress are still intact. There's no way of telling how many of King Arthgal's men are in the fortress, but the Lochlannach are besieging the fortress so there must be something inside that they want badly enough to wait. The surrounding towns and villages have been destroyed. We found survivors, and they're making their way to Alba since we're the only kingdom in Britain that's not under Lochlannach control."

Causantín nodded thoughtfully. "We only have seven thousand soldiers and four hundred horsemen in addition to the horsemen you took with you. How are we supposed to defeat ten thousand Lochlannach?"

"Actually, My King, Ciaran had some ideas about that," Raibeart said, motioning for Ciaran to come forward.

Looking at Ciaran, Causantín said, "I'd like to hear your ideas, Ciaran. Let's go into my tent, and we can talk while we eat."

The King led Raibeart and Ciaran into his tent and gestured for them to sit down. The King called for a servant to bring food and drink, and after the servant left to obey his King, Causantín asked Ciaran to present his ideas. The King listened carefully as Ciaran outlined his plan to trick the Lochlannach into thinking that the Albans had only a small force instead of their entire army. Ciaran also discussed his ideas of harassing the Lochlannach at night, destroying their ships and supplies while killing as many of their warriors as possible.

"Is there any way to coordinate our attacks with the forces inside the fortress?" Causantín asked.

"I'm not sure how we'd do that, My King," Ciaran answered. "There's no way to get near the fortress. Perhaps the men in the fortress might realize what we're doing and launch a night attack when they hear us attacking."

The servant returned with the food and drink, and Causantín ordered him to send word to all earls and chiefs to join him in one hour. The servant left, and Causantín motioned for Raibeart and Ciaran to eat.

When the earls and chiefs arrived, Causantín had Raibeart and Ciaran repeat their report and suggestions. There was much discussion regarding how to help the Alt Cluts break the siege. In the end, the Alban leaders realized that a pitched battle against the Lochlannach would be disastrous and would invite a general invasion of Alba if it failed.

After the meeting was over, each leader returned to his camp and informed his soldiers to be ready to move south at first light. Ciaran and Raibeart asked for directions to their camp and soon were surrounded by the men from Airer Goídel. Word of the situation at Dumbarton had already been spread by Caitlin and Ringean. Ciaran told everyone to be ready to leave at first light, and he then went to take care of his horse.

As he led his horse to the nearby stream, his children followed him. "Father," Maol-Chaluim began, "is the Bishop with the King?"

"I didn't see him. Why?"

"Because Iain mac Mànas has been making a pain of himself ever since we left home, and I thought that if we had a word with the Bishop, the Bishop might have a word with Iain and get him to calm down."

"What's Iain saying that's so terrible?" Ciaran asked.

"He's still going on about Caitlin and some of the other women coming with the army. He's saying we'll all be damned for not keeping women in their proper place, and he can't pray for the souls of anyone killed during battle in the company of women. He's trying to turn the men against you. The men saw right through him, and they're not listening, but he's still talking."

"We're not the only clan to bring women along who want to fight," Ciaran pointed out. "Is Iain going to ask the Bishop to excommunicate all of us from the church because he's upset that women are fighting?"

"I don't know, Father," Maol-Chaluim answered. "What do you want to do about Iain?"

Ciaran sighed. "Bring him here," he said finally.

"Yes, Father."

Maol-Chaluim left to find Iain, and Ciaran continued watering his horse and talking with his two younger children. Twenty minutes later, Maol-Chaluim returned with Iain, who didn't look happy to be summoned from whatever he had been doing.

"You asked to see me?" he said with an air of self-importance.

"Yes I did," Ciaran replied. Looking to Maol-Chaluim, he said, "Son, hand me your sword."

Maol-Chaluim drew his sword and handed it to his father.

"Thank you," Ciaran said. "Please take Iain and bend his neck over that rock."

Maol-Chaluim grabbed Iain by the shoulders and pushed him over to the rock where Ciaran was pointing. He forced Iain to his knees and held the priest down with Iain's chest on the rock and his neck exposed.

Ciaran rested the flat side of the sword blade on Iain's neck. "Didn't we have a conversation already about you speaking out against me and my decisions, Iain?"

"Yes, My Chief," Iain said, his voice shaking with fear.

"And is it true that you continued to speak out against my decision to allow women to accompany the men into battle, even though you had agreed not to?"

Iain squirmed, but Maol-Chaluim put his knee in Iain's back to hold him down. "You said that you'd only banish me," he cried out.

"If you can't keep your word to me, how do you expect me to keep my word to you?" Ciaran asked, moving the sword blade back and forth along Iain's neck.

Iain shuddered as the sword moved, and he thrashed about, trying in vain to break free of Maol-Chaluim's grip. "You can't kill a priest!" he said finally.

"I'm not killing a priest, I'm killing a traitor. When you betray your chief by trying to get the men of the clan to turn against him, you're a traitor. A priest would never break his word.

You did, so you can't be a priest. Give me one good reason why I should let you live after what you've done?"

"The Bishop will never let you get away with murdering a priest."

"Maybe he won't and maybe he will. You'll still be dead if you don't give me a reason to let you live."

Iain's mind when completely blank from fear. He couldn't think of a single thing to say in his defense. He knew that it has been a risk condemning Ciaran's decision to the men of the clan with the Chief's son nearby, but at the time, he believed he had been right.

Ciaran watched Iain's trembling body for a few minutes, and then he said, "I'll make you a deal, Iain. I rule this clan and my word is law, understand? You're responsible for the salvation through Christ of the people in the clan. You may continue to instruct the people in the clan about Christ and the Apostles and about how to live their lives in conformance with the word of God. You may not, however, contradict me in front of anyone, challenge my decisions or the way I lead the clan, speak out regarding the role of women in our clan, or preach the rules of the church of Rome if they aren't the words of our Lord, his apostles, or the prophets. Understand? I'll let you live if you swear to this. But know this: if you don't swear, I'll have your head right here and now. And if you ever break your word, I'll have your head the same day. Nod if you understand."

Iain nodded.

"Swear."

"I swear," Iain said.

"Good." Ciaran nodded to Maol-Chaluim, who released Iain.

Iain stood up and wiped off the dirt from his clothes as Ciaran returned the sword to his son. "Would you really have killed me, Ciaran?" the priest asked nervously.

Ciaran nodded. "Just as I'd kill anyone who tried to turn the clan against me. I have no time for traitors when there are two Lochlannach invasion forces less than a day's ride from here."

Ciaran led his horse back to the camp, followed by the priest and his children. No one spoke. Ciaran's children had never

54

seen their father take such drastic action to make a point before, and they were surprised that he'd go to such lengths to make Iain start behaving himself. Caitlin had been in favor of banishing the priest, but Ciaran wanted to give Iain one last chance.

Iain was deeply affected by what had happened by the stream. He was so caught up in what he saw as his role in clan society, that he forgot he still lived under the rule of men. Part of him wanted to ride immediately to see the Bishop, but he knew that he'd never be able to return home if he did that. If he caused the Bishop to condemn Ciaran, the entire clan would rise up and hunt him down along with the Bishop.

I got into this mess by breaking my word once. Maybe this time I should just keep my word. He reached up and felt where the sword had rested on his neck, deciding that keeping his word was probably the best course of action.

At dawn the next morning, the army of Alba moved south toward Dumbarton. More soldiers had arrived during the night, as had refugees from Alt Clut, who told the same story as Raibeart and Ciaran had about the towns and villages of Alba's neighbor.

King Causantín rode at the head of the main column of soldiers. Raibeart and Ciaran rode with the combined force of horsemen, many of whom were serving as scouts to alert the army if any Lochlannach should be sighted. They made their way slowly, in case they stumbled upon the enemy.

Late in the afternoon of the first day, riders spotted a large group of refugees heading north. They were being led by King Causantín's sister, who was married to Prince Rhun. The refugees were led to the spot where the Alban army was camped for the night.

The King was relieved and happy when he saw his sister. She told the Alban leaders about the night attack used to allow the villagers of Dumbarton to escape and about the Lochlannach attempt to block the source of the fortress' well.

The next morning, the refugees were given supplies and an escort to take them to Alba. The army continued its journey south. Shortly after sunrise two days later, the King and his earls stood on the same hill where Raibeart and Ciaran had stood, looking down at the ruin of Dumbarton and the invasion force surrounding the fortress.

"Heaven help us," Causantín said softly.

Chapter 7

King Causantín immediately understood why Ciaran had recommended using trickery to break the siege around Dumbarton. His army wasn't large enough to attack Amlaíb and Ívarr's combined forces, but if he could wipe out a portion of the Lochlannach invaders, then any subsequent pitched battle would be more evenly matched.

He wasted no time getting ready for the initial attack. He ordered one of his northern earls to advance a force of about two thousand men. Causantín planned to hide in the woods to the east with the rest of the foot soldiers while Raibeart hid in the woods to the west with the horsemen.

Causantín's orders were clear. If the Lochlannach threw in their full force, the northern earl was to withdraw from the field, and the army would regroup and try the plan again another day. However, if the Lochlannach threw in only as many warriors as they felt they needed to defeat two thousand soldiers, then Causantín and Raibeart would attack from the sides once the battle started, and they'd flank the Lochlannach warriors, destroying them. Then the army would either advance or withdraw, depending on how the remaining Lochlannach warriors responded.

Raibeart led the horsemen of Airer Goídel and the other clans to a place between two hills to the west of the northern Earl's position. Causantín led the rest of the foot soldiers to the tops of two hills to the east. Within an hour, the northern Earl moved his forces down the hill toward the monastery and the ruins of the town of Dumbarton, making no attempt to conceal his presence.

"My King," the guard said to Amlaíb as he rushed into the monastery, "Soldiers are approaching from the north!"

"How many?" Ívarr asked.

"Perhaps two thousand, My King," the guard answered.

"Are they from Alt Clut or Alba?" Amlaíb asked.

"They appear to be from Alba, My King."

"Ha!" Ívarr roared. "Are these all the soldiers Causantín can spare for his neighbor? He must think he's next to be invaded."

Ívarr shouted to one of his leaders to assemble a force of equal size and meet the Albans in battle. Looking at Amlaíb, he added, "You keep your men on the siege of the fortress in case King Arthgal tries anything. I'll take care of these Albans."

"Yes, Ívarr," Amlaíb replied.

As Ívarr left the monastery, Amlaíb looked troubled. *Why did the Albans send so few soldiers?*

Causantín watched from his hiding place on the edge of the woods as the Lochlannach warriors formed ranks to the north of the monastery. He saw the huge blond-haired fighters moving forward, and he estimated the force was only slightly larger than the one his northern earl was leading.

"I think they're doing exactly what we hoped they'd do," he said to the earls watching with him.

The northern Earl watched the Lochlannach force approaching and gave the order for his men to stop and hold their position. He wanted to make the Lochlannach cross the open fields so reinforcements would be farther away when Causantín and Raibeart attacked.

Ívarr led his men forward toward the Alban soldiers. His men were expert fighters, and he knew that it would be easy to defeat the Albans. When the soldiers halted their advance, Ívarr thought it was because they were afraid of his warriors. He didn't want the Albans to change their minds and leave the field, so he ordered his warriors to charge and ran with them toward the enemy, holding his great axe ready to personally kill the leader of the Alban army.

Raibeart watched the Lochlannach warriors move closer to the waiting soldiers. His instructions were to wait until all of the Lochlannach warriors were fully engaged with the soldiers before riding out and attacking from the west, cutting off the Lochlannach retreat and preventing reinforcements from coming to the aid of the warriors. He saw the soldiers brace themselves for the attack, and then he heard the familiar crashing sound as the warriors' weapons struck the soldiers' shields.

He watched for several more minutes as the front line of soldiers broke and the melee began. Then he turned to his horsemen and gave the signal to advance.

Caitlin rode with her father and brother near the front of the column of horsemen. She checked the two leather straps that held the shield in place on her arm. She had tightened the straps shortly before Raibeart gave the signal to attack, and she wanted to be sure that the shield wouldn't come loose during the battle. Satisfied that the shield was secure, she drew a long dagger with her shield hand so she could attack and defend herself at the same time. She then drew her sword. Many of the horsemen from her clan did the same, and the blades caught the sunlight as the horsemen left the safety of the trees and broke into the open fields.

Ívarr had just pulled his axe out of the chest of the earl leading the Alban soldiers when he saw movement out of the corner of his eye. Looking west, he saw the horsemen advancing on his position. He shouted to his warriors, but he found himself facing two soldiers and had no time to order his warriors to prepare for the horsemen's charge.

Causantín saw Raibeart riding out of his hiding place and gave the order for the army to advance. A thousand of his soldiers remained in hiding in case they were needed, but three thousand soldiers left the safety of the trees and moved quickly toward the battle.

Two of Ívarr's warriors came to his assistance and helped him kill the soldiers who had attacked him. He looked around for the horsemen and saw them moving into position behind his warriors, cutting off the way back to the encampment. Then he saw the rest of the Alban army approaching from the east.

"It's a trap!" he yelled to his warriors. He turned and started desperately fighting his way toward the horsemen. *We need to get back to the city!*

Causantín's army struck before Ívarr reached the horsemen, and soon the Lochlannach were surrounded and being torn apart by the Alban army. Realizing their position was hopeless, twenty warriors formed a circle around Ívarr to protect their King and to help him retreat back to the monastery. They fought bravely, but by the time they reached the horsemen, there were only ten warriors remaining.

Raibeart saw a group of warriors trying to escape and sent a squad of horsemen to intercept them. The warriors fought ferociously, and eventually four of the warriors broke through and ran back toward Dumbarton with the horsemen chasing them all the way.

The horsemen saw more warriors approaching the field, and wheeled their horses about and rode back to inform Raibeart that reinforcements were coming.

Raibeart ordered his horsemen to turn and attack the reinforcements while King Causantín's soldiers finished off the last surviving warriors. Only a few hundred warriors had reached the fields, and when they saw Raibeart's six hundred horsemen riding toward them with their swords raised, they held their ground for as long as possible before breaking and running for the safety of their encampment.

In the distance, Raibeart saw the berserkers approaching, and he knew it was time to withdraw. He gave the order to turn around, and he and his horsemen rejoined Causantín and his soldiers.

When they reached King Causantín, not a single Lochlannach warrior was still alive. The northern Earl had been killed, as had four hundred Alban soldiers and twenty horsemen. Hundreds more were wounded but were able to make an orderly retreat back to the safety of the hills and the trees. The Alban losses were surprisingly light, considering they had fought a pitched battle with over two thousand of the fiercest warriors in that part of the world.

Caitlin hadn't been injured, and she had killed two warriors during the initial attack on the Lochlannach flank. Her father and brothers were also unhurt, and her clan suffered no losses at all.

By the time Amlaíb and a large part of his forces had arrived on the battlefield, all that remained were the dead bodies of the Norsemen killed by the Alban army. The Albans had removed the bodies of their own dead and were gone. He thought about pursuing them, but he wasn't sure how many soldiers might be hiding behind the hills and waiting for him to do just that.

He ordered his men to start carrying the bodies of the fallen back to the encampment. *They fooled us once already. I'm not going to risk them fooling us a second time.*

That night, the funeral fires for the Lochlannach dead lit up the sky along the river. Causantín felt a great sense of satisfaction as he watched from the safety of the woods. He had reduced the Lochlannach numbers by two thousand. *Now we have almost the same numbers.*

He gave the signal for the horsemen and the thousand soldiers he had held in reserve to advance. He knew that the Lochlannach would never expect a night attack on the same day as a pitched battle, and he wanted his enemy to begin feeling fear.

Caitlin followed her father and brother carefully in the darkness. The horsemen were to create a diversion and protect the soldiers, who would be firing flaming arrows at the longships beached along the ruined city. She saw the lanterns carried by each squad of soldiers to ignite the arrows, but the horses kept the Lochlannach guards from seeing the light.

Three hours after sunset, the horsemen attacked the area where the Lochlannach were storing their supplies. They killed dozens of guards before entering one of the larger encampments and killing anyone within reach of their swords.

When the flaming arrows started flying toward the longships, the horsemen turned and attacked the men who were racing toward the ships to put out the fires. Once the ships were beyond saving, the horsemen rejoined the soldiers and retreated to the north.

Caitlin had just turned her horse to follow her father when a Lochlannach warrior attacked her. She barely had time to raise her shield to deflect his spear thrust. The sudden attack nearly knocked her off her horse. In the light of the burning ships, she saw the young warrior. She raised her sword and struck, hitting his shield and knocking him backward a few steps. She saw what looked like three bears on the shield with a hammer at the bottom, but she stayed focused and turned her horse to attack the guard again.

From her new angle, she saw the young warrior's face clearly. His helmet had been knocked off, and he was struggling to position his spear for the next attack. He looked up at her and stopped in his tracks. For a moment, the two just stared at each other, but the sounds of other Lochlannach approaching forced Caitlin to turn her horse again and ride off after her father and brother into the night.

Asbjorn watched her disappear and then turned to retrieve his helmet. He ran for the ships to help put out the fires, but most of them were already burning out of control. His cargo ship suffered only minimal damage, but twenty-five other ships were destroyed in the raid.

As he worked through the night to save the remaining ships and take inventory of the damaged or destroyed supplies, his mind kept going back to the face he saw in the firelight. *The Alban was a woman! She fought well. I wonder if all Alban women are fighters... and so beautiful.*

For the next several weeks, the Albans continued attacking at night. They never attacked the same part of the Lochlannach encampment twice, making it hard for the leaders to know where to place their warriors. On two occasions, the defenders inside the fortress joined in the battle once the Alban attacks had started, and Ívarr and Amlaíb were beginning to realize that the Albans and Alt Cluts had a combined force larger than the invasion force.

Thorleik continued working as quickly as possible to move the rocks protecting the source of the fortress' well to block the Alt Clut's water supply. Amlaíb wanted the siege to end as quickly as possible now that the Norse forces no longer had the advantage of numbers.

After about two months, the final capstones were successfully removed and the source of the well was uncovered. Thorleik immediately had his men fill in the tunnel with dirt and rocks.

King Arthgal and Prince Rhun watched the Lochlannach block the source of the well. For weeks, the defenders inside the fortress had been storing water in casks, cisterns, and anything else usable for storing water. Arthgal estimated that they could easily last another two months with the water on hand, and he believed that the Lochlannach might abandon the siege and sail back to Ireland if the Albans continued to harass the invaders and reduce their numbers. He couldn't think of another way to save his kingdom.

Three nights after the well had been blocked, King Arthgal made his rounds along the fortress' parapet. He saw a light rising into the sky and then falling inside the fortress walls. Soon other lights were rising and falling all around. He looked down and saw fires breaking out all around the fortress.

"They're shooting flaming arrows," Prince Rhun cried as he ran to his father and pulled him down from the walls.

Hundreds of flaming arrows rained down inside the walls, igniting fires all around the fortress. Smoke filled the courtyard, and Arthgal knew that his men would either choke on the smoke or have to open the gates and flee the fortress if the fires weren't put out soon. But the only way to put out the fires was to use the water that they had stored for drinking when the well was blocked.

He had to admire the Lochlannach strategy. *They planned this perfectly. Put out the fires and run out of water, or keep the water and be overcome by the flames and smoke. Either way, the siege is over.*

"Break open the casks and put out the fire," he ordered when he reached the courtyard.

"But Father, we'll run out of drinking water if we do that," Prince Rhun protested.

"And we'll all burn if we don't," his father countered. "There's no choice, son. If we don't put out the fires, we'll die. If we run out of water, some might be spared."

Prince Rhun nodded and left his father to join with the men who were battling the fires all around. King Arthgal stood in the center of the courtyard, wondering if there were any other options still open to him.

King Causantín watched the fires appear along the walls of the fortress. "They're making Arthgal waste his water putting out fires," he commented to his earls who were standing with him.

"Do you think they've blocked the source of the well?" Raibeart asked.

"I think the fire attack proves that," Causantín replied. "Arthgal can't hold out much longer."

"What can we do to help?" one of the eastern earls asked.

"Only what we've been doing," Causantín said. "The more ships we burn, the less tribute and fewer prisoners they can take back with them. And the more of their warriors we kill, the longer it'll take before they invade us as punishment for helping Alt Clut."

"When do you want us to attack again?" Raibeart asked.

"In an hour," Causantín replied.

Two days later, three captured Alt Clut guards were marched up the causeway to the gates of the fortress along with six Lochlannach warriors.

"They want to discuss terms for our surrender," one of the captives shouted to King Arthgal, who was standing on the wall overlooking the gates.

"What are their terms?" Arthgal shouted down.

"First, you must surrender yourself and everyone else in the fortress. Second, you must surrender the fortress. They'll select prisoners to be taken back to Ireland, but you may pay tribute to buy the freedom of some of the prisoners. Then you must agree to pay an annual tribute to them, and if you fail to pay the tribute, they'll return and subjugate the kingdom and make it part of the Lochlannach kingdoms of Britain."

"Will they guarantee our safety if we surrender?"

"No, My King," the captive replied.

"I see," Arthgal said. "May we have time to think about their demands?"

"No, My King. They want their answer now. They say if you don't surrender immediately, they'll burn the fortress down with you inside and subjugate the kingdom immediately."

Turning to his son, Arthgal said, "It doesn't look like we have any choice, does it?"

"No, Father. The Alban army isn't large enough to break the siege, and we're running out of supplies. At least this way some will live."

"Agreed," his father said.

Turning to the captives, he shouted, "Very well. We surrender. We'll come down the causeway and surrender our arms to their leaders."

The captives and the warriors returned to the base of Dumbarton Rock to inform the Lochlannach leaders of the surrender, and King Arthgal turned to address his men and inform them of his decision.

An hour later, King Arthgal led his men down the causeway to the base of Dumbarton Rock. They surrendered their weapons and were immediately taken prisoner by the Lochlannach. Warriors ran up the causeway and ransacked the fortress, seizing all of the treasure and other tribute that the soldiers had tried to hide. When the fortress was emptied of everything of value, the Lochlannach set it on fire and let it burn. The heat from the fire cracked the stone walls at the base of the fortress, and by the next morning, a few burned and scorched walls lying in ruins along the summit of the hill were all that remained of the once mighty fortress.

King Arthgal was held with the prisoners who'd be taken back to Ireland, but Prince Rhun was released on the condition that he'd ensure the annual tribute was paid. A ransom amount was set for the prisoners, and Prince Rhun was able to free several hundred of them from the remnants of the royal treasury that was kept hidden in case of attack. But he was unable to purchase his father's freedom. That would have to wait until the first tribute payment was made.

Ívarr was pleased with his share of the tribute but was furious to discover that only the soldiers remained in the fortress. Women fetched a much better price at the slave markets, but this expedition had yielded few women. He wanted to search the countryside for where the women might be hiding, but the presence of the Alban army nearby made that impossible.

Finally, he realized that it was time to be satisfied with the victory over Alt Clut and start for home. He had been gone for more than a year and was ready to see Áth Cliath again. He ordered his longships to start loading for the trip back to Ireland, and he instructed Amlaíb to take care of getting the prisoners home.

As he watched his longship being prepared to leave, he glanced to the north. *Alba is the only part of Britain that's not under my control. It's time to start planning for the next expedition. All of Britain will be mine, and I swear to Odin that no Alban army will deny me my destiny!*

CHAPTER 8

The night that Ívarr's fleet left Alt Clut, the Alban horsemen attacked again, hoping to destroy more longships and free some of the prisoners waiting to be carried back to Ireland. Amlaíb anticipated the move, however, and had a large force hiding in the shadows.

King Causantín sent in almost two thousand foot soldiers and all of the horsemen to burn ships and rescue prisoners. At the same moment the soldiers began shooting flaming arrows at the longships along the river, the Lochlannach attacked with the berserkers in the lead.

The berserkers attacked anything that moved or carried a weapon, including other berserkers and many Lochlannach warriors. The Alban soldiers fought bravely, and started using the archers with their flaming arrows on the berserkers to gain an advantage in the fight. Many berserkers were killed, and the light helped to locate and attack the nearby Lochlannach warriors.

Caitlin knew that fighting at night was difficult for any army, and she worried that the horsemen from her clan would have a hard time identifying friend from foe in the low light. *I hope I don't accidently kill one of my own clansmen.*

Caitlin and the horsemen from her clan fought with the warriors guarding the prisoners. She killed five warriors, but then she found herself surrounded and cut off from the rest of her clansmen. She hacked with her sword at the warriors, killing two more. She turned her horse to ride back to the safety of the other horsemen when she felt herself being grabbed and pulled to the ground. Her horse bolted, and she was alone with the spear of a Lochlannach warrior pressed against her throat.

"Drop your sword," she heard a voice command.

She obeyed and felt the spear lift off her. A strong hand grabbed her arm and pulled her to her feet. Looking at her captor, she recognized him. It was the same warrior she had fought on her first raid. She saw in his face that he recognized her as well. They stared at each other for a moment before her captor spoke.

"You are my prisoner. Do you understand?" Asbjorn asked.

"Yes," Caitlin answered, hoping to be rescued by any members of her clan who were still nearby.

Asbjorn motioned for her to walk forward toward a holding pen filled with prisoners. She heard the battle in the distance, but from the sounds, she knew it was moving further away from her.

As she walked to the holding pen, she saw that a few ships had been burned, but not as many as the Albans had hoped to destroy. Given the number of prisoners in the holding pen, it was clear that no prisoners had been freed.

Caitlin stopped at the gate to the holding pen, and her captor spoke to an older warrior in the tongue of the Lochlannach. The older warrior nodded and then opened the gate.

"You are the prisoner of Asbjorn Thorleikson," her captor said as he pushed her through the gate. "Your fate belongs to me. Remember that and accept whatever happens. Do you understand?"

Caitlin turned and looked at him. "I understand, but I'll never rest until I escape and return to my people."

Asbjorn smiled. He was impressed to see a woman warrior with the Albans, and her determination made her even more attractive. "Perhaps I'll keep you for myself," he said as he closed the gate. "But if you try to escape, you'll be sold at the slave markets, and you'll never see this land again."

Caitlin watched him walk away and started trembling. When she had asked to join her father and her clan in battle, she never considered the possibility of being captured and carried away to Ireland as a prisoner and a potential slave. She looked around at the faces of the Alt Clut prisoners and saw the look of total defeat in their eyes. She saw the guards surrounding the holding pen, and knew that escape would be difficult.

I have to find a way out of here.

"Where is your sister?" Ciaran asked Ringean when the horsemen returned to their camp later that night. "I have unhappy news for her."

"What news, Father?" Ringean asked.

"Her betrothed is dead. One of the berserkers killed him in the attack tonight. She needs to know."

"I haven't seen her since we returned to camp. I'll help you look for her."

For the next two hours, Ciaran and Ringean looked for Caitlin among the horsemen and foot soldiers of their clan. As the sun rose the next morning, it was clear that she was nowhere to be found.

"Do you think she was captured, Father?"

"I hope so," Ciaran replied grimly. "If she's still alive, she can be rescued."

Caitlin woke up the next morning and saw several dozen Alban prisoners with her in the holding pen, including four from her own clan. She walked over to them and was grateful that they weren't injured.

"Is there any way we can escape from here?" one of them whispered to her.

She shook her head. "We're too well guarded. Our only hope is if another raid creates enough confusion for us to slip past the guards."

Over the next several days, Caitlin saw Asbjorn a number of times. He was one of the guards who selected the prisoners that would be loaded into longships and taken to Ireland. She wondered why he never selected her but was grateful to be one of the last loaded.

I wonder if he's going to put me on his own ship.

Asbjorn captured a total of six prisoners during the expedition. Thorleik was proud of his son. He was also surprised to discover that one of the prisoners was a young female Alban fighter.

"What do you intend to do with her?" Thorleik asked when he came to see his son shortly before the rest of Amlaíb's forces were to leave Alt Clut.

"I'm thinking of keeping her for myself, Father," Asbjorn replied.

Thorleik laughed and slapped his son on the shoulder. It was not uncommon for Norsemen to take wives from among their captives, and he knew that Asbjorn was at the age when he needed to be thinking about taking a wife and starting his own family. The tribute he'd earn from the expedition and from the sale of his other prisoners would allow Asbjorn to start a comfortable life, and a few more successful expeditions would earn him the lifestyle due a warrior from an important family.

Bjornkarl had also learned of Asbjorn's prisoners, and when Bjornkarl heard from his father that Asbjorn planned to keep the female prisoner for himself, he knew that he finally had something to take from his younger brother.

On the afternoon before Bjornkarl's ship sailed back to Ireland, Asbjorn saw his brother walking toward the holding pen of the prisoners. Bjornkarl had gone there many times to find female prisoners to have his way with, but Asbjorn knew that there was only one female prisoner remaining in the holding pen. He grabbed his spear and ran for the holding pen as fast as he could.

Bjornkarl motioned for the guard to open the gate of the holding pen. Bjornkarl walked over to where Caitlin was sitting with the other members of her tribe. He looked at her with an evil grin, savoring the moment. He hated his younger brother, for reasons even he didn't fully understand, and he knew that taking this female prisoner would hurt Asbjorn considerably.

Smiling with his usual twisted smile, he grabbed Caitlin and roughly pulled her to her feet. He clutched her arm tightly as he led her back to the gate.

Bjornkarl led Caitlin toward the tents. She struggled to break free, suspecting for the first time what was about to happen. They had reached the far end of the holding pen when she heard a familiar voice behind her.

"Bjornkarl, she's mine! Let her go!"

Bjornkarl spun around, skill clutching Caitlin's arm. Asbjorn stood there with his spear in his hand, looking enraged as he tried to catch his breath.

"Who are you to tell me what I can and cannot do?" Bjornkarl asked contemptuously.

"Not her, Bjornkarl. She's mine."

"I'll do whatever I want to whoever I want. Understand, Asbjorn?" Bjornkarl snarled.

"Not with her you won't." Asbjorn said, tightening his grip on his spear.

Caitlin didn't understand the language of the Lochlannach, but it was clear what was happening. The warrior who was clutching her arm planned to rape her, but Asbjorn was trying to prevent that from happening. Her captor was now her protector. She remained still, looking for a way to escape should the two warriors decide to start fighting over her.

"Put down your spear, brother," Bjornkarl said coldly. "I'm a berserker, and you have no right to stop me from doing whatever I want to any prisoner."

"Not with her," Asbjorn repeated.

Bjornkarl laughed. Then he turned away and led Caitlin toward his tent.

Asbjorn threw down his spear and launched himself at Bjornkarl's exposed back. Caitlin was thrown clear as Bjornkarl fell forward. She wanted to run away, but as she moved clear of the two warriors, she saw several Lochlannachs approaching to see what the commotion was all about. She had no choice but to stay where she was and watch what was happening.

Bjornkarl got back on his feet and faced his brother, furious that Asbjorn would attack him in front of others. Asbjorn ducked the first swipe of Bjornkarl's fist. Bjornkarl stepped forward quickly, and the second swipe sent Asbjorn flying backward. Asbjorn rolled away to avoid Bjornkarl's kick to his ribs and got back to his feet.

Bjornkarl ran for Asbjorn, but Asbjorn slipped past him. Before Bjornkarl turned around, though, Asbjorn jumped on his brother's back and reached his arm around Bjornkarl's neck. Bjornkarl tried to flip Asbjorn over his shoulder as he had done before, but Asbjorn stayed on his back and kept tightening his grip on Bjornkarl's neck.

Bjornkarl launched himself backwards and fell on top of Asbjorn. The fall and the weight of his brother on top of him knocked the wind out of Asbjorn, and he released his grip on Bjornkarl's neck. Bjornkarl leapt to his feet and kicked Asbjorn in the head and the chest repeatedly.

Asbjorn was nearly unconscious and bleeding heavily. Bjornkarl drew his dagger and knelt over his brother. He was about to plunge the dagger into his brother's chest when he was slammed into with enough force to knock him to the ground away from his brother. He turned to face his new attacker and found himself face to face with his father.

"Odin's Ravens and Thor's Hammer, Bjornkarl!" Thorleik shouted at his eldest son. "That's the second time I've had to stop you from killing your brother. Are you mad to dishonor my name and our house like this?"

"He attacked me first, Father. It's my right."

"Why?" Thorleik demanded.

Pointing to Caitlin, he said, "I was taking one of the prisoners to my tent and he tried to stop me. No one may stop a berserker from doing as he wishes with a female prisoner. He knew that, and he attacked me anyway from behind. He deserves to die."

"You know the law perfectly well, Bjornkarl. That prisoner belongs to Asbjorn, and he already stated his intention to keep her for himself. That makes her your brother's property, and you have no rights or claims to any property of a member of our family. I've told you this before. You know the only reason you tried to take her was to hurt your brother and make him attack you. You bring shame on me, my house, and my family by your treachery towards your brother."

"I'm a berserker, Father..." Bjornkarl began.

"And I'm your father and a member of Amlaíb's council!" Thorleik shouted, interrupting his son. "Your warrior rank doesn't change the law or your place under my rule. I've warned you before to leave your brother alone, and this is the last time. Make any attempt to harm your brother or take something of his again, and I'll have you banished. Do you hear me?"

Bjornkarl stared at his father in disbelief. Berserkers had been banished before, but it was rare and never when the berserker was the son of one of the Norse leaders. He looked at his brother, who was slowly getting to his feet, and then back to his father.

"You wouldn't dare!" Bjornkarl snarled.

"Yes I would," Thorleik answered coldly as he stared angrily at his oldest son.

Seeing no way to win the situation, Bjornkarl shrugged. "Very well, Father, but you make sure that he stays away from me from now on. The next time I see him and we're alone, I promise you one of us won't survive the meeting."

"And if you kill your brother while I'm alive, Bjornkarl," Thorleik said, "I won't rest until you're dead by my hands. Are we clear?"

Bjornkarl stared at his father with a look of amusement and contempt on his face. His mouth curled into a familiar sneer. "Yes, Father," he said finally, his voice filled with sarcasm.

With that, Bjornkarl turned and strode back to his tent. Thorleik checked to make sure Asbjorn was all right, and then left to follow Bjornkarl.

Caitlin walked over to Asbjorn and hesitatingly reached out her hand and touched his arm. "Are you all right?" she asked.

Asbjorn looked at her and nodded with a faint smile. "It hurts, but I'll heal."

"Who was that?"

"That was my brother, Bjornkarl. My father, Thorleik, is the one who stopped the fight."

"Thank you for saving me. I guess I'm the reason for the fight."

"Yes, but it's an old fight. He has everything he wants, but what he wants the most is what I have. He's one of the berserkers, and they feel entitled to everything. They raped most of the women prisoners that we took, but there was no way I was letting him have you."

"Why not?" Caitlin asked.

Asbjorn looked at her for a moment and then said, "Because I was planning to keep you for myself. I don't want you to be sold as a slave in some faraway land."

This surprised Caitlin, but she said nothing. She looked around and noticed that most of the guards had gone back to their duties. She knew that she could escape with little effort, but something kept her from running.

Asbjorn looked in her eyes and knew what she was thinking. He wondered if she'd run, but he knew that it would be too hard for her to get away while the sun was up. He was attracted to her, but he also knew that any life with him included the probability of Bjornkarl trying to finish what he started. As badly as he wanted Caitlin, he didn't want her to be put in that position again.

He heard a sound above him and looked up to see two ravens flying in circles. A moment later, one of the ravens flew north, leaving the other behind. Understanding the ravens' message, he said softly, "You and I will go for a little walk, and when we get far enough from ships, start running as fast as you can. Your people should be able to reach you before the other guards can."

"You're letting me go free?" she asked, sounding shocked.

Asbjorn nodded. "Don't ask me why. Just go and don't let yourself get captured again. Your next captor won't be kind to you."

"What about the other members of my clan?" she asked.

"I can't do anything for them. I'm sorry. I'm taking a big enough risk letting you escape."

Asbjorn retrieved his spear. He took Caitlin by the arm and led her toward the longships. When they reached the ships, he turned and led her along the riverbank away from the city and the ruins of the fortress. The sun was setting on the other side of the river as the two reached a point well away from any of the Lochlannach warriors who were patrolling the area.

"I want you to push me down and kick me," he said as he loosened his grip on her arm. "Then start running. I'll make it look like I'm injured so no one will ask any questions when I come back without you."

"Thank you again," Caitlin said. "I owe you my life."

"I hope it's a long and happy one," Asbjorn said. "Now go."

Caitlin spun around and pushed Asbjorn to the ground. Not wanting to hurt him, she kicked the dirt next to his head several times and then ran across the fields toward the safety of the trees.

Asbjorn sat up and watched her run for a minute before struggling to his feet and slowly making his way back to the longships and the holding pen. He looked back a couple of times, and saw Caitlin disappear in the distance. None of the warriors chased after her, and Asbjorn was confident that no one had seen her escape.

By the time he reached the holding pen, he had his story worked out about what happened to his prisoner, but no one asked. While Asbjorn had been away, Amlaíb had given orders to break camp, load the rest of the prisoners, and be ready to sail shortly after noon the next day. The expedition was over, and the warriors were returning home.

Raibeart stood next to his horse just inside the trees when he saw a figure running across the field toward him. He looked at the figure for several minutes before he realized that it was Caitlin. He quickly mounted his horse and galloped out to meet her.

When he reached her, he held out his hand. She caught it, and he pulled her onto the back of his horse. Then he turned and rode back to the trees as fast as he could. When they reached safety, he turned and said, "You gave us quite a scare, Caitlin. Your father will be very happy to see that you're still alive."

"Thank you, My Lord," she said, tightening her grip around his waist. "I'm happy to still be alive, too."

"I'll take you to your father, but I want to hear all about what happened."

Raibeart rode as quickly as possible through the trees and underbrush until he reached the camp of Caitlin's clan. Raibeart shouted for Ciaran, who came running immediately along with his two sons. When Ciaran saw Caitlin on the back of Raibeart's horse, he reached up and pulled Caitlin off, hugging her and laughing with joy for her safe return.

That evening, Caitlin had to tell the story of her capture and escape several times for her clan. "I don't know why he let me go," she said when she was finished telling the tale, "but it was clear that he didn't want his brother or anyone else hurting me, and he didn't want me taken far away from here to be sold as a slave."

"Well, whatever his reasons, he has my gratitude," Ciaran said.

"He couldn't risk letting the others from our clan escape, though," Caitlin added. "They're still being held as prisoners, and most of the prisoners have already been taken away to Ireland."

"Should we go after them, Father?" Maol-Chaluim asked.

"What do you think, Raibeart?" Ciaran asked.

"I think I can convince the King to let us attack the holding pen tonight," Raibeart replied confidently. "Let's go get our men back!"

CHAPTER 9

Amlaíb sat at the table in the center of the monastery's main chamber, enjoying his final supper in Alt Clut before returning home. He looked up when Prince Rhun was ushered into the chamber.

"Welcome, Your Highness," he said through an interpreter from Alt Clut as he gestured for the Prince to sit down.

Prince Rhun sat on the wooden bench opposite Amlaíb and stared at the Lochlannach leader in silence. This amused Amlaíb, who continued eating. Finally, Rhun said, "Is there something you wanted of me other than to watch you eat?"

"Yes there is. We're leaving tomorrow, but before we go, I want to make sure you understand a few things. First, your father has already been taken back to Ireland, and we'll be holding onto him until next year when your first tribute is due. If you meet our ransom demands and your tribute is sufficient, we'll return your father to you. Otherwise, we'll return only his head. Second, I want to make sure you understand what will happen if you miss paying your tribute or if it's not the amount set by Ívarr."

"I understand," Prince Rhun said bitterly. "You'll come back in force, take our lands, and kill everyone you left alive."

"That's correct," Amlaíb said, taking a drink. Some of the liquid ran down his beard, and he wiped it off with the back of his hand before slamming the tankard down on the table.

"We'll send a ship back here in a year to pick up the tribute," he continued. "And if we don't receive the right amount, or if the ship we send doesn't make it back within a week, we'll be back with every warrior we have to take your entire kingdom."

"I think we understand each other perfectly well," Prince Rhun said.

"Good. Keep your people well away from our ships, and don't attempt to free any of the remaining prisoners. For every prisoner we lose between now and when we leave, we'll take ten in his or her place... starting with you."

"You won't have any problems from my people," Prince Rhun assured him. "We just want you to leave."

"Very well, Your Highness. You may go now," Amlaíb said, taking another bite of the meat on his platter.

Prince Rhun stood and stared at Amlaíb a moment before turning and leaving the monastery. Amlaíb reached for the tankard and watched the Prince leave the chamber.

Something tells me we'll be back here within a year or two.

Raibeart and Causantín watched the Lochlannach preparations later that night from the safety of the trees. "They're definitely getting ready to leave," the King said. "They've moved their tents closer to the longships, and there are more guards around the supplies and the prisoners."

Raibeart nodded. "It looks like most of the prisoners have already been taken away to Ireland, and they're taking no chances with losing the remaining ones."

"I'm not sure another night attack will be worth the losses we'll have," the King said, turning to face Raibeart. "There are too many guards, and the warriors are too concentrated near the river to risk it."

"I agree," Raibeart said sadly. "I wanted to get our men back, but I'm afraid there's no way we can."

"I didn't say we wouldn't attack them," Causantín noted. "I said we couldn't attack them tonight."

"Then when do you want to attack?" Raibeart asked.

"If they start leaving tomorrow, the cargo ships will be the last to leave with the supplies and the remaining prisoners. Once most of the ships with the warriors have sailed, we'll attack the rest of the ships and kill as many of their warriors as we can. Your horsemen will lead the attack with the archers, and the foot soldiers will be close behind. Once the Lochlannach see the size of our force waiting on the shore, they won't risk turning around for a fight. It'll hurt them, and maybe we can rescue our men at the same time."

"That's a lot of ground to cover for an attack," Raibeart pointed out.

"That's why we're going to start moving into position tonight," the King replied. "Your horsemen will stay here because there's no way to hide the horses. The archers and foot soldiers will deploy after midnight and hide in the tall grasses around Dumbarton until your horsemen start the attack. The archers will provide cover for you, and you'll bring lanterns with you so the archers can light their arrows. By the time the Lochlannach realize it's a full scale attack, it'll be too late, and their losses should be quite high."

Raibeart nodded in admiration. "An excellent plan, My King," he said.

A little after midnight, the soldiers and archers moved into position. The soldiers moved to the east to surround the ruins of Dumbarton while the archers moved south toward the Lochlannach camps and the longships. It took almost four hours for all of the soldiers to reach their designated places, but by the time the sun rose in the east, there was no sign of the danger lying so close to where the Lochlannach were preparing to leave.

The horsemen were camped just inside the trees, waiting for the signal to begin their attack. Ciaran had told Caitlin earlier that she wouldn't be joining the rest of the horsemen for the attack, but she protested loudly.

"There's no way I'm staying behind, Father," she said, standing with her face close to her father's.

"Caitlin, be reasonable. You were captured and you escaped once. I don't want you in that kind of danger again."

"Are Maol-Chaluim and Ringean staying behind?" she asked.

"No, they're both part of the attack."

"Then how can you ask me to stay behind when the rest of my family is going into battle, Father? Or has Iain finally convinced you that my fighting is a sin against God and the church?"

"You know perfectly well he hasn't convinced me of that, young lady," Ciaran snapped. "I want you safe, that's all."

"And I won't be safe until the Lochlannach are gone, Father. If I can help make them leave or kill the ones who don't leave, then I'm doing more to keep myself safe than I would by hiding in the woods like a frightened child. Besides, they owe me for the life of my betrothed, and I claim the right of vengeance against them."

Ciaran looked at the determination on the face of his daughter and realized that he wasn't going to win this argument. "Will you at least promise to stay as close to me as you can?" he asked finally.

"Yes, Father," she said with a twinkle in her eye.

Causantín and a company of mounted guards waited on top of a nearby hill to survey the Lochlannach activities. Prince Rhun, who had gone searching for the Albans in case they were still in the area, stood with his brother-in-law on the hilltop accompanied by three companies of soldiers who'd join the Albans in the attack.

"I wish we'd found a way to coordinate our attacks before the fortress fell," Prince Rhun said to Causantín as they waited and watched. "We might have broken the siege and forced them all to swim home."

"I know," Causantín said. "We just couldn't find a way to get information to you. What was it like being trapped inside the fortress?"

"Bad enough. We were helpless to defend our people, and we had to watch hundreds of our men, women and children loaded onto the longships and taken away to Ireland. We hid most of the treasury from them, but they took quite a bit, and it'll be a long time before we recover from this raid. You should see the ransom demand they have for my father!"

"Steep?" Causantín asked.

"Beyond that," Prince Rhun replied. "It'll take most of the treasury we have left to have him returned alive, and that's in addition to the annual tribute that we have to pay to keep from being invaded again."

"Are you going to pay the ransom?" Causantín asked, looking at his brother-in-law.

"What do you mean by that?" Rhun demanded.

"I mean are you willing to wipe out your treasury for one man? You're ready to be king, and you'll make a good one. I'll give you whatever help you need, and thanks to your marriage with my sister, our two kingdoms will be closer than ever. I can't understand why you'd risk all you have just to get back a king when there's someone ready to take his place right here."

"You're taking about my father!" Rhun protested.

"No, I'm talking about what's best for your people. Is depleting your treasury what's best for them? I don't think so. You're king now while he's gone, so your people have a leader. You have a treasury to use for rebuilding your country. Would you throw it away just to bring your father home? What kind of home would he have waiting for him? A broken wasteland? You can't risk your kingdom and your subjects for one person, even if that person is your father. If you're going to be a king, then you need to start thinking like a king. Your people come first. I'm sorry about your father, but he's not worth the loss of your kingdom."

"They'll kill him if I don't pay," Rhun said, shocked at what Causantín was suggesting.

"We all die in the end," Causantín reminded his brother-in-law. "Your job is to provide for your people, not the Lochlannach."

Rhun knew Causantín was right, even though he didn't like the idea of betraying his father in this way. Arthgal had been a good king and a good father. Rhun knew that he was ready to be king, and knew he and Causantín would work well together to rebuild and defend both kingdoms. *Am I really ready to let the Lochlannach kill my own father just to be king?*

No, not just to be king, but to help my people rebuild.

Looking at Causantín, Prince Rhun nodded and said, "I hate it, but you're right. I need to do what's best for my people, and that doesn't include paying the ransom for my father."

"You're making the right decision, *King* Rhun," Causantín said with a smile. *And when you die in a few years with no children old enough for the throne, I'll use your wife as the reason to annex your kingdom into mine, adding your people and lands to Alba. The kingdom of Alt Clut won't survive you, brother.*

81

Amlaíb's longship pulled into the main river and made its way toward the channel shortly before mid-morning. The longships for his council members and the berserkers were the next to depart. All along the riverfront, the warriors were busy loading cargo, tribute, and prisoners onto the remaining longships – too busy to notice the Alban soldiers creeping closer to the riverfront through the tall grass.

The north wind blew briskly, and Asbjorn hoped it would help the fleet get home more quickly. He was busy getting the rest of the unused supplies loaded onto his cargo ship before loading the remaining prisoners that he had been guarding. He wished there were more warriors to help defend against an attack by the Albans, but he knew Amlaíb wanted to vacate Alt Clut as quickly as possible.

Over half the fleet was sailing toward the channel when Causantín gave the order for the attack to begin. Raibeart led his horsemen from their hiding place toward the longships along the riverfront. Several of his horsemen carried lanterns for the archers to use to ignite their arrows, but the rest had their swords ready for the attack.

It was a while before the warriors loading the longships noticed the horsemen approaching, and when they started to shout and point, the archers rose up from their hiding place and filled the sky with arrows. The warriors grabbed their shields to protect themselves from the deadly hail of arrows landing all around them, and then they saw the foot soldiers rise up and advance on their position.

Knowing that they were hopelessly outnumbered, the warriors abandoned their supplies and climbed onto their longships, hoping to push off and reach the safety of the main river before the soldiers reached the riverfront.

Raibeart's horsemen reached the archers and gave them the lanterns before taking a position just north of the longships. The archers fired their flaming arrows at the exposed decks of the longships, which caught fire quickly. The warriors worked feverishly to put the fires out, but the archers kept firing and soon several of the longships were burning out of control. The sound of timbers cracking from the heat of the fires could be heard above the shouts of the Lochlannach on shore and onboard the longships.

Warriors attempting to escape the infernos jumped back to shore and ran to the undamaged longships, hoping to secure passage on those ships rather than having to face the soldiers approaching the riverfront.

Asbjorn's ship and the other remaining cargo ships were too damaged to salvage. He followed the warriors who were trying to reach the other longships, but the sound of riders behind him told him that he'd never reach safety in time. He and the warriors with him turned to fight, but when they saw the size of the force approaching them, they opted to surrender and hope for mercy from the Albans.

Asbjorn threw his shield and spear down and knelt on the ground. He then took off his sword belt and placed it on his shield. A squad of Alban horsemen surrounded the surrendering warriors as the rest of the horsemen continued on toward the warriors who were still trying to escape or who had turned to fight.

Nearly forty ships had to be abandoned because of fire, and the ships that did manage to get away were filled with more than twice their usual number of warriors. More than a hundred warriors had been killed, and there were almost fifty taken captive during the assault. The remaining prisoners in the holding pen were freed, including all of the Alban prisoners from Caitlin's clan.

By the time Causantín and King Rhun arrived at the riverfront, the battle was over, and the last surviving longship was sailing out of sight. The other longships were floating downriver and burning out of control, or were beached and burning. The north wind blew the thick black smoke away from the Alban army and the captured Lochlannach.

"What do you want done with the captives?" Causantín asked King Rhun.

"Kill them all," Rhun replied, leaving Causantín to check on his people.

Raibeart rode up to Causantín with a smile. "Your plan worked perfectly, My King," he said.

"Thank you, Raibeart. All of the surviving Lochlannach were captured by your horsemen. To you goes the honor of dispatching them to their gods."

"Yes, My King. I'll see to it at once!"

Raibeart rode off to tell his men to bring the captive Lochlannach to the holding pen for execution. Causantín turned his horse and rode after King Rhun. Riders would need to be sent to inform the local villages and the refuges that the Lochlannach threat was over, and Causantín would need to work out a plan to withdraw the Alban soldiers from Alt Clut as soon as possible.

Raibeart's men led Asbjorn and the other captives to the holding pen where the prisoners had been kept since the expedition into Alt Clut began. He wondered what his fate would be at the hands of the Alban army, but he assumed the worst. *Why did I surrender? I don't mind dying in battle, but I don't like the idea of dying like a caged animal.*

He looked around the holding pen at the faces of the other captives. Many were the younger warriors like himself, but a few were older warriors who had seen many successful expeditions. His friend, Hundulfr Játmundsson, sat on the ground several feet away, holding his arm. He was injured during the attack, and Asbjorn saw blood on Hundulfr's arm, one of his legs, and his face.

Asbjorn heard a familiar sound, and when he looked up, he saw a raven land on the railings of the holding pen. "Have you come to tell me that I'm going to die here?" he asked the raven as it stared at him from its perch. A moment later, it was joined by another raven flying in from the north. Asbjorn wondered if these were the same two ravens he had seen when he allowed his female prisoner to escape.

The ravens cocked their heads, but didn't make a sound. "Did you come to tell me that I'm *not* going to die?" he asked, surprised that they were just staring at him. The ravens beat their wings, but still made no sounds. Asbjorn found himself more confused than before, but he kept an eye on the ravens, looking for a sign from them about his future.

After what seemed like hours, the horsemen surrounded the holding pen and started removing the captives five at a time.

Asbjorn watched as the captives were forced to their knees. Five Albans stepped forward and swung their large swords, removing the captives' heads from their bodies. Then the next five captives were selected to meet the same fate.

The Albans continued taking five at a time and beheading the captives before returning to the holding pen for the next group. There were only four captives remaining when they came for Asbjorn. The ravens were no longer on their perches, and Asbjorn wondered if those were the last messengers from Odin that he'd ever see.

Asbjorn found himself going numb from the realization that he was about to die. He felt the hands grabbing him and leading him to the place of execution, and he saw the bodies and the blood all over the ground, but somehow it didn't seem real to him. He was pushed to his knees, and he looked up at his executioner, curious. *Will I feel the blade take my head? Will it hurt? Will the Valkyries come looking for me among the slain?* These were the thoughts running through his mind as he watched the executioners step forward to send him and his companions to their fate.

A shadow crossed in front of him, and he saw the two ravens fly low to the ground and then begin circling above Asbjorn and his executioner. Asbjorn's brain registered that the ravens were there, but he had no idea why Odin would bother to send his messengers just as Asbjorn was about to die.

Asbjorn heard a shout and saw a figure running toward him. The sun was at her back, making her outline glow and hiding her face in shadow. *Has the executioner done his job already? I didn't feel a thing. Does death come that easily?*

The glowing vision moved closer, and Asbjorn couldn't take his eyes off of her. *Is this a Valkyrie? Have I been found worthy to be chosen after only one expedition?* Asbjorn stared at her as she stopped in front of him. *Thank you, almighty Odin.*

He looked up at her, and as a cloud crossed in front of the sun, he saw her face clearly. But it was not the face of a Valkyrie he saw. It was the face of the prisoner that he had set free.

CHAPTER 10

"Stop," Caitlin cried when she recognized Asbjorn. She dismounted from her horse and ran towards him.

The executioners stood still and didn't raise their swords. They looked at Raibeart in confusion, waiting for him to tell them what to do.

"What are you doing, child?" Raibeart demanded, standing next to Ciaran who looked equally confused.

"This is the Lochlannach who set me free," Caitlin said, standing next to Asbjorn. "You said you were grateful to him. If you are, then show it now and spare his life."

Raibeart looked at Ciaran. "What do you want to do?" he asked.

Ciaran turned to Caitlin. "And what would he do if we spared him? He's far from his home and he's in a country that wants him dead. It would be more merciful to kill him now and send him to his gods. How will he survive here? He won't even be able to communicate with anyone."

"He speaks our language, Father," Caitlin said. "He can communicate with us just fine."

Looking at her father and at Raibeart, she saw they were skeptical about the wisdom of saving this young Lochlannach warrior. Finally, she said, "At least give him a choice. If he's willing to live as one of us, then he should have the chance. It's a life for a life. He saved my life, and I owe him his life. But, if he'd rather go to his gods, then he can follow the others into death and my obligation to him is satisfied."

"What's his name?" Raibeart asked.

"Asbjorn Thorleikson," Caitlin replied.

Hearing his name snapped Asbjorn's consciousness back to what was going on. He looked up and recognized Caitlin's face. She smiled at him and he smiled back.

"Asbjorn Thorleikson, stand up," Raibeart said.

Asbjorn stood and faced Raibeart.

"Do you understand what I'm saying to you?" Raibeart asked.

"Yes, sir," Asbjorn replied.

"How do you know our language?"

"My grandmother was a Dalriadan Scot from Ireland, sir. She taught me the Alban tongue."

"Did you allow this girl to escape?" Ciaran asked.

"Yes, sir. I captured her and I released her."

"Why?" Ciaran asked.

"Because my brother had plans for her that I wouldn't wish on anyone. I didn't want her sold as a slave, either. I can't explain why, but I felt it was right to let her go free."

Turning to Ciaran, Raibeart said, "It's up to you, Ciaran. She's your daughter so the life debt falls on you as well."

Ciaran stared at Asbjorn for a minute. Then he said, "Asbjorn Thorleikson, because you freed my daughter and spared her from your brother's plans, I give you a choice. You can die here with the others, you can try to swim back to Ireland, or you can stay with my clan and agree to live as one of us. But I warn you: if you betray any of our people, or if you attempt to help any Lochlannachs who invade Alba or Britain, you'll lose your head the same day, and I'll feed your body to the dogs. Do you understand?"

Asbjorn nodded. He looked over at Hundulfr, who stared at Asbjorn with fear in his eyes. Then Asbjorn saw the executioners step forward again, and the fear in Hundulfr's eyes changed to pleading. A moment later, the last of the Lochlannach captives were dead.

"That's the fate awaiting you if you betray us or if you wish to follow them to your gods, Asbjorn Thorleikson," Ciaran said. "What is your choice?"

Asbjorn thought about his father, his mother, his brother, and the rest of the people he knew from the longphort. He knew that he couldn't swim home, so he'd never see his people again. *I could die as a Norse warrior taken prisoner. There's no shame in this. Death at the hands of an enemy is considered an honorable death.*

He looked at Caitlin and realized that he was being given a choice that would allow him to be near her, although he doubted that he'd ever be allowed to be with her in the way he wanted. Still, it was a chance to live and to get to know her better. *I want to live, but can I turn my back on my family – on the only way of life I've ever known?*

Looking up, he saw the ravens were still there, circling the place of execution. As he watched, the ravens cried out and flew to the north toward Alba. *I guess you were messengers from Odin after all.* Taking the ravens as a sign from Odin to live and go to Alba, he made his decision.

"I wish to live, sir," he said to Ciaran. "I will obey you in all things."

Ciaran nodded and Raibeart ordered the men to take apart the holding pen and use the timbers to build a funeral pyre for the executed and slain Lochlannach. Asbjorn watched as the bodies and heads of his friends and fellow warriors were dragged closer to the river. Then he watched the holding pen dismantled and the timbers piled around the grisly remains. Raibeart lit the pyre, and soon Asbjorn's companions were being sent with honor into the next world.

Rest in Valhalla, my friends. May the Valkyries take you to your reward. Almighty Odin, lead me and protect me as I follow the path you've set before me.

After a while, he turned to Caitlin and Ciaran, who were standing near him. "What happens to me now?" he asked.

"You'll come with us," Ciaran said. "It won't be easy for you. My people won't trust you. But you have my protection for as long as you obey me. You'll learn the ways of the Albans, and you'll learn the ways of Christians. We'll see how things go for a while, and then we'll decide what to do with you."

Over the next several days, Asbjorn found himself in the company of Caitlin and her brother, Ringean. Ciaran had assigned them the tasks of making sure that Asbjorn didn't escape and protecting him from any angry Alt Cluts who were returning to Dumbarton to rebuild their city.

Ringean was irritated at having to watch Asbjorn, but as time passed, he didn't mind it so much. Ringean was fascinated by the information Asbjorn was sharing so freely. It was Ringean's first conversation with someone who had such a different perspective on the world.

"What does your name mean?" Caitlin asked toward the end of the first day.

"Well, 'Bjorn' means bear and 'As' is one of our words for the gods, so Asbjorn means bear-god. My father's name is Thorleik, which is why I'm called Thorleikson or 'son of Thorleik.' His full name is Thorleik Meginbjornson. Thor is our warrior god of battle, so his name means battle-god-like. Meginbjorn means bear-strength, so you would translate his name as 'battle-god-like son of bear-strength.' Bjornkarl is my brother, and his name means bear-hunter."

"So you're bear-god son of battle-god-like, your brother is bear-hunter son of battle-god-like, and your father is battle-god-like son of bear-strength?" Caitlin asked.

"In our way of naming people, yes," Asbjorn replied. "My father is one of the members of Amlaíb's council, so you would call him a nobleman. Names are important to the noble families, so you'll see Bjorns and Thors throughout my family."

"And your brother is a berserker?" Caitlin asked.

"Yes."

"What exactly is a berserker?" Ringean asked.

Asbjorn hesitated for a moment. *How much about our ways do I share with these Albans? Am I betraying my people – my family – by answering their questions?*

Then a new thought came to him. *I betrayed my people and my family when I decided to live instead of dying with my fellow captives. But didn't Odin send his ravens to tell me to live and return to Alba with these people? He must have a plan for me, and it's with the Albans. If I'm going to make a place for myself with them, I can't hold anything back.*

"What's a berserker?" Ringean repeated himself, sounding insistent.

"Our society is broken into two main groups," Asbjorn began. "Warriors and everyone else. Within the warriors, there are several distinctions. Berserkers are the highest class of warrior. They are the bravest and the most powerful. They go into battle first, and their job is to strike fear into the enemy and break their front lines so the rest of the warriors can attack."

"Why do they wear animal skins?" Caitlin asked.

"Mostly to make the enemy think that they're shape-shifters who are actually transforming into either bears or wolves. They drink an elixir just before battle that's made from strong liquor and these peculiar mushrooms that we have growing all around. The elixir makes the berserkers go mad, and they start acting like bears and wolves. They don't feel pain when they're drinking the elixir, and they won't stop fighting as long as they're still alive. Sometimes they even kill each other during battle."

"How do you control warriors like that?" Ringean asked.

"You don't," Asbjorn admitted. "They're not supposed to drink the elixir except before and during battle, but they drink it all the time. They're the most respected of all the warriors, and our society lets them get away with anything because they're so fierce in battle. They kill our own people over the slightest perceived insult, and they feel entitled to take whatever they want from anyone except the king or his council. The elixir gives them an appetite for women, though, which drives them to rape constantly. They rape women during battle, they rape prisoners, they rape the wives and daughters of their closest friends, and they even rape brides on their wedding night. Sometimes it gets so bad they have to be banished, but that's rare. Mostly, everyone just turns a blind-eye to what they do and tries to stay out of their way."

"Is your brother like that?" Ringean asked.

"Worse. He's a naturally mean person, so the elixir makes him even more dangerous. He almost killed me twice for trying to stop him from taking my things. The first time was a few months ago when he tried to steal the knife that my father gave me for my birthday. The second time was when I kept him from raping your sister. My father had to stop him both times."

Caitlin shuddered at the memory of Bjornkarl. "Would you ever want to be a berserker?"

Asbjorn shook his head. "No, I just wanted to be a warrior so my father would be proud of me and so the people would be proud of my father's house."

"Why do you invade other people's lands and take their money and people?" Ringean asked, changing the subject.

Asbjorn shrugged. "It's just what we do. We believe our gods demand that we prove ourselves in battle. The best of the fallen warriors are taken to Valhalla and made part of the army of the gods. They have the honor of defending creation in the battle against chaos at the end of the world. It's the goal of every Norseman to be selected. But fighting is expensive, so we have to pay for our battles somehow. We explore and conquer new lands, but it takes a long time to extract wealth from new lands, and there are no battles to fight in uninhabited places. So we fight with people who are strong and wealthy, prove ourselves to our gods, and pay for the expeditions with tribute and prisoners, who we sell as slaves."

"I think it's despicable to take things that don't belong to you," Caitlin said, sounding irritated by Asbjorn's lack of remorse for his people's actions.

"May I ask you a question?" Asbjorn inquired.

"Yes," Caitlin replied stiffly.

"Are you a Pict or a Dalriadan Scot?"

"I know I have Pictish blood in me, but we're Dalriadan Scots."

"And how did the Dalriadan Scots come to be in Alba?"

"They came over from Ireland and settled near our village. Their main fortress of Dunadd is near our lands."

"And if you were a Pict when the Dalriadan Scots arrived, how would you feel about them?"

"What do you mean?" Caitlin demanded.

"My grandmother was a Dalriadan Scot, and she told me that the Scots invaded Pictland and set up a kingdom on their lands. I'm guessing the Picts thought about the Dalriadan Scots the way you think about my people. Your people took their lands and eventually seized their entire kingdom. Most of Britain has been taken by other peoples over the centuries. The Romans took land from the Britons, the Saxons took land from the Britons after the Romans left, and my people are taking land from the Saxons.

Everyone takes something from whoever was there before, and it'll be taken again by someone else who comes later. It's the nature of the world. We're not very different from the Dalriadan Scots, except that we aren't here for conquest. We leave when we're done. Your people stayed."

Caitlin stood up angrily and stormed off, leaving Asbjorn alone with Ringean. "I guess she didn't like the comparison," Asbjorn commented.

Ringean smiled. "I don't think she liked it at all."

Asbjorn didn't see Caitlin for the rest of the day, but the next day she seemed to be in a better mood. She and Ringean explained the structure of Alban society to Asbjorn, including the role of the clans.

"Clans aren't exactly family groupings, although many in our clan are related," she stated. "Clans occupy territories around Alba. Each clan has a chief who rules the territory. The chiefs fall under earls who answer to the king. My father is our chief, and our territory is where the old kingdom of Dalriada was located."

"Is it normal for women of Alba to fight alongside men?" Asbjorn asked.

Caitlin shook her head. "It was in Pictish society, but the Christian church doesn't think women should do anything except prepare food, serve their husbands and fathers, and make babies. I don't happen to agree with that. Women have to fight to defend the villages when invaders come, so what's the difference between defending one's home and fighting in the field against the enemy? It's still fighting, isn't it?"

Asbjorn nodded. "For centuries we had women warriors, who were called 'shield maidens,' but you rarely see women fight anymore. I'm not sure why since our gods never said anything about women not fighting. Many of our goddesses are also warriors."

"How many gods and goddesses do you worship?" Ringean asked.

"It depends on who you ask," Asbjorn said. "I think there are at least a dozen major gods and goddesses, but there are lesser gods and goddesses who are mentioned from time to time.

Sometimes I think that we absorb the gods of people we conquer, but it's hard to tell. I've never seen any of it written down."

"Well, you're going to find the same thing with Christianity when Iain starts instructing you in the mysteries of the Church of Rome," Caitlin said. "There are things written down, but in a language only the priests and Bishops can understand. And some of the stories we have sound like stories you have in your religion. The battle against chaos at the end of the world sounds like the Christian stories about the end of the world that Iain taught us."

"I look forward to learning from him." Asbjorn always liked to learn new things, and the chance to learn an entirely new religion interested him greatly.

A week later, Raibeart announced that the Alban horsemen would begin withdrawing from Alt Clut the next day to return home. The presence of Lochlannach warriors on the islands surrounding Alba made it important for the army to return to Alba before the seas froze. Lochlannach raids in the dead of winter were common since the warriors simply walked across the ice and attacked more easily than they could by boat.

Caitlin and Ringean had been teaching Asbjorn how to ride a horse, and he was getting more comfortable with handling the large beasts. The night before they were to leave, Ciaran returned Asbjorn's sword and the knife that Thorleik had given Asbjorn for his birthday. His shield and spear had been destroyed as part of the funeral pyre for the fallen Lochlannach on the day Asbjorn had been spared.

"Thank you, sir," Asbjorn said as he accepted the return of his weapons. "I will only use this sword in your service and in the service of your clan."

The next morning, Asbjorn rose early and prepared to leave. Caitlin found him with his horse and watched as the young warrior prepared the horse for the journey home. After he was finished, Asbjorn looked up and saw Caitlin watching him.

"Good morning, Caitlin," he said. "I didn't know you were there."

"Good morning, Asbjorn," she said. "It looks like you're anxious to get started."

"Anxious, excited, nervous, scared… I like new situations, but the unknown can still be frightening. I don't know what to expect once we reach your village. I don't know where I'm going to live or what I'm going to do. All I know is that I'm going. For you, it's home – the end of a journey. For me, it's a strange place I've never been to before – the beginning of my next journey. I don't know if I'll ever feel like I'm home again."

Caitlin nodded. "You're experiencing what I almost experienced when I was your prisoner. The only difference is: you had a choice and I didn't."

"I hope you don't still hold it against me that I took you as my prisoner," Asbjorn said.

She shook her head. "No, you set me free and that made up for taking me prisoner. I guess I should be grateful that you didn't kill me."

"I would never have killed you unless there was no way to avoid it," Asbjorn commented.

"Why?" Caitlin asked.

"Because alive you were worth a great deal of money, not to mention the honor I'd receive for taking a prisoner in battle. Dead, you would be worth nothing."

Caitlin glared at Asbjorn for a minute. Then she saw a faint smile on his lips.

"Is that the only reason you didn't kill me?" she asked, ignoring the smile and pretending to be angry. "The way you were showing me off to your father and the other guards made me think that you had something else on your mind."

Asbjorn started blushing, and Caitlin had to suppress a laugh when he turned red. She knew he had mentioned keeping her for his own on one occasion, but they had never spoken about it again.

"I had thought about taking you as my wife," he said hesitatingly, "before I realized it would make Bjornkarl want you even more."

"Do your people normally take wives from among your prisoners?"

"Actually, it happens frequently," Asbjorn admitted.

"But if you had kept me, you'd have received no money for me, right?"

94

Asbjorn nodded. "I'd still have the honor from capturing you during battle, but I'd lose the tribute from your sale as a slave."

"Would that have been a lot of money?" Caitlin asked.

"Yes. Women, especially young women, fetch the highest prices."

"And you were willing to lose all that money by keeping me?"

Asbjorn nodded.

"I'm flattered, Asbjorn. I probably would've killed you in your sleep on our wedding night, but I'm still flattered."

"Then I guess I did the right thing by setting you free," he said. "I'm still alive."

"I hope you stay that way," she said. She started to smile at Asbjorn, but then she turned away quickly and motioned for him to follow her back to camp. "Come with me. You need to eat something before we leave."

Chapter 11

Amlaíb's fleet made good time on the return to Áth Cliath. The north wind blew strongly for the entire voyage, allowing the overloaded longships to cut through the water of the channel faster than usual.

Most of Ívarr's fleet had been unloaded and his longships beached upriver to give Amlaíb's fleet room to land and begin unloading. Thorleik guided his ship to shore and ordered his men to secure the longship with ropes. He was the last person to leave his ship and jump down onto the soft sand of the harbor beach. Looking around, he saw his wife, Bergdís, waving to him from the crowd gathered to watch the victorious Norsemen return home. He waved to her, and then he ordered his men to start unloading the longship.

More and more longships arrived and were beached all around the harbor. Thorleik kept a close watch for the cargo ships, which he knew would arrive last. It was mid-afternoon when the last longship finally arrived in the harbor, and Thorleik knew there were many longships missing.

He checked with the captains of the last few ships to return and heard the same story from each of them. The longships had been attacked by the Alban army and many were destroyed. Hundreds of Norsemen were killed or captured in the battle. Thorleik knew the fate of Norse prisoners in Alba, and he felt a knot growing in the pit of his stomach. *Where is Asbjorn?*

By nightfall, most of the Norsemen had returned to their homes or gathered in the longphort to hear the tales of the expedition repeated to cheering crowds. Thorleik remained on the beach, hoping some of the missing ships might still make it back.

He had been staring out across the harbor for more than an hour when he felt a hand gently touch his arm. Turning, he saw

Bergdís standing there. "What are you doing here?" he asked, putting his arm around her shoulder.

"You didn't come home for supper," she replied softly. "I knew something must be wrong, so I came looking for you."

Thorleik turned back toward the harbor. "The Albans attacked the fleet as we were leaving Dumbarton. We lost several longships. I was waiting to see if any of the missing ships made it home."

"We lose longships all the time, my husband," she stated. "Why are you so concerned about these?"

Thorleik didn't answer, but Bergdís saw his jaw trembling. After a moment she whispered, "Asbjorn?"

Thorleik nodded.

Bergdís began to cry. Thorleik pulled her closer and held her as they grieved for their son.

As the morning sun rose over the harbor, Thorleik knew that there would be no more ships returning from Alt Clut. Asbjorn was among the missing. Amlaíb, hearing that Thorleik hadn't left the harbor since his arrival, came down to check on what was keeping his old friend from joining in the celebration of their victorious return.

"There you are, Thorleik," he said as he reached Thorleik's ship around mid-morning. "What are you still doing here?"

"We're missing a lot of ships, Amlaíb," Thorleik said, still facing the mouth of the harbor. "I estimate almost forty haven't returned."

"How can that be?" Amlaíb asked, standing next to Thorleik.

"The Alban army attacked after many of our ships had left Dumbarton. The last few ships to return here were overloaded with warriors trying to escape after their own ships were destroyed. None of the remaining cargo ships survived the attack, and the casualties were high."

"Were any prisoners taken?" Amlaíb asked.

"I've heard that there were, but you know the fate of prisoners at the hands of the Albans."

Amlaíb remembered that Asbjorn had been assigned to one of the cargo ships. "Was your son on one of the missing ships?" he asked.

Thorleik nodded, and Bergdís began crying softly again.

"I'm sorry, old friend," Amlaíb said, putting his hand on Thorleik's shoulder. "He was a fine young man and a credit to your house. If you wish vengeance, I'll permit you to execute the Alban prisoners we took."

"The Alban prisoners never left Alt Clut," Thorleik said. "They were to be loaded onto Asbjorn's ship. I'm sure they were freed during the battle along with the remaining Alt Clut prisoners who hadn't been sent back here already."

Amlaíb was angry at this news. The loss of the men and ships was a terrible thing, but it was a risk every Norseman faced on an expedition. The loss of the prisoners meant there would less money from the expedition for replacing the ships and training new men.

"I'll send a few ships north to see if any of the missing ships ran aground or were too damaged to complete the voyage home," Amlaíb said to Thorleik.

"I want to go with them," Thorleik said.

"Fine, but remain in the channel. Do not approach Dumbarton under any circumstances. The Alban army will be there, and I can't afford to lose you."

Thorleik's longship, accompanied by three other longships, left the harbor the next morning and turned north once they reached the channel. They rowed against the wind for three days, but there were no signs of the missing longships. Thorleik maneuvered his longship around the mouth of the river leading to Dumbarton, but he obeyed Amlaíb's instructions and stayed in the channel. After two days, he ordered the ships to turn for home.

Bergdís was waiting for him on the beach when his longship entered the harbor. He jumped down and walked over to her after his men had secured the longship. The look in his face told her everything she needed to know. She started crying again. Thorleik put his arm around her, and they walked back to the longphort to inform Amlaíb that there was no sign of the missing ships.

Thorleik thought about Asbjorn as they walked. Normally, the young warriors assigned to the cargo ships had the safest duty of any warriors on an expedition. It was difficult to accept that Asbjorn was dead, and Thorleik chided himself for allowing Asbjorn's cargo ship to be one of the last ships to leave Alt Clut. *If only I had sent him home a few days earlier with the prisoners.*

Bjornkarl stopped by a few days later, and it was clear that he had been drinking heavily since his return from Alt Clut. "I hear Asbjorn never came home," he said as he entered his father's house.

"Not now, Bjornkarl," Thorleik said. "I'm in no mood to hear what you have to say about your brother."

"I wasn't going to say anything, Father," Bjornkarl said with his usual sneer. "I just wanted to see if the stories were true."

"The stories are true. His ship was destroyed when the Albans attacked. He was either killed in battle or executed afterwards."

"And what became of his prisoners?" Bjornkarl asked.

"None of them made it back here."

"Including the girl?"

"Yes, including the girl. She was going to be brought back on Asbjorn's ship. I think he wanted to make sure that you didn't intercept her before he claimed her for himself."

"Pity," Bjornkarl said as he turned to leave his father's house. "She really was a lovely creature."

"It's disturbing to me that you're more upset over a girl you wanted to rape than a brother who you'll never see again," Thorleik said as Bjornkarl reached the door. "But then again, you never did care about your brother or your family, did you?"

"I have always cared about my family, Father," Bjornkarl said as he stepped outside. "In my own way I've always cared."

Thorleik heard the sound of Bjornkarl's laughter fade into the distance and fought to control the rage boiling up inside him. He'd never understand why Bjornkarl hated his younger brother so much, but he realized that it no longer mattered. Bjornkarl had no younger brother anymore.

Thorleik sat down on the bench near the door and buried his face in his hands, feeling the loss of Asbjorn more strongly than ever before. *I hope the gods treat you with honor, my son.* Thorleik found himself wishing it were Bjornkarl he was mourning over, rather than Asbjorn.

Asbjorn found the journey back to Airer Goídel an easy one. The foot soldiers had left two days earlier because it would take them longer to reach the village. Maol-Chaluim was in the lead and looked forward to being with his family again. His younger brother Ringean also looked forward to seeing his betrothed and finishing the wedding plans upon his return.

Caitlin never spoke about the loss of her betrothed, and Asbjorn made sure never to broach the subject. He remained silent and listened to what others were saying around him. He remembered Ciaran warning him that he wouldn't be welcomed when they returned to Airer Goídel, and he was determined to keep from giving anyone cause to hate him more than they already might. He knew that he was under the protection of Ciaran and his family, and he wanted to honor Ciaran's generosity by never giving Caitlin's father a reason to question the wisdom of letting a Lochlannach invader live.

Three days after leaving Dumbarton, the horsemen of Airer Goídel reached home. The foot soldiers were already there and waiting for their chief to return. Overall, the clan had suffered few losses in the fighting against the Lochlannach. Only thirty-five of the foot soldiers and fifty horsemen had been killed or wounded, and the wounded would recover fully. All who had been taken prisoner had been rescued.

Ciaran spoke a few words to the assembled crowd, and then introduced Asbjorn, letting everyone know that he had helped Caitlin escape and was now under Ciaran's protection. Asbjorn felt nervous when the entire village glared at him. He was grateful when Ciaran led him away from the icy and angry stares of the crowd.

"You'll be staying in my barn until we can find a better place for you to live," Ciaran said as they led the horses to Ciaran's home. "There's a loft that will work for now. It's warm and dry. We'll get you some new clothes in a day or so, and then start working to make you part of the clan."

"Thank you again for all you've done for me," Asbjorn said as they reached Ciaran's home, which was a farm with several buildings clustered close together.

"Just keep your word and that'll be thanks enough," Ciaran said.

A week after arriving at Ciaran's farm, Asbjorn woke up in the early morning darkness feeling disoriented. For a moment, he couldn't remember where he was or what he was supposed to be doing. He sat up and looked around, and then remembered he was in the loft of Ciaran's barn.

He dressed quickly and climbed down the ladder, making sure not to disturb the horses and other livestock still asleep. He stepped into the chilly pre-dawn air and looked up at the sky. He estimated that it was still about an hour before sunrise, but he felt the need to walk around and stretch his legs.

A sound made him look up quickly, and he saw the silhouette of a raven flying overhead. *Are you another messenger from Odin?* The last several times he had seen ravens, they had helped him do what he needed to do. For no other reason than that, he decided to follow the raven. It seemed to be leading him north.

He walked through the village. No lights shone through any of the windows, and the only wisps of smoke from the chimneys came from fires left unattended for several hours. His feet made a crunching sound in the frost on the ground, but apart from that, the night was silent.

In the darkness, Asbjorn saw the outlines of the village buildings clearly. Most of the members of Ciaran's clan were farmers who spent the bulk of their time tending to their crops, flocks, and horses. But as the clan grew and prospered, many of the younger families built houses in the village, rather than on their families' farms. Many of the craftsmen had houses and shops in the village as well, including stonecutters and blacksmiths. Asbjorn walked through the village, passing stables, workshops, granaries, and the inn that served as the primary gathering place for the villagers.

When he reached the northern edge of the village, he heard the call of the raven ahead. It was still heading north. He walked through fields and along streams, and he followed a wide path through a forest as black as a cave. He wasn't sure why he kept walking, but he felt compelled to follow the raven's call.

As he left the darkness of the forest, the sky lightened in the east, signifying that it was almost sunrise. He looked up and saw the raven flying in circles in front of him. He walked toward it, and in the field in front of him, he saw the shadows of large shapes all around. Moving closer, he reached out and touched one of the shapes. It was a wooden log standing upright in the ground. It had been smoothed down, and there was no bark, branches, or leaves left on it. As he ran his hands along the wood, he felt carvings all around, but there wasn't enough light to determine what the carvings represented.

Other logs stood nearby, and in the low light, he saw that they were arranged in a circular pattern. Inside the circle, though, were much larger shadowy shapes. He walked toward them, curious. He put out his hand when he reached the first one, and discovered it was stone. He remembered seeing stone circles in Ireland and wondered if this stone were part of a large stone circle like those he had seen before.

The stone circles in Britain and Ireland were hundreds if not thousands of years old. No one knew who had built them or for what reason, but Asbjorn was certain it wasn't a place for Christian worship. Not even the Norsemen used them for worship, preferring the sacred groves and other special places. Asbjorn wondered if there were still non-Christians in Alba who used the stone circles for ceremonies.

He heard a noise nearby and realized it wasn't the raven. He peered around the stone and saw a figure kneeling and facing toward the east. Asbjorn remained hidden behind the stone. *I doubt that's a Christian rite he's practicing. Do they still practice the old rites here in Alba? Are there laws against it? What will he do if he finds me here?*

Asbjorn pressed himself against the stone on the opposite side from where the person was kneeling. *Why did the raven lead me here? Whoever's inside the circle doesn't want to be discovered, so what do I do? If I try to leave the circle, I might be seen or heard. The sun is rising. If I stay here, I might still be seen. I'm a stranger in this land. What if he doesn't know that I'm under the protection of Ciaran? What if he doesn't care? I wish I had my sword with me.*

The first rays of the morning sun appeared over the horizon, and Asbjorn carefully peered around the stone to see what the person inside the stone circle was doing. He saw what looked like a sacrifice in a bowl sitting on top of a large flat stone in the center of the circle. A long knife was next to the bowl, and there appeared to be blood on its blade.

The person kneeling said something Asbjorn didn't understand, but he was certain that he recognized the voice. Then the person looked up at the rising sun and Asbjorn saw his face. It was Ciaran!

Ciaran heard Asbjorn gasp and looked over at the young warrior. For a moment, Asbjorn thought Ciaran might grab the knife and come after him, but Ciaran just smiled.

"How long have you been standing there, Asbjorn?" he asked, getting to his feet.

"Only a few minutes, sir," Asbjorn replied. "I woke up well before dawn and wanted to stretch my legs. A raven led me here."

"A raven? Why would a raven lead you here?"

"The ravens are messengers from Odin, the greatest of our gods. I've been led by the ravens before, and they haven't led me astray yet."

"I imagine you're wondering what I'm doing here," Ciaran said as he cleaned off his knife and put it back in the sheath on his belt.

"I assume it's a religious rite of some sort," Asbjorn answered cautiously.

Ciaran nodded. "This circle has been here for as long as anyone remembers. The stones are ancient, but the timbers have to be replaced every few years. Some of the villagers, and especially our village priest, want the circle destroyed since it represents something other than Christ, but it's stood here long before we arrived and will still be here long after we're gone."

"I thought you were a Christian, sir," Asbjorn said, walking into the center of the circle.

"I am, but I also respect the gods who were here before Christ was ever preached in this land. I don't pray to them, but sometimes I make offerings and tell them about what's going on in the world outside the circle. I was telling them about our victory against your people when you arrived."

Asbjorn looked around the circle, and in the sunlight, he saw how immense the circle truly was. There were dozens of stones and hundreds of timbers forming multiple circles that radiated out from where Asbjorn and Ciaran were standing.

To the northeast and south of the circle, there were the remnants of an ancient forest, thick and dark green. Rocky peaks jutted above the trees to the northeast, and Asbjorn wondered if it were even possible to reach those peaks through the dense undergrowth of the forest. To the east and west of the circle, the land had been cleared so the sunrise and sunset would be unobstructed by the trees. In the center of the circle lay a large stone in the ground with several smaller stones around it and what looked like steps going down underneath the large stone.

"What's this in the center?" Asbjorn asked, wondering if it might be an underground temple of some sort.

"I think it's a tomb, but I'm not sure," Ciaran replied. "No one knows the true history of this place."

Ciaran pointed to the carvings on a couple of the stones. "These carvings are on several of the stones, and there's writing on most of the stones as well. I don't know what the carvings mean or what the writings say, but when I'm here, I feel like I'm in the presence of something very old. I come here to think since most Christians are afraid of the stone circles and avoid this place."

Turning to Asbjorn, he said, "I don't want you to mention this to anyone, Asbjorn. There are many who wouldn't understand and might use this against me. I've never been challenged for leadership of the clan, and I don't want that to change."

"I won't say a word, sir."

"Good." Looking around, Ciaran added, "I think it's time to be getting back to the farm. We need to eat, and we need to start working on finding a way for you to contribute to the clan so people will come to accept you faster."

They walked back through the forest south of the circle toward the village in silence. In the sunlight, Asbjorn saw the dense foliage forming a natural wall on either side of the path they were following. Asbjorn felt it would be easy to get lost in the forest, and he wondered what great unseen beasts made it their home.

As they left the forest behind them and approached the village, Asbjorn saw much thicker smoke from the chimneys and knew that people were rising and building up the fires for cooking and for warmth against the cold air. A few people were working outside, and Ciaran called out to each of them and wished them a good morning.

Asbjorn felt some of the people staring at him, but he kept looking forward and followed Ciaran through the village to his farm, which was down the hill from the village and close to one of the many streams cutting through the area and providing water for farming and livestock.

When they reached Ciaran's house, Asbjorn looked at the buildings making up the farm. There was the large main house, where Ciaran and his second wife, Beathag, lived with Caitlin. Maol-Chaluim and his wife, who was expecting a child any day, lived in a smaller house on one side of the main house. Ringean lived in a house, which was nearing completion, on the other side of Maol-Chaluim's house. The house was to be finished before Ringean's wedding, which would take place in the spring. The other buildings were storage sheds and barns for the livestock and the harvested crops.

In the distance, there was another large house, which belonged to Dùghall mac Unen, Ciaran's younger brother. Dùghall's wife had only produced daughters, who were married and lived with their husbands in other parts of the village. In the absence of a male heir, Ciaran and Dùghall had merged their farms together, and Maol-Chaluim ran both of them well.

Caitlin and Beathag were busy working on breakfast when Ciaran and Asbjorn entered the main house. Beathag knew Asbjorn had captured and then released Caitlin, but she was still cautious whenever Asbjorn was around.

"I am pleased to meet you, ma'am," Asbjorn had said to her when they were first introduced to each other. "I hope my being here won't make you uneasy in any way."

"You have manners I see," Beathag had replied. "If you act as well as you speak, we'll get along well enough."

105

In the days since their initial meeting, Beathag had come to accept Asbjorn, and Asbjorn felt the tension between them lessening.

Asbjorn greeted Caitlin and Beathag as he and Ciaran entered the house. Asbjorn looked over at Caitlin, who just smiled and kept helping Beathag with the cooking. *She was a warrior when I first met her. I don't think I'll ever get used to seeing her doing domestic things.* He tried to keep from staring. She looked different than she had when she was his captive, and he found himself even more attracted to her than before.

After breakfast, Ciaran asked, "So now that you've been here for a week, what do feel you can do to help around the farm or the village, Asbjorn? What skills do you have?"

"I wasn't raised on a farm, sir," Asbjorn replied. "I was taught how to handle the longboats and longships from an early age, and I was taught to hunt and to fight. My father was a nobleman, so I was being groomed to be a warrior and nothing else. I did help load and unload cargo, so I can do heavy lifting. But I'm a quick study and can learn anything that someone teaches me."

"I think I can teach you some of the work we do on the farm, and then we'll see if there's other work that suits you. We'll be planting crops in the spring, so for now all we do is care for the horses and the animals in the barn. I'm also thinking it would be good to know more about how your warriors are trained so we can defend ourselves better when they raid us. You and I need to discuss that further and see what needs to be done to update how we train our people to fight and defend our lands."

"Yes, sir," Asbjorn said, feeling uncomfortable about teaching Albans how to defeat his people. *Former people,* he reminded himself. *Ciaran and his clan are my people now.*

CHAPTER 12

Asbjorn did his best to be useful around the farm, helping to keep the livestock in the barn fed and watered. He also spent several hours a day cutting firewood and bringing water up from the stream for drinking and cooking. It didn't take long for everyone to settle into a comfortable routine with the newest resident of the farm, and Asbjorn felt more at ease each day, even though the villagers who called on Ciaran made it clear that they weren't happy about the young Lochlannach's presence.

Maol-Chaluim's wife gave birth to a boy two weeks after Asbjorn arrived. Asbjorn saw little of Caitlin and Beathag for several days after that.

Three weeks after Asbjorn arrived in Airer Goídel, Ciaran called for a meeting of the village elders and ranking soldiers. He had Asbjorn explain how the Lochlannach warriors trained and what their weaknesses were. Asbjorn also explained about the berserkers and the elixir. "They always have a leather bag on them holding the elixir," he said. "If you can cut it open or take it away from them, they won't be able to keep fighting like animals. It'll make them easier to defeat when the effects of the elixir start to wear off."

Caitlin walked up to him the next morning. "I hear you've been teaching the men how to defeat your people," she said.

Asbjorn nodded. "I told them about how we train, how our warriors are organized, and the secrets about the berserkers and their elixir."

"How did it feel giving the men that information?"

"I won't lie to you; it was uncomfortable. I know you're my people now, and I owe it to the clan to help in any way I can, but it felt like I was betraying my father. It was the right thing to do, but I'm not sure I liked doing it."

"I wonder if I would have felt the same way if you had taken me to Ireland," she commented.

"Probably, although there would be major differences."

"What differences?"

"Well, you'd be my wife. Your role in our society would be well defined and you'd be immediately accepted. I have no idea what my role is, I'm not accepted, and I feel like I'm alone here."

"I guess it's harder for you than I imagined," Caitlin said. "I'm sorry you have to go through this, but I didn't want them to kill you."

"The life debt?" Asbjorn asked.

"No... well, yes, there was a life debt, but that's not the whole reason. It's not just because you let me escape. You were kind to me when you didn't have to be, and you protected me against your brother, nearly getting killed for your trouble. That tells me that you're a good person inside, and I didn't want to see a good person die just because he was born into a life that's different from mine."

Caitlin started blushing, and she quickly turned away from Asbjorn, hoping he wouldn't ask her any more questions.

Two days later, Ciaran went to find Iain mac Mànas. It was time to start Asbjorn's education, and Ciaran couldn't think of anyone better suited than the village priest to handle the young Lochlannach's instruction.

Predictably, Iain was furious at the prospect of having to teach a Lochlannach anything other than how to die a violent death.

"I won't do it!" he said for the third time as his voice got higher and louder.

"Why not?"

"He's a pagan and a Lochlannach. He should be crucified, not treated like one of our own. Look at what his people have done to us!"

"He saved my daughter's life and agreed to live with us peacefully. He even agreed to become a Christian. This is your chance to save a pagan from damnation. Surely that's not too big of a task for you."

Iain's face was getting redder by the minute. "Of course it's not too big of a task for me," he snapped. "I just don't see why it has to be done at all."

"Because I gave my word to him just as he gave his word to me. As long as he keeps his word, then he's under my protection. We can't judge one young man based on the deeds of his people just because he was born a Lochlannach. We must look at his deeds alone, and he saved Caitlin's life. That's the only deed I care about."

Ciaran let this sink in before continuing. "Iain, there's no one else here who can teach him as well as you can, and I need you to do this. It'll be difficult, but I think you're up to the challenge. He needs to learn the ways of Christ and be baptized. Do this and you won't have to be bothered with him anymore. Please Iain."

Iain looked at Ciaran with surprise. In all the years they had known each other, Ciaran had never said "please" to him. While he hated the thought of having to be in the presence of a Lochlannach, Ciaran was right about one thing: it would be a challenge, and Iain liked challenges when it came to saving men's souls.

"Very well," he said finally. "I'll try. But if he won't give up his pagan ways, his soul will need to be purged."

"Thank you, Iain. Let's see how things go before deciding what needs to be done. And keep me informed about how it's going. I need to know if he's truly keeping his promise to me."

"Rest assured, Ciaran, I'll update you regularly."

Iain spent many days instructing Asbjorn in the tenets of Christianity and teaching Asbjorn about Jesus, the apostles, and the prophets. Asbjorn was a quick study, but there were some things Iain taught him that just didn't make sense. One day, after several weeks of lessons, Asbjorn felt he had to ask some questions, and he hoped Iain wouldn't get offended.

"I don't understand, sir," Asbjorn began, feeling frustrated.

"What's confusing you, Asbjorn?" Iain asked, sounding annoyed.

"If I heard you correctly, God impregnated Mary and she gave birth to Jesus, but Jesus the human was actually God in human form?"

"Right."

"And then the Jews captured Jesus and had the Romans torture and kill him?"

"Right."

"How can you kill a god?"

"Jesus was crucified by being hung on a cross," Iain explained, misunderstanding what Asbjorn was really asking.

"No, I mean how can a god be killed at all?"

"Well," Iain began, pausing to think of the best answer. "He rose again on the third day, proving he was God."

"But he rose in human form, right?"

"Yes."

"Then how does coming back to life in human form prove that he's a god? If he came back to life in the form of a god, that would prove he was a god, wouldn't it? But to be killed as a human and come back as a human just proves that he was a human who was more powerful than death."

"That's what proves he's God!" Iain stated. "What human can be more powerful than death? Remember, after he came back in human form, he was carried up to heaven."

"Which is where he came from before he impregnated Mary?" Asbjorn asked.

"Right."

"I don't understand."

On the day after Asbjorn attended his first mass, he was feeling even more confused. He went to search for Iain, and found him sitting near the stream.

"What is it now, Asbjorn?" Iain said irritably when he saw Asbjorn approaching.

"Forgive me for intruding, sir, but I wondered if I might ask some more questions," Asbjorn replied.

"Come and sit down," Iain said after a moment. "Ask your questions."

Asbjorn sat down on the rock next to Iain. "I don't understand what you were saying at mass," Asbjorn began. "And I don't understand the purpose of sitting there and listening to something I can't understand. How am I supposed to learn anything from that? How can I be saved by what you're saying if I don't even understand what's being said?"

"The service is in Latin," Iain replied. "It's the official language of the church."

"Do I need to learn Latin to be saved?"

"No one speaks Latin anymore, Asbjorn. It's what people used to speak in Rome."

"So it's not the language Jesus spoke?"

"No, Jesus was a Jew, so he spoke either Hebrew or Aramaic."

"So the ceremonies are the words of Jesus translated into Latin?"

"Well, no," Iain answered. "The ceremonies aren't the words of Jesus."

"Then what are they?" Asbjorn asked.

"The ceremonies commemorate what Jesus said and did on earth."

"Like what?" Asbjorn asked.

"Well, the wafer and the wine we take at the end of the ceremony are from the Last Supper, which is the night before Jesus was captured."

"So you commemorate the last thing Jesus did before he was killed? What about what he said and did before that? Or do you only commemorate his death?"

Iain was exasperated, but he had to admit that Asbjorn asked a good question. So much of the doctrine of the church was based on the death of Jesus. Even the use of the cross, which was an instrument of terribly slow execution, was in reference to the death of Jesus. Iain had never thought about it before, and he wished the Bishop were there to give him the proper answer.

Changing the subject, Iain asked, "So what else confuses you?"

"I don't understand why the church says women are inferior to men. The women I've known are strong, brave, and good fighters. They seem equal to men to me."

"They're *not* equal," Iain spat out angrily. "They are weak, and they are evil."

"Why?"

"Because of Eve. She was tempted by the devil, and then she tempted Adam, causing both of them to be cast out of paradise."

"So the action of a woman thousands of years ago makes all women inferior?" Asbjorn asked.

"Exactly."

"But Eve was tempted by the devil, right?" Asbjorn asked.

"Yes."

"And Adam was only tempted by Eve?"

"What do you mean, 'only'?" Iain asked, feeling even more irritated.

"Well, if Adam and Eve were to be tempted, wouldn't the devil go after the stronger one and let the stronger one then tempt the weaker one? If Eve were the weaker one, could she have tempted Adam so easily? What if Eve was the stronger one and the devil went after her because he knew that tempting Adam would be too easy?"

"That's blasphemy!" Iain said strongly.

"Why?"

"Because it goes against what the church says."

"So blasphemy is anything the church doesn't like?" Asbjorn asked.

"Yes. The church says that women are inferior, so they are inferior."

"It sounds to me like someone in the church was jealous of women and decided to make them inferior to feel better about himself."

"How can the church be jealous of women?" Iain demanded, getting angrier.

"Well, didn't you teach me that Jesus appeared to Mary Magdalene when he first rose from the grave?"

"Yes," Iain replied, not knowing where Asbjorn was going with this line of questioning.

"Would he appear to someone inferior and evil as his first act after he overcame death and came back to earth alive? Why would he waste his first appearance on an inferior and evil creature? He'd first appear to someone he held in high importance, wouldn't he?"

Before Iain answered, Asbjorn continued. "And he impregnated a woman to enter into this world in human form. Would he have consented to be inside an inferior and evil creature just to be born? From what you taught me, his mother was there with Mary Magdalene below the cross as he was dying, and they regularly visited his grave – something his other followers never did. It seems to me that those women were superior to the men who followed Jesus, so I don't understand how the church can say women are inferior and evil when there are two women you taught me about who seem quite superior. Don't you pray to Mary the mother of Jesus?"

"Mary the mother of Jesus is also divine."

"Really?" Asbjorn asked. "I thought only pagans believed in the goddess."

"What goddess?" Iain demanded.

"She's known as the earth mother to some religions. My grandmother was Irish, and many of the old Irish religions have a mother goddess who gave birth to all of creation. I didn't realize the Christians had a goddess as well."

"We don't," Iain said. "We only have one God, and that's Jesus."

"Then how is Mary divine if she isn't a god?" Asbjorn asked, sounding more confused than before.

"Because the church declared her to be divine," Iain stated to end the argument.

"But how can a church, made up of men, declare who is divine?" Asbjorn asked.

"Because the church was created by Peter, who was one of the apostles of Jesus."

"So it was Peter who declared that Mary is divine?" Asbjorn asked.

"No, that came much later," Iain replied. "There was a council of Bishops five-hundred-and-forty-five years ago in a city called Nicaea, which is in Asia Minor. They met to clear up some points of disagreement and settle on a single doctrine for the Christian church."

"All of the Christian Bishops attended this council?"

"Well, no. Only the principal Bishops in the Roman Empire attended."

"And the Pope presided over the meeting?" Asbjorn asked, fascinated at the idea of a council of men to define the articles of faith of a religion. "Why wasn't the meeting held in Rome?"

"The meeting was presided over by the Roman Emperor Constantine."

"And he was a priest?" Asbjorn asked.

"No. In fact, he wasn't even a Christian yet. He didn't convert until he was near death, many years later."

"Wait a minute," Asbjorn said with a bewildered expression on his face. "A pagan emperor called a meeting of Roman Bishops and decided what the doctrine of the Christian church would be?"

"Yes," Iain replied. "He was tired of his Bishops arguing, and he knew that Christianity would be the best way to help him hold the empire together. Rather than keeping the empire in line by the sword, he'd use faith to keep the Roman citizens behaving the way he wanted them to. At Nicaea, he listened to his Bishops give their opinions, and then he chose the ones everyone would follow from then on."

"So is the church an instrument of God or an instrument of the Roman Empire?" Asbjorn asked.

"It's always been an instrument of God," Iain stated with his usual air of superiority.

"But its teachings were dictated by a pagan emperor who wanted the church to help him politically control the citizens of his empire?"

"Yes."

"And the church has declared that anyone who holds to a different belief from what the church teaches is a criminal?"

"A heretic and a blasphemer," Iain corrected him.

"And the penalty of being a heretic and a blasphemer is death?"

"Yes," Iain said proudly.

"Did Jesus kill people who disagreed with him?" Asbjorn asked.

"Of course not! He was a teacher who tried to show man the way to live according to God's will, and he was a healer. He

114

even healed one of the soldiers who came to arrest him when Peter cut the soldier's ear off."

"Then the apostles killed those who disagreed with him?"

"No, the apostles were teachers as well," Iain replied.

"Then who decided that unbelievers should die if it wasn't God and it wasn't his apostles?" Asbjorn asked.

"The church decided it."

"Why? If the church is trying to save the souls of men, wouldn't it try to reform the heretic or blasphemer first? If the church just kills the person, the person has no chance to be reformed, and his soul is damned forever, isn't it?"

"It's not about saving the soul of the heretic or blasphemer," Iain said irritably. "It's about keeping others from following the heretic or blasphemer by showing them what awaits all heretics and blasphemers."

"And was this decided by the church or by Emperor Constantine?"

"Both, I guess. The church needed to be organized and end all disagreements between the bishops about the articles of faith, and Constantine needed a way to better control the citizens of the empire."

"So then the church really is just an instrument of the Roman Empire," Asbjorn concluded.

"No, it's the instrument of God," Iain insisted loudly.

"I don't understand."

"He's an insolent heretic and blasphemer, and he should be put to death immediately," Iain said to Ciaran later that day as they two men walked through the village together.

"Why? Because he asked you some questions that you didn't like or couldn't answer?" Ciaran stopped walking and turned to face the priest. "Look, Iain, you and I were born Christian. There are things we've known since we were children, and we take for granted that others know just as much as we do. The lad was raised with different beliefs, and I'm sure our beliefs are as strange to him as his beliefs are to us. Frankly, I'm encouraged that he's asking questions. It means that he's actually trying to learn and understand so he can be a good Christian. I'd be more worried if he weren't asking questions at all."

Ciaran put his hand on the priest's shoulder. "Try and understand things from his perspective, Iain. He's a stranger in a strange land, he's trying to learn a new religion and unlearn the ways of his people so he can fit in with us. He's alone, he's afraid, and it's only our patience, our understanding, and our commitment to helping him that's giving him the strength to honor his oath to us and live as one of us here. I can't imagine how difficult it must be to try to teach the ways of Christ to someone who wasn't born a Christian, but that's your great task, and I'm asking you to keep trying. If he's asking questions, then you're getting through to him. Help him, Iain. Help him to be a Christian. I have to believe that the rewards in heaven will be greater for someone who teaches with love rather than threatens with death."

Iain thought about this for a moment as the two started walking again. He tried to remember what it was like when the Bishop first revealed the history and mysteries of the church to him many years earlier. It was only the confident faith of the Bishop that helped him rationalize some of the conflicts he felt existed between what Christ preached and what the church did.

Maybe if I have the same confidence in my faith, the lad will be more inspired to accept what I teach him.

"Very well, Ciaran. I'll continue teaching Asbjorn. But he tries my patience."

"We each have our own cross to bear," Ciaran said, smiling at Iain's discomfort.

CHAPTER 13

Early one afternoon, a few weeks after Ringean's wedding, Caitlin found Asbjorn sitting by himself inside the stone circle north of the village. She walked up to him and stood there silently until he looked up and saw her.

"What are you doing here, Asbjorn?" she asked. "I thought only my father came here."

"I come here to think sometimes," Asbjorn answered, motioning for Caitlin to sit down.

"What are you thinking about?" she asked as she sat next to him.

"Home," he replied.

Caitlin looked at him. She understood why Asbjorn had been thinking about home recently. A week earlier, three Lochlannach longboats from the islands around Alba had sailed up the Abhainn Fìne River and attacked the village in search of plunder. Asbjorn joined the men of the village in fighting off the raiders, killing three of the Lochlannach including the leader of the raiding party.

Even though Asbjorn fought against the raiders, the men of the village still showed no sign of accepting him as a member of the clan. The next morning after the raid, Asbjorn overheard some of the men talking to Ciaran, suggesting that Asbjorn was the cause of the raid and was still working with the Lochlannach in spite of his promise. Ciaran defended Asbjorn and sent the men away, but Asbjorn knew his presence at Ciaran's farm was causing problems for the clan's chief.

"I guess you still miss your family and your people," she commented softly.

"Yes and no," Asbjorn said, continuing to stare off into the distance. "Sure, I miss my family and friends, but more than that I miss the feeling of belonging somewhere. I know your father is dealing with problems because of me. The villagers don't want me here even though I've done everything I can think of to prove that I'm honoring my word. I can't leave without breaking my word to your father, and I can't stay without risking your father's position with the clan. I don't know what to do."

Caitlin thought about this for a while. *Father believes in Asbjorn. So do I. But the villagers are slow to forget that he was born a Lochlannach, even though he fought and killed Lochlannach raiders side-by-side with us only a week ago. Father will continue defending Asbjorn, but the villagers won't have any reason to let go of their mistrust until someone else outside of our family starts defending him. But who could that be?*

She thought about the people in the village for several minutes. Then an idea came to her. *There's one person who might be able to defend Asbjorn and make others stop mistrusting him.* She was excited at the idea and decided she'd speak to this person the next morning. She was so focused on what to say to the other person that she didn't realize she had put her hand on top of Asbjorn's.

The two of them sat next to each other in the middle of the stone circle until the sun set in the distance, lost in their own thoughts and unaware that they were holding each other's hands.

"Caitlin, I understand that you like Asbjorn, and you want him to be accepted by the clan, but what you're asking me is quite impossible."

"Why?" Caitlin asked.

"Because I don't trust him," Iain replied firmly. "How can I make the people trust someone I don't trust? That would make me a hypocrite."

"Tell me why you don't trust him," Caitlin pressed, unwilling to give up on her idea.

"He's a Lochlannach," Iain stated as if that explained everything. "You can't trust the Lochlannach."

"Even if he were a Christian?"

"But he's not a Christian," Iain reminded her.

"But if he were, would you trust him and defend him?"

Iain thought about this. He instinctively hated all Lochlannach, but he also fervently supported all brothers and sisters in Christ. Iain saw that the real problem he had with teaching Asbjorn the ways of Christianity was that it might force Iain to change the way he thought about Asbjorn. *I hate Lochlannach and love Christians. But what if a Lochlannach became a Christian? Would I hate a Christian because he was a Lochlannach, or would I love a Lochlannach because he was a Christian? Which is more important to me: how a person was born or how a person chooses to live?*

After a while, he answered Caitlin's question. "Yes, I'd trust and defend him if he were a Christian."

"Then what's stopping him from being a Christian?" Caitlin asked, surprise with Iain's admission.

"He needs to be baptized."

"And what do we need to do to have him baptized?"

Iain stared at Caitlin, wondering why she was pushing so hard. Then he said, "He needs to convince me that he's ready to surrender himself completely to Christ."

"And how can he do that?"

"I need to evaluate how much he's learned and how much he believes in the one true God," Iain replied slowly, thinking back to the criteria the Bishop had given him years earlier.

"Then there's no time to waste," Caitlin stated. "When can you evaluate him?"

"You did what?!" Ciaran demanded when Caitlin relayed her conversation with Iain to her father.

"I asked Iain to baptize Asbjorn and publically defend him with the clan," Caitlin repeated. "Asbjorn's having a hard time. He knows the risk you're taking in defending him, and he feels terrible about it. But he also wants to honor his word to you by not running away. I thought that if someone else were to start defending him from outside the family, it would help the villagers to start accepting Asbjorn more."

"What makes you think Iain will ever defend Asbjorn? You know how much he hates all Lochlannach."

"Because he loves Christians more than he hates Lochlannach," Caitlin replied. "If Asbjorn is baptized, Iain will see

Asbjorn as a Christian first. Then Iain can influence the rest of the clan to see Asbjorn that way."

"And Iain agreed to this?" Ciaran asked. He was stunned that Caitlin had found a potential solution to the problem that Asbjorn's presence was causing with the clan.

"Provided Asbjorn can prove that he's ready to be baptized, yes."

"You are an amazing young woman," Ciaran said, giving his daughter a hug. "I'm proud of you."

"Thank you, Father," Caitlin said, smiling in her father's embrace. Then she said, "I need to find Asbjorn and let him know what's happening. Do you know where he is?"

"Yes, he's down by the stream. I asked him to water a few of the horses and let them stretch their legs."

Asbjorn kept a tight grip on the rope of one of the horses when he heard someone running toward him. He turned and saw Caitlin coming down the hill from the farm with an excited look on her face. The horse, recognizing its usual rider, stopped trying to pull away from Asbjorn, and started moving toward Caitlin, hoping for a treat.

"What are you doing here?" Asbjorn asked as she reached her horse.

"Looking for you," she said, patting the side of the horse's neck. "I think I have a solution to your problem."

"Which problem is that?" Asbjorn asked.

Caitlin told Asbjorn her conversation with Iain and her father. Asbjorn listened to every word, wondering why she had gone to the trouble to help him.

"When does Iain want to test me?" he asked when she was done explaining the plan.

"Tomorrow afternoon. Some of the clan elders will be there to make sure the examination is done properly, but you should have no problems convincing them you're ready. If you pass, Iain will baptize you the next day. From that moment on, you'll be a Christian to him and not a Lochlannach. He can then use that to help the rest of the clan stop mistrusting you."

Asbjorn was surprised at what Caitlin had accomplished. "Thank you, Caitlin," he said. "But why did you do all this for me?"

"Because I want you to feel like you belong here," she said. "I don't want you to feel like you have no place in the world to call your own."

Before he knew what he was doing, Asbjorn reached forward and gave Caitlin a hug. When he realized what he had done, he was about to pull back when he felt her put her arms around him. They stood there for quite a while as the horse nudged its rider, still waiting for its treat.

"I baptize you, Asbjorn Thorleikson, in the name of the Father, the Son, and the Holy Spirit," Iain said as he pushed Asbjorn's head underneath the icy water of the stream running along the northern side of the village. Many of the villagers and Ciaran's entire family were there to watch the ceremony. Caitlin couldn't stop smiling.

For most of the previous afternoon, Iain and the village elders had questioned Asbjorn regarding his faith. At the end of the examination, they were forced to admit that Asbjorn had learned a great deal about the Christian way and seemed genuinely ready to abandon his worship of the Lochlannach gods and begin worshiping Christ. Unable to find a reason to refuse, Iain consented to baptize Asbjorn the next day.

As Iain pulled Asbjorn's head out of the water, he said to the gathered members of the clan, "Today, Asbjorn Thorleikson, who was once an enemy of our people, joins us in the brotherhood of Christ. He has proven himself worthy to receive the blessings of the Church and is now under the protection of the Church, just as all faithful Christians are. Whatever doubts you may have had regarding this young man, cast them away. He is a Christian and belongs in our fellowship just as each of you belongs. I know what is in this young man's heart, and, like our Chief, I know him to be a fine addition to our clan. His soul belongs to almighty God. Rejoice with me."

Iain's words sent a shock through the crowd. Caitlin was beaming with joy. Asbjorn stood next to Iain in the stream, dripping wet but feeling elated that someone else was finally standing up for him. Asbjorn still had questions regarding the doctrine of the church and some of its inconsistencies, but for the first time since leaving Ireland, he was starting to feel like he belonged somewhere. He looked over to Caitlin and saw her expression. He flashed her a quick smile, but their eyes remained locked on each other as the villagers slowly moved forward to welcome Asbjorn into their fellowship.

Over the next several months, Asbjorn and Caitlin had the opportunity to spend more time together. Several days a week, they went riding so Caitlin could help Asbjorn learn about the surrounding territory. They frequently visited the stone circle where Asbjorn still liked to go to think. They also walked together almost daily.

Toward the end of summer, a Lochlannach raiding party attacked the village with four longboats, and Asbjorn fought alongside the members of his clan. At one point during the fighting, Iain became surrounded by five of the raiders. He swung his sword in wide arcs to keep the raiders away, but he was tiring rapidly. Asbjorn, seeing the priest in trouble, ran through the melee and charged the raiders, shouting at them in the tongue of the Lochlannach, which caused them to hesitate long enough for Asbjorn to reach Iain.

He killed two of the raiders before they realized that he wasn't there to help them. He pushed Iain out of the way and attacked the three remaining raiders. They fought as well as the men under the command of Asbjorn's father, but in the end, they were no match for the young man who stood between them and the priest. Four of the raiders lay dead on the ground and the fifth was severely wounded. He tried to escape when another member of the clan finished him off.

"Thank you, Asbjorn," Iain said, grateful to be alive.

"You're welcome, Iain," Asbjorn said. The cross Caitlin had given him on the day he had been baptized was visible on his chest. It was covered with the blood of the raiders, but Asbjorn refused to hide it under his tunic. It was the first gift Caitlin had given him and the first gift he had received as a Christian. He intended to wear it openly and proudly for the rest of his life.

Caitlin, Ringean, and some of the other horsemen rode into the village a few minutes later and engaged the raiders who were still fighting. Soon, only three of the raiders were still alive. Asbjorn spoke to them and told them to surrender or be killed. They lowered their swords, and were soon sitting on the ground with their hands bound behind them.

With Asbjorn translating, Ciaran interrogated the prisoners until he was satisfied that the Lochlannach raiding party was not part of a larger invasion force. Then Ciaran had the prisoners killed and the bodies taken back to their boats. Once all the bodies had been loaded onboard, the longboats were set on fire and pushed out into the river, which took them west toward the sea until the ships and the dead were consumed by the fire and sank below the waves.

Several of the villagers came up to Asbjorn and thanked him for his help during the battle. Iain made a point to tell everyone how Asbjorn had saved his life. For the first time, Asbjorn felt truly accepted by the clan.

Several days later, Ciaran and Caitlin were walking across the fields to the east of the farm. After a while, Caitlin asked, "Why did you want to walk with me today?"

Ciaran kept walking in silence and Caitlin had to repeat her question several more times. "I wanted to talk to you about your betrothed," he said finally.

This was the first time Ciaran had brought up this topic since telling Caitlin that her betrothed was killed during one of the attacks against the Lochlannach at Dumbarton. Caitlin wondered why Ciaran was bringing it up.

"What about him, Father?" she asked cautiously.

"It's been eight months since he was killed in Alt Clut. I think that's sufficient time to mourn him. We need to start thinking about finding someone else to be your husband."

"Do you have someone in mind, Father, or are you just preparing me that you're going to start looking for someone to marry me off to?" Caitlin asked.

"I haven't selected anyone yet," he replied. "I wanted to know if you had any thoughts on the matter."

It was unusual for a father to consult a daughter in the matter of marriage, but Ciaran and Caitlin had the kind of father-daughter relationship where Ciaran valued Caitlin's opinions. "Why now?" she asked, avoiding the question for the moment.

"It's unseemly for someone your age to be unmarried," Ciaran stated. "You're a beautiful young woman and the daughter of the clan chief. Anyone would be lucky to have you, and I'd like to see you married by the spring."

"Do any of your friends have sons who'd be 'suitable'?" she asked, trying not to sound sarcastic. "Or do you want to use me as part of an alliance with one of the other clan chiefs?"

"I'm sure they do, and I'm sure I could. That's certainly an option, but I want to know if you have any thoughts about potential suitors. Is your heart leading you somewhere that I should know about?"

"Like where?" she asked.

Ciaran stopped walking and turned to face his daughter. "Caitlin, I've seen the way you and Asbjorn are when you're together. If you have feelings for him, I want to know before I make any decisions about your future."

Caitlin was shocked. "Would you let me marry a Lochlannach?" she asked.

"No, but I don't consider Asbjorn a Lochlannach anymore. He's part of our clan, and he's proven his loyalty to us many times since you spared his life. And unlike another suitor, you know he'd die to keep you safe. He's proven it already. If you have feelings for him, just tell me. If not, then I'll look elsewhere."

Caitlin thought about Asbjorn and the time they had been spending together. *He protected me from his brother. He's kind and gentle, and he's a fearless warrior. He's also handsome!* She never thought that her father would let them be together, so she never gave serious thought to a relationship with Asbjorn before. Now that it appeared to be an option, Caitlin found herself liking the idea very much.

"What if he doesn't want me as a wife?" Caitlin asked.

Ciaran looked at his daughter and laughed. Caitlin blushed, and then started laughing with her father. There was no doubt that Asbjorn wanted to be with Caitlin, but he'd never betray Ciaran's trust by acting on it.

"I don't think that's an issue, do you?"

"No, Father," Caitlin replied.

"So, are you saying that you want me to pursue this with Asbjorn?" Ciaran asked.

"I think so, Father. Are you sure it's what you want? Would the clan accept this?"

"I think they would, and if they don't then that's their problem. I think Asbjorn will make a fine son-in-law, and I know he'll make you happy. If this is what you want, I'll see about making it happen."

"Do you want me there when you talk to Asbjorn?"

"No," Ciaran said. "The first conversation should be man-to-man. After that, you and he should talk, and then all three of us should talk. Since he has no family here but us, there's no need to discuss this with his parents. I'll just need to discuss it with Iain to make sure that he has no objections."

"Something tells me Iain won't object," Caitlin said. "The way he talks about Asbjorn these days, I'm sure he'd be happy to help do anything for the man who saved his life."

"Something tells me you're right," Ciaran said as he turned and started walking back toward the farm.

Later that afternoon, Asbjorn found Ciaran sitting in the middle of the stone circle.

"Excuse me, Ciaran," he said as he entered the center circle. "Caitlin said you wanted to talk to me."

"Yes, Asbjorn. Please sit down across from me."

Asbjorn sat down and faced Ciaran, curious about the summons. He heard a sound above him and noticed a raven sitting on one of the great stones just over Ciaran's shoulder.

"I need to talk to you about Caitlin," Ciaran began.

"What about her?" Asbjorn asked, taking his eyes off the raven.

"In our clan, a young woman of her age would normally be married or at least betrothed by now. She was betrothed last year, but he died at Dumbarton, and I've been giving her time to mourn his loss. The mourning is now over, and it's time for me to find her a husband."

"Why are you telling me this?"

"Because I see the way the two of you are together, Asbjorn. You allowed her to escape and saved her from your brother, she spared your life, and the two of you have been spending time together. I'd think that any decisions I make about her future would affect you."

Asbjorn didn't respond, and Ciaran continued. "Normally, the daughter of a chief would be betrothed to the son of one of the clan elders, or to the son of one of the other chiefs to build a stronger tie between the two clans."

"Is that what you're going to do?" Asbjorn asked, realizing that he might never see Caitlin again.

"It's not my first choice," Ciaran admitted. "Caitlin is special to me, and I wanted her thoughts on the matter before I made my decision."

"What did she tell you?" Asbjorn asked, curious.

"She has someone in mind that she wouldn't object to marrying. He's a good person and has already proven himself to her in ways most suitors couldn't until after they had been married for several years. I have to admit that I think the union would be a good one, not only for her but for the family and for the clan."

Asbjorn felt his heart sinking lower and lower. It was one thing to know that he'd never be with her, but it was something altogether different to know that she might belong to someone else.

"Asbjorn, look at me," Ciaran said.

Asbjorn lifted his head and looked at Ciaran.

"Caitlin has said that she wants to marry you, and I support her decision. I believe there's love there, which is a rare and precious gift. You've proven yourself to her and to me. I've come to respect you and to think of you as part of the family. A marriage to my daughter would make it official. But I first need to know if you want to marry my daughter."

Asbjorn blinked. *Did I hear Ciaran correctly?* "You're asking me if I want to marry Caitlin?" he asked feeling dazed.

"Yes, Asbjorn. I'm asking if you want to marry her."

Asbjorn thought back to when he had first seen Caitlin on her horse during the siege of Dumbarton Rock. He remembered seeing her for the second time and making the decision to capture her and take her back to Ireland to keep her for his own. He remembered letting her escape after Bjornkarl tried to take her. He remembered when she spared his life. He remembered all the time they had spent together since returning to Alba, and he realized that he loved Caitlin very much. He glanced up and saw the raven still sitting on the stone, staring at him. It clocked its head, and then spread its wings and flew away to the south.

"Yes, I wish to marry your daughter," he said finally, believing the raven had delivered its message.

Ciaran smiled. "Then it shall be done," he said. "We can work out the details later, but for now, I'll get ready to make the announcement to the clan. You should go talk to Caitlin and let her know that we talked and what we decided. I think she'd like to hear it from you."

"I will, Ciaran, Thank you!"

Before he knew that he had even stood up, Asbjorn found himself running to find Caitlin. He reached the farm and saw her walking toward the barn. She was already inside when he caught up to her.

"I just talked with your father," he said, out of breath.

"How did it go?" Caitlin asked casually.

Asbjorn put his arms around her and pulled her close. He leaned in, and soon his lips touched hers. They held each other for what seemed like hours.

When he finally pulled back, Caitlin looked at him and smiled. "I guess it went well."

"Yes it did," Asbjorn confirmed as he leaned in again.

CHAPTER 14

It was almost one year after Asbjorn came to live in Airer Goídel when the finishing touches were completed on the house that he and Caitlin would live in after their wedding. The winter had been a mild one, allowing completion of the house's construction before spring. Ciaran chose the location for the house – sheltered next to a grove of trees halfway between Ciaran's house and the house of Dùghall, Ciaran's brother.

Asbjorn did most of the work on the house under the watchful eye of Ciaran, who knew how to build houses to withstand the weather common to the region. Caitlin also watched the construction with great interest, making a number of suggestions so the house would include everything she wanted.

Ciaran rode over to Dunadd to tell Raibeart mac Stiùbhart personally, both as a sign of respect and as an opportunity to get Raibeart's opinion about the reaction to the news.

Some of the chiefs of the neighboring clans, who had hoped to pursue a marriage between their sons and Ciaran's daughter, were extremely unhappy with the betrothal and sent messages stating they thought Ciaran was making a mistake. The reaction of the clan to the announcement of Caitlin's betrothal was more amusement than surprise. The villagers had seen Asbjorn and Caitlin spending time together during the months prior to the announcement.

Raibeart supported Ciaran's decision and agreed to make it clear to the clan chiefs in his region that the betrothal had his blessing.

"So much of what we do with our children is about politics rather than parenting," Raibeart commented once Ciaran told him about the betrothal. "We forget that our children are men and women in their own right with the same desires we have – to live their own lives as they wish and to love whom they will. You might easily have used Caitlin as a pawn in a political move to increase the influence of your clan, but instead you let her follow her heart and be with a man she already loves. I envy the courage it took to do that, and I think the union between those two young people will produce children who will be both beautiful and fierce warriors."

"So you approve of the betrothal?" Ciaran asked.

"You don't need my approval, old friend," Raibeart replied, "but, yes, I heartily approve. And I'll let the other chiefs know of my approval. That should silence any discontent that may arise when they realize they can't marry one of their sons to Caitlin."

Iain performed the wedding ceremony shortly after noon on a beautiful day early in the spring. The new leaves on the trees were a deep green, and the flowers had already started blooming. Caitlin looked radiant in the dress that she and Beathag had made for the occasion, and Asbjorn couldn't take his eyes off Caitlin for most of the ceremony. At one point during the service, though, Asbjorn looked up when he heard a familiar sound and saw several ravens circling the couple before flying off in different directions. Asbjorn smiled to himself, taking this as confirmation that Odin wanted the marriage to happen. Even though Asbjorn had renounced the gods of his ancestors before he was baptized, there was no denying that the ravens appeared to him when important things were about to happen.

The wedding feast was held in a field between Ciaran' and Dùghall's houses, and it lasted well into the evening. Raibeart and a few of the clan chiefs attended, but the ones most disappointed with Ciaran's decision regarding Caitlin's betrothal left early. Ciaran took no offence at their actions. He was happy to have Asbjorn as his son-in-law, and he didn't care if the other chiefs approved or not.

Ciaran's sons, Maol-Chaluim and Ringean, also supported the betrothal. They had come to know and respect the young Lochlannach, and they were pleased that their sister seemed happy with her choice for a husband. Ringean had helped Asbjorn build his new house, and the two had grown as close as blood brothers.

As the moon rose above the trees, and the feast guests grew sleepy from the food and spirits, Asbjorn and Caitlin excused themselves and walked arm-in-arm through the moonless night to their new home. Asbjorn and Caitlin had moved their belongings into the house the previous day, but this would be the first time either had slept there.

Asbjorn felt both nervous and excited about being alone with Caitlin for their first night as a married couple. Ciaran, Maol-Chaluim, and Ringean had all given him advice about how to be with a woman, but once he was alone with Caitlin, all of the things they told him vanished from his thoughts.

Caitlin also felt nervous and excited about being with Asbjorn. Beathag and Caitlin's sisters-in-law had given her plenty of advice, but Caitlin knew her own mind and knew what she wanted. When she and Asbjorn reached the house, she excused herself and changed out of her dress into a simple gown that stopped just above her knees.

When she returned, she saw Asbjorn react in the candlelight, and she smiled. Sensing Asbjorn's nervousness, she took him by the hand and led him to the bed. She helped him undress and placed his clothes on a nearby chair. Then she put her arms around him and kissed him deeply.

"I love you, Caitlin," he whispered in her ear as he put his arms around her.

"I love you, too, Asbjorn," she said as she pushed him back onto the bed.

Asbjorn looked up at her as she pulled off the gown and crawled into bed next to him. She reached for the fur blanket and covered them with it. Then she put her arms around Asbjorn again and pulled him close.

"I hope you're not too tired, my husband," she purred.

"Not even a little bit, my wife," Asbjorn said, kissing her.

"Good," she said as she pulled him on top of her.

Life over the next several weeks settled into a calm and happy routine as the spring planting and tending the flocks filled most of the days. Asbjorn and Caitlin still found ways to spend time together, and they rode with the village patrols several times a week. There was always the threat of raids now that the weather on the channel had improved.

About three weeks after the wedding, a messenger from Dunadd rode up to Ciaran's farm and delivered an urgent summons from King Causantín mac Cináeda. "The King commands for his earls and clan chiefs to join him with all possible haste," Ciaran read to his entire family over dinner. "He also says we should bring retainers with us."

Looking around the table, he said, "I'm taking Maol-Chaluim and Ringean with me. Dùghall will stay here and keep an eye on the farm and the village while we're away."

Looking at Asbjorn, he added, "Asbjorn, I want you to come with me as well."

"Of course, Ciaran," he said, looking over to his wife with a smile. "When do we leave?"

"We ride to Dunadd tomorrow to meet with Raibeart and the other chiefs from his region. Then we'll all ride to the King two days after that. We should be gone about two weeks altogether."

The ride to the King's council was easy and uneventful. Asbjorn noticed the disapproving looks that he received from some of the other chiefs and their sons, but he ignored them. He was happy with his new wife and too excited about being included in the council to care what anyone else thought.

Asbjorn had seen King Causantín from a distance at Dumbarton, but doubted that the King had given him any notice at all. When Ciaran presented Asbjorn to the King upon their arrival at the council meeting, Asbjorn felt the monarch staring intently at him as he dropped to one knee and bowed.

"I understand that you chose to remain here in exile from your countrymen," the King said, "and that you've taken a wife from your new clan."

"Yes, My King," Asbjorn said, still looking down.

The King put his hand on Asbjorn's shoulder and motioned for him to stand. He saw the cross Caitlin had given Asbjorn as a baptismal gift and raised his right eyebrow. "You're a Christian?"

"Yes, My King."

"You took your vows freely and sincerely?"

"Yes, My King."

The King thought about this for a moment. He looked at Raibeart and asked, "Then this is a man to be trusted?"

"He is, My King," Raibeart and Ciaran both answered.

"Very well. Welcome to this gathering," the King said to Asbjorn.

Once everyone had arrived, the King addressed the earls, chiefs, and retainers. "Ívarr has sent us a message from Ireland. He demands tribute, and if it's not paid to him in two months, he claims he will invade Alba. He also demands an annual tribute be made or he'll bring his fleet across the channel and conquer us, adding Alba to his ever-growing kingdoms in Britain."

The earls, chiefs, and retainers responded angrily and loudly to this news. The King let them shout for a few minutes before holding up his hand for silence.

"We are of like mind," he said. "I have no intention of paying tribute to Ívarr or any other Lochlannach, and Alba will never pay tribute as long as I and my heirs are Kings of Alba. But not paying means war, and if Ívarr intends to make good on his threat, we need to start preparing now. I believe Ívarr won't wait two months. He'll be here in one month, and we need to be ready to meet him wherever he lands."

Asbjorn was barely listening anymore. *Will Amlaíb and his men join Ívarr on this expedition? Will my father, my brother, my kin and my friends be there? Will I have to face them on the fields of battle? I knew there might come a time when I'd have to fight against my father's men, but I never thought it would be so soon.*

"I think we can assume that Ívarr and his forces will sail up the Abhainn Fìne River, My King," Raibeart was saying when Asbjorn started listening again. "It's the first major waterway leading into the interior of Alba, which is why the Dalriadans picked it when they first invaded Pictland. If we set up our defenses in Airer Goídel around Dunadd, we can control the engagement from a place that's strong, easily defended, and commands both banks of the river. And if Ívarr comes a different way, there are good roads leading from Dunadd that we can use to move our forces quickly to meet him."

"I agree," the King said. "We need to concentrate our forces at Dunadd and wait for Ívarr there. We must keep him from getting past Airer Goídel to the interior of Alba. I need all of you to raise your armies and bring them to Dunadd as quickly as possible. One decisive victory might keep us free from invasion for several years, but a loss or a draw would invite another invasion within the year and potentially put us under the yoke of making tribute to the Lochlannach for the rest of our lives."

Asbjorn felt Ciaran watching him closely on the ride back home. Finally, he turned and asked, "Why do you keep staring at me, Ciaran?"

"I'm wondering how you're feeling," his father-in-law replied.

"I'm fine. Why?"

"Because I saw the look in your eyes when you heard that we're going to defy Ívarr's demand. You're worried about facing your father and your people, aren't you?"

Asbjorn nodded. "Once I agreed to stay here, I knew there might come a day when I'd have to face in battle the people I grew up with, but I was hoping it wouldn't be so soon."

"Look, why don't you stay behind and handle the defense of the village in case raiders decide to attack while we're dealing with Ívarr's forces? That way you won't have to worry about whether your father or his men are coming with Ívarr."

"There are many in the clan who can defend the village from raiders," Asbjorn replied, "but not as many who know how Lochlannach deploy for battle. I can do more good by being with you at Dunadd than by being left behind on the farm."

"I know you can, Asbjorn," Ciaran said softly. "I'm just trying to make the situation easier on you."

"I appreciate that, Ciaran," Asbjorn said with a faint smile. "But it's going to happen sooner or later, so it might as well be sooner. Even if we defeat Ívarr, he'll be back, and my father and my people will most likely be with him. I can't hide from who I was forever. I'm your son-in-law and I'm a Christian living in Alba. You are my people now, and I need to be with my people to defend my home against Ívarr and any other invaders."

"Very well, Asbjorn. As long as you're sure."

"I am, Ciaran. Thank you for the suggestion, though. It's good to know you care."

"Of course I care, Asbjorn. Even if you weren't Caitlin's husband, I'd care and be concerned for you. You've proven to be a remarkable young man that I'm proud to have in my clan."

Asbjorn nodded gratefully. Even though there was the strong possibility that Thorleik would be with Ívarr's forces, Asbjorn thought of Ciaran as his father now, and he knew his place would be at Ciaran's side in the fight to come.

When they returned to the village, Ciaran sent word for the foot soldiers and the horsemen to gather as quickly as possible for the march to Dunadd. Asbjorn went to find Caitlin and told her what was happening.

"Your father suggested that it might be easier on me if I stayed here to defend the village," Asbjorn told her after explaining what had been discussed at the gathering. "I'm grateful for the offer, but I know my place is with the soldiers standing against Ívarr's expedition. I'm sure my father and his men will be there, including Bjornkarl, but I can't stay here just to spare myself the discomfort of facing them."

"I know you can't, my love," Caitlin said, taking his hand in hers. "You need to go. I'll stay here and keep an eye on things. If raiders come to the farm, I'll make sure they wish they hadn't."

The next morning, Asbjorn joined the rest of the horsemen shortly after sunrise. Soon, he was riding to Dunadd between Ringean and Ciaran. Maol-Chaluim was leading the foot soldiers and would be leaving for Dunadd later in the day. Dùghall remained behind to lead the defense of the village from raiders with some of the older men and the women who knew how to fight. Iain, who was with the foot soldiers, didn't protest Ciaran's decision to allow women to fight to defend the village. He had learned his lesson about starting battles with his chief.

Raibeart, the Earl of Airer Goídel, presented King Causantín with a strong defensive strategy against Ívarr's fleet on the Abhainn Fine River. "Forests run alongside both banks, both upriver and downriver of Dunadd. The landing area below the fortress is narrow and won't give Ívarr's fleet room to beach all of the ships at the same time. It'll take a while to unload the ships and get his warriors into position, and the clearing stretching from the river to

134

the fortress is long and narrow because of the forest. This will prevent the Lochlannach from being able to spread out and attack along a wider front. It'll also make them more vulnerable to an attack from the sides of the clearing."

"How can we be sure the Lochlannach will land here at Dunadd?" the King asked.

"We'll hide archers in the trees both upriver and downriver of the fortress. If the longships attempt to sail past the fortress, the archers upriver will attack, driving the invaders back. The archers downriver will then attack the fleet from behind, forcing the Lochlannach to beach the longships near Dunadd. The foot soldiers and horsemen will be hiding behind the trees on either side of the clearing. The terrain will give us a distinct advantage in the battle, and we'll force the Lochlannach to withdraw and attempt to escape back downriver. The archers waiting downriver will harass them all the way to the channel."

The King nodded. "Let's hope Ívarr brings his fleet up the river so your plan will work."

"Even if he doesn't," Raibeart said, "we'll make him regret coming on an expedition against your kingdom."

It took two weeks for the bulk of the Alban forces to arrive at Dunadd. Asbjorn and the horsemen from Airer Goídel were ordered to wait just inside the forest to the south. This would put them in a position to attack the Lochlannach from the rear. All of the other Alban forces were deployed in the forest and along the river, waiting for the signal that the longships had been sighted.

The King set up a series of watchers and beacons to alert him if the Lochlannach decided to approach from a different direction. He looked for the longships and the beacons daily, but so far, there had been no sight of the expected fleet.

Asbjorn, like the other horsemen from his clan, waited anxiously inside the forest for the invasion fleet to arrive. Scouts rode to Alt Clut and northern Britain to see if the Lochlannach forces were moving north overland, but there were no signs of armies anywhere in the south. The horsemen made sure that their weapons were sharpened and their horses were rested for the anticipated battle, but there was little else to do besides wait.

Asbjorn had told Raibeart about the berserker elixir, and Raibeart had passed this information to the King. The King selected three companies of Alba's best archers to shoot at the elixir bags as soon as the berserkers came into range. Asbjorn gave the archers detailed information about the bags and where the berserkers kept them so the archers would know where to aim.

Shortly after dawn on a misty morning about five weeks after the King's council meeting, one of the sentries posted downriver rode quickly to the fortress with urgent news. Ivarr's fleet had been sighted on the river.

CHAPTER 15

King Causantín wasn't surprised when he heard the sentry's report. *Ívarr's fleet includes over a hundred longships. I assumed he'd be prepared for us to resist his demands. It looks like he decided to bring a large enough force with him to either frighten us into paying the tribute peacefully or break our resistance and take the tribute by force.*

The Alban forces along the river and around Dunadd were well-hidden, and the longships showed no signs of slowing down as they came into view of the fortress. From his hiding place in the forest, Asbjorn saw that the longships hadn't fastened their shields to the sides. *They're not expecting an attack on this part of the river. Ívarr must think that we don't know he's coming early.*

The lead ships were well past the landing area when the archers upriver opened fire on the fleet. The hail of arrows from both banks caught the warriors in the lead ships off-guard. One arrow narrowly missed Ívarr's shoulder and killed the man standing directly behind him. Several arrows hit Thorleik's longship and killed twenty of his rowers.

    The rowers quickly mounted their shields along the longship railings to protect them from the archers. Seeing this, the archers switched to flaming arrows. The wooden shields and deck timbers caught fire easily, and soon several ships were burning on the water. The fire raged across the center deck of Ívarr's ship, sending his warriors scrambling to put out the flames before the fire spread out of control. Seeing no way to continue upriver safely past the archers, Ívarr ordered the longships to reverse direction and row downriver.

The rowers quickly turned around on their benches and started rowing in the opposite direction without turning the longships around. This aspect of the longship design gave the fleet the ability to get away from an enemy with great speed.

As the lead ships of the fleet rowed downriver to escape from the archers and their deadly hail of flaming arrows, Ívarr faced another problem – the rest of the fleet was still moving upriver. The captains of the ships moving upriver, seeing the lead ships suddenly change direction, ordered their ships to stop and reverse course to row downriver as well.

The archers hiding downriver from the fortress were waiting for this to happen. They opened fire on the rear of the fleet, killing and injuring many of the warriors. The archers then switched to flaming arrows, and the captains of the longships under attack downriver ordered their rowers to change direction and start rowing upriver again.

Soon, the river was choked with longships sailing into each other from opposite directions as their captains tried to get away from the archers. Thorleik's longship accidently rammed into a much smaller ship, breaking the hull timbers of the smaller ship. The smaller ship started to sink, and Thorleik's rowers had to pull in their oars and help rescue the warriors who jumped into the river with all of their weapons and supplies.

The archers continued firing at the Lochlannach ships. The fleet fell into complete confusion, and nothing Ívarr did could restore order.

Seeing no alternative, Ívarr ordered the fleet to beach near the fortress. He needed the men to extinguish the fires on the ships and run off the archers so the fleet could continue moving upriver and reach Scone, the capital of Alba.

When landing in enemy territory, Ívarr always deployed his berserkers first, then his seasoned warriors, and lastly his least experienced warriors. However, because of the unexpected and devastating attack by the archers, the least experienced warriors panicked and landed their longships first, making it difficult for the berserkers to reach the shore. There was a limited area for landing because of the forests along the river, so the longships already on shore had to move to allow the remaining longships to land.

By the time Ívarr reached shore, he was frustrated with the deployment of his warriors. He was also surprised that there were no Alban forces from the nearby fortress rushing out to engage his men. In fact, apart from the archers upriver and downriver, who were still firing on the longships, there was no sign of life anywhere along the river or around the fortress.

Once the berserkers finally reached land, Ívarr ordered them to form a perimeter around the landing area. Then he ordered two groups of his experienced warriors to deal with the archers who were hiding in the forests along the river.

King Causantín and Raibeart watched with satisfaction from the upper wall of the fortress as Ívarr beached his longships and tried to get the confused warriors organized. When the two groups of warriors moved away from the landing area to hunt down the archers, Raibeart nodded to a nearby guard, who gave the first signal to the waiting Alban soldiers.

Ívarr heard the signal horn sound and turned to face the fortress. The clearing between the landing area and the fortress was still empty and completely silent. Ívarr looked at Thorleik, who was standing next to him with a concerned look on his face.

"What was that?" Ívarr demanded.

"It sounded like a signal horn, but I don't know who or what it was signaling," Thorleik replied, looking around for any sign of Alban soldiers.

Suddenly, the gates of the fortress opened, and Alban soldiers poured down the causeway with the King and Raibeart in the lead. Ívarr saw the soldiers form ranks at the base of the fortress. He sent runners with instruction for his warriors to forget about the archers and move forward to engage the soldiers.

The berserkers took their position in front and moved forward toward the waiting soldiers. The berserkers reached for their elixir bags to drink and begin the fighting frenzy. The companies of archers, who had worked with Asbjorn and who were waiting on either side of the clearing for this, opened fire on the berserkers. Many of the berserkers, who were not yet under the elixir's influence, fell when the first hail of arrows hit. Many others discovered their leather elixir bags were damaged and leaking. The berserkers started drinking the elixir as quickly as they could, but wave after wave of arrows cut down their ranks faster than the Lochlannachs expected.

"It looks like the archers are shooting at the elixir begs," Thorleik said when he saw the berserkers trying to save the leather bags they all carried. "How is it possible they know to aim for that?"

"I don't know," Ívarr confessed. "But this is starting to look like a well-laid trap."

"How did they know we were coming?"

"Causantín must have guessed that I'd send the fleet early to collect the tribute," Ívarr surmised, looking around. *This isn't ground that I would have chosen for a battle, but there's no way I can back down from this fight. I wish I had waited for Amlaíb to return before setting out on this expedition. I need him here with me now.*

Resigning himself to the situation, Ívarr ordered Thorleik to send his warriors to flush out the companies of archers who were targeting the berserkers. Then he ordered the rest of his warriors to deploy for battle.

The least experienced warriors stayed with the longships and tried to put out the fires caused by the archers, who were still firing flaming arrows from the opposite bank of the river. Several longships had to be pushed out into the river to keep their fires from spreading to the other ships along the shore.

Thorleik's warriors moved toward the companies of archers who were still firing at the berserkers. Just before they reached the archers, though, another signal horn sounded, and the companies of archers stopped firing and retreated to the fortress. Thorleik ordered his warriors to join the surviving berserkers and move against the Alban soldiers.

King Causantín waited until the Lochlannach had almost reached his soldiers, and then he gave the order to signal the rest of his forces to attack.

Foot soldiers ran from their hiding places in the forest and attacked Ívarr's warriors on both sides. As the warriors tried to regroup to face the soldiers charging in on their flanks, King Causantín ordered the soldiers at the base of the fortress to attack.

Ívarr found himself being attacked on all sides. He looked around for a way to escape, but there was none. The archers, who were deploying in a ring around the warriors, fired again. The warriors hid beneath their shields, giving the approaching Alban soldiers an advantage. The soldiers attacked the Lochlannach raiders ferociously. The battle became a melee as the ranks of soldiers and warriors broke down into clusters of fighting all around the clearing.

Ívarr was furious as he swung his great battle axe at the attacking soldiers. *How is it that the Albans are so well-prepared for us? Thor, help us be victorious this day.*

Asbjorn watched the battle begin and waited for Ciaran to give the order to attack. *I thought I was ready for this. I thought I could fight Ívarr's warriors and kill them as invaders. I fought against the raiders who attacked our village, but this is different. These are my people. If I fight them, I betray my family and can never go home. If I don't fight, then I betray Ciaran and Caitlin's trust, and I can't stay here in Alba with my new family.*

He glanced over at Ciaran and Ringean. *The ravens led me here, so they must want me to be with the Albans. That means I have to fight the warriors.* He steadied himself and prepared for the order to charge.

Ciaran led the horsemen from their hiding place and attacked the warriors from the rear. Asbjorn and the horsemen from his clan slammed into the rear of Ívarr's forces at the same time that the King and his foot soldiers reached the front ranks of the warriors. Asbjorn swung his sword at anyone within reach, but his blows caused only minor injuries. *I'd rather not kill any of them. I used to be one of them. I'll defend myself, but I don't want to kill.*

The warriors, unprepared for the ferocity of the mounted attack, broke and ran in an attempt to get to safety. The horsemen wheeled around and attacked the warriors defending the longships. The inexperienced warriors who were trying to get the fires under control were forced to abandon the longships and join in the fight.

The warriors, who broke and ran from the horsemen, regrouped and attacked when they saw the longships in danger. They knew that the fleet needed to be protected at all costs if they were ever going to see home again.

Asbjorn and the other horsemen heard the warriors approaching and turned to face them. The warriors reached the horsemen, and after a few minutes, Asbjorn and the others found themselves surrounded. *There's no longer a choice. If I don't kill them, they'll surely kill me.*

He grimly looked around at the warriors around him. *I was raised believing that a warrior's highest goal was to be chosen for Valhalla to join the army of the gods. Perhaps Odin needs me to be with the Albans to send him more warriors. Either way, it looks like that's what I'm going to do. Forgive me, Father.*

Asbjorn hacked at the warriors with his sword, and, fortunately for him, they weren't able to get past his defenses. Two members of Asbjorn's clan rode up to support him, and soon the attacking warriors were pushed back. Asbjorn and his companions pressed forward, killing and wounding as many warriors as they could.

Thorleik and his warriors were pushed back toward the center of the clearing, but their experience and discipline kept the Albans from breaking their ranks or getting past them. Fresh soldiers attacked from the sides, though, and after an hour of difficult fighting, Thorleik's ranks finally broke, and the Albans poured through the breach toward the center of the Lochlannach forces. Thorleik rallied his men and attempted to reach the Alban King, but they were pushed back and eventually retreated to where Ívarr and his personal guards were fighting.

The battle raged for several hours before Ívarr finally admitted that the battle couldn't be won. His forces were never able to get organized, and the Albans were slaughtering his warriors on all sides. Most of the berserkers were dead or wounded, and as the elixir wore off, the surviving berserkers found themselves unable to sustain their fighting strength.

King Causantín stayed in the most intense parts of the battle. Many kings would let others lead the charge against the enemy, but Causantín insisted on leading his soldiers. He and his bodyguards fought their way toward the center of the Lochlannach ranks. Causantín wanted to reach Ívarr and personally kill the Norse King of Britain who dared to demand tribute from Alba. Causantín hacked at Ívarr's defenders until he was only a few feet away from the King of the Lochlannachs.

Causantín leapt from his horse and ran at Ívarr with his sword raised for a killing blow. Ívarr, seeing the movement out of the corner of his eye, turned and barely managed to duck out of the way as the sword swung for his exposed neck. He raised his axe and attacked Causantín. Causantín rushed forward and slammed his fist into the side of Ívarr's face, knocking off Ívarr's helmet and splitting his cheek just below the eye. Ívarr fell back, but managed to kick Causantín in the thigh, which prevented Causantín from striking Ívarr on the ground. Using his axe to help him stand, Ívarr got back to his feet and circled Causantín in the center of the melee.

Several of Causantín's soldiers rushed forward to attack Ívarr, but the King motioned for them to stay back. This fight was between Causantín and Ívarr alone, and only one would walk away from it alive. Most of Ívarr's bodyguards were dead, and the soldiers kept any of the other warriors from coming to the aid of their leader.

Thorleik watched as Ívarr and Causantín fought. A quick assessment of their fighting styles told him that Ívarr was at a disadvantage. *Ívarr stayed away from the hard fighting as much as possible. Causantín led his soldiers into battle and has been fighting for hours, but he doesn't appear tired at all. The Alban King seems to be getting stronger at the prospect of killing Ívarr, and Ívarr can't hold on much longer.* Thorleik and his warriors pushed their way toward Ívarr, but the Alban soldiers surrounding the two kings made it impossible for Thorleik to offer any help.

Causantín picked up a fallen shield, but Ívarr broke it with his axe. Causantín threw the shield away and rushed Ívarr before the Lochlannach leader brought his axe back around. Causantín thrust with his sword, and Ívarr's eyelids and mouth opened wide as the blade ran him through. He dropped his axe as his knees buckled. Causantín pulled out his sword, and blood poured out of Ívarr onto the ground. Ívarr gasped one last time, and then fell face down onto the ground.

Thorleik and his warriors cried out at the loss of their leader. Thorleik heard Causantín order for Ívarr's head to be hacked off and put on a pike for all to see. Thorleik shouted for the surviving warriors to push toward the river and the waiting longships. It was time to make their escape.

Asbjorn's shield was torn from his arm by an axe-wielding warrior, but Ringean suddenly appeared and killed the warrior before Asbjorn was harmed. Asbjorn and Ringean, who were each on their third horses, continued attacking the warriors who were trying to get to the longships on the riverbank. Asbjorn had several cuts along his arm and upper leg, but his wounds didn't slow him down.

When Asbjorn and Ringean saw Causantín raise Ívarr's head on a pike, they heard a great shout from the Alban soldiers near the center of the clearing. Then Asbjorn saw Ringean fighting another warrior. He moved to help his brother-in-law, but the Lochlannach warrior pulled Ringean off his horse, causing him to drop his sword. Asbjorn raced forward, and used his sword to block an axe blow aimed for Ringean's head. He hacked at the warrior, giving Ringean time to retrieve his own sword and kill the warrior.

Asbjorn then heard a familiar voice shouting in the tongue of the Lochlannach. Turning, he saw Thorleik leading the warriors who were fighting their way back to the longships. *Father must have taken command of the Lochlannach forces when Ívarr was killed. Why isn't Amlaíb taking charge of the expedition?*

The archers, who had attacked the berserkers, took position between the Alban soldiers and the retreating warriors. They fired wave after wave of arrows at the Lochlannach. The archers on the opposite bank of the river had exhausted their supply of arrows. They moved upriver in case the Lochlannach tried to simply cross the river and deploy their warriors on the opposite bank from the Alban army.

Ciaran shouted for the horsemen to regroup and prevent the retreating Lochlannach from seeking refuge in the forest. Asbjorn reached out his hand and lifted Ringean onto the back of his horse. He wheeled around and followed the other horsemen back toward the edge of the forest. When he turned to face the warriors again, he saw many of the berserkers running for the longships. He recognized Bjornkarl, and part of him was disappointed that his brother had escaped to fight another day.

"Thanks, Asbjorn," Ringean said as he got down from Asbjorn's horse. "I thought that Lochlannach was going to kill me."

"Any time, brother," Asbjorn said, smiling at his brother-in-law. "You had my back when I lost my shield, and I wanted to return the favor."

Ringean ran off to find another horse. Asbjorn watched the Lochlannach warriors reach the longships and try to escape. He knew the longships faced more archers as they rowed downriver, and he knew the archers would make sure that no Lochlannach jumping out of a burning longship made it to shore. *I wonder how many more of the warriors will die before the longships make it back to Ireland.*

Asbjorn looked back at the clearing and saw the dead and dying warriors all around. *These were my people. I used to live among them. Some of them were my friends. Some were even family! And now they're dead and waiting for the Valkyries to come and choose who will go to Valhalla, and I'm fighting with the soldiers who killed them. Is this what Odin wanted me to do here today?*

Asbjorn turned back toward the river. *No. Alba is my home now, and Caitlin and her kin are my family. Father always said that you must do what is necessary to protect your family, and that's what I did here today.* Asbjorn knew he had done what needed to be done, but the Lochlannach in him felt sad about the day's work.

Asbjorn watched as Thorleik's ship rowed out of sight. The sun was getting lower in the afternoon sky as the last longship pushed away from the shore and started rowing downriver toward the channel and safety.

The waiting archers opened fire on the longships, but Thorleik ordered the fleet to row as fast as possible toward the channel. Flaming arrows fell all around. Thorleik shouted for anyone not rowing to put out the fires and ordered the rowers to increase speed to get clear of the archers.

Ciaran and the horsemen rode along the riverbank to make sure that the surviving longships didn't try to land somewhere else. The archers waiting downriver killed hundreds of Lochlannach and set fire to at least twenty more longships that eventually sank. The horsemen followed the longships until it became too dark to see the path, but the lanterns and torches on the longships were seen getting smaller and smaller in the distance until they finally disappeared when the fleet reached the mouth of the channel and turned south toward Áth Cliath.

The horsemen returned to the fortress the next morning. Foot soldiers and local villagers were still working to identify the dead and save the wounded Alban soldiers injured during the battle. The Lochlannach wounded had been killed, and the funeral fires were still burning close to the river, making a terrible smell that no one present would soon forget.

Maol-Chaluim had been injured when he became surrounded shortly after the men of the clan attacked Ívarr's right side, but the wound was clean, and he was expected to make a full recovery. Ciaran checked on Maol-Chaluim, and then he checked on the rest of his clansmen before leaving Asbjorn and Ringean to find Raibeart.

"Did you see your father?" Ringean asked Asbjorn as they waited for Maol-Chaluim to regain consciousness.

"Yes. He took charge after the King killed Ívarr. He ordered the retreat. I saw Bjornkarl as well. They both looked uninjured, but I don't know if the archers changed that."

"Are you glad that you didn't have to fight them?"

Asbjorn nodded. "I would have fought them if there were no choice, but we were too far away from them."

Later that day, Ciaran found them and gave them an update from the King. "It looks like we killed almost half of Ívarr's forces. We estimate that there were almost twenty-five hundred Lochlannach killed either by the archers or during the battle, and the fires destroyed fifty longships. Our forces lost about seven hundred altogether, but close to a thousand more were wounded. It's the most serious defeat of the Lochlannach in years, and with Ívarr dead, it'll be a long time before they'll be ready to attack us again."

"I wouldn't be so sure," Asbjorn said. "Ívarr's dead, but Amlaíb wasn't here. When he gets the news, he'll proclaim himself to be the Norse King of Britain, taking all of Ívarr's conquered lands as his own. That's a lot of land and a lot of wealth that he'll control – enough to build a new fleet and train new warriors. We hurt them badly today, and they won't forget it. But it won't be enough to keep them from trying again. In fact, it'll make them more determined than ever before to invade us. Remember, Lochlannachs believe that their gods require them to do battle with strong enemies to prove themselves worthy of Valhalla. It probably won't be next year or the year after, but I believe they'll be back within three years, and it'll be the largest fleet that Áth Cliath has ever sent against an enemy."

"Are you sure, Asbjorn?" Ciaran asked.

Asbjorn nodded. "I have no doubts. Yesterday's loss will drive them mad, and Amlaíb won't rest until the killing of his kinsman is avenged. It's their way."

"Then I'd better tell Raibeart and the King about this," Ciaran said. "We need to make sure we're ready since I doubt Amlaíb will repeat the mistake of announcing that he's coming here to receive tribute."

"I think you can depend on Amlaíb attacking us unannounced," Asbjorn said. "He never cared for Ívarr's arrogance. He knows Alba will be hard to take and harder to hold. He won't attack until he's sure he can defeat us and keep us from defying him ever again."

CHAPTER 16

At the same time that Ívarr realized the Alban King had set a trap for the Lochlannach warriors at Dunadd, Amlaíb and his fleet of cargo ships rowed into the harbor at Áth Cliath. They were returning from the slave markets in southern Europe, where they successfully sold all of the prisoners taken on the last several expeditions.

Amlaíb looked around the harbor and was surprised that it seemed deserted. *Where are the longships? Where are the warriors? Ívarr was planning to sail to Alba to collect tribute, but my men and I were supposed to be part of the expedition. Ívarr's fleet wasn't supposed to leave the longphort until I returned with the empty cargo ships.*

Amlaíb jumped ashore as soon as his ship beached along the banks of the harbor. He strode quickly to the longphort to find out why the fleet was gone. "Where is the fleet?" he demanded of one of the guards at the longphort's gate.

"Ívarr and the fleet sailed three days ago," the guard said.

"Madness!" Amlaíb muttered as he pushed past the guard and continued to the great house that served as his palace. He glanced back once to make sure that the treasure was being unloaded from the cargo ships. When he reached the great house, he ordered the servant to summon his council.

"The council members aren't here," the servant said. "They sailed with Ívarr and the rest of the fleet."

"You mean Ívarr took my warriors on his expedition without me?" Amlaíb snarled.

"Yes, sir. He took about a hundred ships altogether."

Amlaíb was furious that his council members would abandon the agreement and sail without their leader, but he knew his kinsman was of higher rank and had the authority to force

Thorleik and the others to obey. "I can't believe Thorleik would go without telling me," he said.

"Thorleik sent three ships to find you," the servant commented. "They haven't returned yet."

Amlaíb nodded. The winds had been especially strong on the voyage back to Áth Cliath, and the empty cargo ships were blown off course several times. It made sense that Thorleik's ships might have missed Amlaíb's fleet.

Amlaíb spent the rest of the day overseeing the division of the shares of the treasure from the slave markets. Warriors received a portion of the sale of each of the slaves they captured, and Ívarr, Amlaíb, and the nobles and council members each received tribute. Hundreds of slaves had been sold, and the gold and silver coins from their sale were bagged and labeled for distribution once the fleet returned from Alba.

The next morning, Amlaíb was still furious that Ívarr had sailed with the fleet a month early. *Even if he reaches the Alban capital, King Causantín's army shouldn't be underestimated. Ívarr doesn't have enough men with him to take on the Albans yet. He should have waited at least a year until we finished replacing the longships and the warriors we lost at Dumbarton.*

Amlaíb spent most of the day pacing the walkways along the top of the longphort walls, watching for the returning fleet. *I hope Ívarr didn't send a messenger to Causantín demanding tribute. He should've just sail to Alba, captured the capital, and demanded a ransom for Causantín and the rest of the city before the Alban army could be summoned.*

Amlaíb felt that Ívarr had too much flare for the dramatic and too little common sense. Ívarr was a fearless warrior on campaign, but Amlaíb knew that his kinsman took too many chances. Ívarr had a habit of making his intentions known to his enemies, and it was only because of the skill of his warriors that his enemies were defeated anyway.

The sun had already set when a servant came to find Amlaíb on the walls. "You need to eat," the servant said to Amlaíb. "The guards will let you know as soon as the fleet is sighted."

Amlaíb nodded and followed the servant back to the great house. *If all goes well, the fleet won't return for another week.* As they walked in the darkness, he tried not to think about what might cause the fleet to return sooner.

It was late in the morning two days later when a guard burst into the great house and informed Amlaíb that the fleet had been sighted. Amlaíb followed the guard back to the harbor and watched as the longships rowed closer to the shore. Looking around, he noticed that Ívarr's great longship was nowhere to be seen. He also noticed that the fleet was much smaller than it should have been. There were fewer than sixty ships rowing into the harbor from the channel, and Amlaíb saw fire damage on most of them.

Thorleik's ship beached first, and Thorleik jumped down and quickly approached Amlaíb.

"Tell me Ívarr didn't tell the Albans in advance that he was coming to demand tribute," Amlaíb said.

Thorleik couldn't look Amlaíb in the eyes. He just nodded.

Amlaíb clenched his fists and shouted at the sky. Thorleik looked at his leader without saying a word, waiting for Amlaíb to calm down. Amlaíb shook his head as more longships beached themselves along the harbor. The warriors jumped down onto the beach looking tired and defeated.

Turning back to Thorleik, Amlaíb said, "Where's Ívarr?"

"He died at the hands of the Alban King. I took command and ordered the retreat. They were ready for us, and the enemy was determined to crush our forces. We lost half our strength before we were able to get back to the ships. I've never seen a battle go so badly."

As the other surviving members of his council walked up, Amlaíb gestured for them to follow him back to his great house. "I want to hear it all," he said as he led them through the gates of the longphort.

For the rest of the afternoon, Thorleik and the other members of the council gave Amlaíb a detailed report of the expedition and the battle at Dunadd. They told him about the archers along the river who forced them to beach the longships, and how they found themselves surrounded by the Alban army.

Thorleik told Amlaíb about how the archers targeted the berserkers. "It's as if someone told them about the elixir," he said.

150

"The archers were shooting at the berserkers and targeting the elixir bags. I don't know why they would have done that unless someone told them what was in the bags and how the elixir works. We lost more than half of the berserkers before the real fighting even started. The Albans knew exactly what to do and where to hit us the hardest."

"Do you suppose any of the prisoners they took at Dumbarton talked?" Amlaíb asked.

"I think some of them must have as a way to try to avoid execution," Thorleik responded. "Most of the warriors we lost were the less experienced ones, and the young fear death more than those of us who have seen battle before."

"Even knowing what the gods expect of them?" Amlaíb demanded.

"What do the young really know of the gods and their expectations?" Thorleik replied bitterly. "We fill their heads from an early age with the stories of Valhalla, glory, tribute, and praiseworthy lives, but until they're hardened by battles, they're still just children who know nothing about life and death. If a sixteen or seventeen year-old watches his fellow prisoners being beheaded by the enemy, who's to say he wouldn't tell everything he knows to avoid the same fate?"

"Do you think Asbjorn might have done that?" Amlaíb asked.

Thorleik was silent. He had been wrestling with that question on the voyage back to Áth Cliath, and it troubled him. *If Asbjorn exchanged information to save his own life, then he might still be alive. But if that information helped the Alban King give Ívarr his worst and final defeat, then Asbjorn would be responsible for the loss of hundreds of his own people.*

Finally, Thorleik said, "I hope not."

"So do I," Amlaíb agreed. "We lost many warriors as we were leaving Dumbarton. Chances are good that it was one of the others who gave up the information."

Thorleik nodded, but he also knew that Asbjorn spoke the tongue of the Albans. *That makes it more likely that Asbjorn exchanged information to save his own life.*

Then he remembered the young female his son had taken prisoner. *Is it possible she induced him to betray his own people?*

This thought disturbed him, and he shook his head to clear the thought. Amlaíb was still asking questions about the battle and Ívarr's death, and while Thorleik did his best to answer, he kept seeing the image of his son and the female prisoner in his mind.

Once the surviving council members had finished relating the events of the raid on Alba, Thorleik asked, "So what are your plans, Amlaíb? You're technically Ívarr's heir, which makes you the new Norse King of Britain."

"And I claim his title," Amlaíb said. "I also claim all of Ívarr's lands, warriors, ships, treasure, and tribute. We're going to use that treasure and tribute to rebuild our fleet and train new warriors."

"I want the largest fleet ever constructed," he continued. "The next time we go to Alba, I want to sail from Áth Cliath with over two hundred and fifty ships and fifteen thousand warriors. Send word to our kinsmen on the islands around Alba that there's tribute and slaves enough for all of them if they'll join with us. And pass the word to all of our ship captains: no more raids along the Alban coastline. From now on, we're preparing for one massive invasion. It won't come this year or even next year, but the year after that we'll sail for Alba and take it all. No one who raises a sword to stop us will survive. We'll put Alba to the axe and grind it into submission once and for all. Then we'll have all of Britain under our rule for the first time!"

The members of the council cheered Amlaíb and his plan. This was an ambitious but workable plan that would give each of them unequalled wealth and glory if they were successful.

"Send word to Ívarr's holdings in Britain that I am now the Norse King of Britain and all tribute must be paid to me on time. Make sure the Britons know that if they defy me or are even a day late with their tribute, I'll burn their lands to cinders and send their entire population to the slave markets."

After the meeting ended, Thorleik returned to his home, only to find that Bergdís, his wife, hadn't been feeling well for several days and was now in bed with a fever. Thorleik stayed by her side for two weeks, feeding her and taking care of her as well as he could.

She put on a brave face for him, but he knew she was slipping away. She saw that something other than her health was troubling him, and she pushed until he finally told her about the battle and his suspicions that one of the warriors captured at Dumbarton had given the Albans crucial information about how to defeat the Norse forces.

"Do you think it was Asbjorn?" she asked.

"I don't know. I hope not, but it's possible. He knew their language…"

"Just because he knew how to speak with them doesn't mean he did speak with them!" she said angrily, causing her to start coughing uncontrollably.

Thorleik held her, wishing he hadn't mentioned anything about Asbjorn knowing the Alban tongue. Bergdís had taught Asbjorn the language of the Albans, and Thorleik didn't want his wife thinking that he blamed her in any way.

Bjornkarl came by to see his mother several days later, but by then Bergdís was delirious and didn't recognize him. Four days after that, Thorleik woke up to find that Bergdís had died in her sleep.

The loss of his wife seemed to drain all of the compassion out of Thorleik. He became quick-tempered and driven to train his warriors longer and harder than anyone else. He also pushed his shipbuilders to construct larger ships faster than ever before. Even Bjornkarl, who wasn't afraid of anyone, became nervous whenever he was around his father. All Thorleik seemed to care about was preparing for the next invasion of Alba.

Amlaíb, seeing Thorleik's way of handling his grief, put the warrior in charge of preparing the entire expedition, including building the new longships and training the new warriors. *If we're successful invading Alba, I'll put Thorleik over Alba and Alt Clut to rule those lands for me. He's earned it, and he'll need a new challenge once the conquest of Alba is finished.*

Caitlin was waiting for Asbjorn when the horsemen returned to the village a week after the battle at Dunadd. Messengers had already informed the village of the great victory against the Lochlannach invaders, and Ciaran sent word to his family that everyone was safe and would be home soon. The clan had suffered a few losses during the battle. Iain, who suffered only minor scratches during the battle, held a special service to give thanks for the victory and for the safety of the clan.

Maol-Chaluim's broken arm and ribs healed quickly, as did the cut on his forearm from a Lochlannach axe. Ringean learned that his wife was pregnant when he returned home, and it was days before he stopped smiling at the news.

Caitlin wanted to hear all of the stories about the battle, and she was especially interested in hearing Asbjorn's thoughts about fighting his former people. *I can see that Asbjorn's troubled about his participation in the battle. I wish there was something I could do to help him get past whatever's bothering him.* After a few weeks, though, the battle faded into distant memory as the day-to-day chores and needs of the farm commanded everyone's attention.

About two months after Asbjorn returned from Dunadd, he noticed that Caitlin seemed to be ill. Every time he saw her, she was throwing up. He was about to send for a Healer when Caitlin finally pulled him aside and told him not to worry.

"I'm not sick, Asbjorn," she said. "I'm pregnant!"

Asbjorn was thrilled at the news and couldn't wait to tell the rest of the family. Everyone was excited, and the women spent a great deal of time talking, planning, and helping Caitlin prepare for the changes that would be happening to her during the pregnancy.

There were several small longboat raids from the nearby islands toward the end of the summer and early autumn, but the men of the village handled them easily. The Lochlannachs who occupied the Alban islands knew about Ívarr's attempted invasion and mistakenly thought that the Albans would be too weak to put up much of a resistance. The men of the village made sure that none of the raiders ever made it back to the islands, giving the Lochlannach on the islands reason to fear the fighting skills of the Albans.

Winter came and seemed to be colder than anyone remembered. Caitlin's pregnancy kept her from doing much around the house.

One morning, shortly before the new year, she woke up and reached for Asbjorn, only to find his side of the bed empty. She looked around, but he wasn't in the house. She was about to get up and look for him when the door opened and Asbjorn entered, carrying two pails of water.

"What are you doing, Asbjorn?" she asked.

Asbjorn put the pails down and smiled at her. "I was just getting us some fresh water."

Caitlin got out of bed and crossed the room to her husband. Putting her arms around him, she said, "That's my job, Asbjorn."

"I know, but you need to rest. I don't mind getting the water."

Caitlin smiled. "But you're already doing most of the work around the house."

"And I'll do whatever is needed to make things easier on you," he said, kissing her cheek. "You need to make sure that you stay healthy for the baby. I'll take care of everything else."

"I knew there was a reason I saved your life," Caitlin said, laughing.

Later that day, while Caitlin repaired the corner of Asbjorn's cloak that had snagged on a rock by the stream, she glanced up and noticed that Asbjorn was staring at her.

"I wish you'd stop doing that, Asbjorn," she said softly. "Every time I look up, you're staring at me."

"I can't help it," Asbjorn said. "You're just so beautiful!"

"I'm not beautiful," she stated. "I'm huge."

"You're beautiful," he said under his breath.

"No I'm not," she whispered.

"Yes you are."

Caitlin went back to her sewing, but she was smiling. She knew that Asbjorn was excited to be a father, and she believed he'd be a good one. She knew from her friends in the village that many of the men were distant with their children and refused to help the women while they were pregnant. She was glad Asbjorn wasn't like any of those men.

Asbjorn stayed close to the farm once spring arrived, knowing that the baby might come any day. Every time he saw anyone approach, he jumped, assuming it was news about the baby. Ciaran and his sons laughed each time, but they were happy that Asbjorn was so excited about becoming a father. It seemed to take his mind off the lingering guilt he felt about the battle at Dunadd.

On a beautiful day just after Asbjorn and Caitlin's first wedding anniversary, Asbjorn received word that Caitlin needed him to come back to the house quickly. When he arrived, the Healer was just coming out. He looked up at Asbjorn and smiled.

"Congratulations, Asbjorn," the Healer said. "Caitlin and the baby are fine. You have a son!"

Asbjorn thanked the Healer. Glancing up, he saw a raven perched on the roof of the house and smiled. *I guess Odin is sending his blessings to my new son.* He entered the house. Caitlin was on the bed, looking exhausted but happy. Next to her, swaddled in a blanket that Caitlin had made during the winter, was Asbjorn's newborn son. Caitlin smiled at Asbjorn, who knelt next to her and gave her a gentle hug.

"How are you, Caitlin?" he asked softly, brushing aside a lock of hair covering her cheek.

"I'm glad it's over," she replied with a tired smile. "Did the Healer tell you it's a boy?"

Asbjorn nodded.

"He's healthy and he's blonde," Caitlin told the new father. "He looks like your son."

"May I hold him?" Asbjorn asked.

Caitlin showed him how and then handed him the baby. The baby's eyes were closed and he appeared to be sleeping. Asbjorn thought that his son was the most beautiful thing he had ever seen.

A short time later, Ciaran and the rest of the family arrived to meet the newest addition to the clan and to Ciaran's family. "What are you naming him?" Ringean's wife whispered when it was her turn to look at the baby's face.

"Alasdair," Caitlin replied.

"That's a good, strong name," Ciaran said, nodding with approval. "It's our word for Alexander, who was a great warrior and king in ancient Greece."

"What will his full name be?" Ringean's wife asked.

"Since my husband decided to keep his Lochlannach name when he was baptized, but has agreed to follow the way we name children, the baby will be known as Alasdair mac Asbjorn," Caitlin said with a smile.

"Alasdair Asbjornsson just didn't sound right for an Alban clansman," Asbjorn admitted.

Everyone laughed softly and congratulated the happy parents several times. The baby, unaware that he was the center of attention, slept peacefully next to his exhausted mother.

CHAPTER 17

In the early autumn, word reached Raibeart mac Stiùbhart of several raids in the northern part of Alba by the Lochlannach who controlled the islands in that area. Raids in the north were common, but these were different. The Lochlannach appeared to be doing more than just looking for plunder and prisoners. They seemed to be probing the Alban defenses and assessing how quickly the Albans responded to their presence. It was as if the raiders were preparing for an invasion, rather than their normal incursions, and King Causantín mac Cináeda was concerned.

Raibeart summoned all of the clan chiefs in Airer Goídel to meet with him at Dunadd to discuss the northern raids. Asbjorn accompanied Ciaran, Ringean, and Ciaran's brother Dùghall to the meeting. Maol-Chaluim remained behind to work the farm and command the defense of the village.

Once the chiefs had assembled, Raibeart informed them about the raids and explained why the raids seemed different. "The King is concerned," he stated before sitting down to let his chiefs discuss the information. "The Lochlannach are up to something, and it's possible that the Lochlannach from the islands around Alba and the Lochlannach from Ireland may be working together for the first time."

"I'd like to know what Asbjorn thinks about this," Ciaran said when Raibeart gestured for the chief to speak.

"So would I," Raibeart said as Ciaran sat down. "Is there an alliance between the Lochlannach of the islands and Amlaíb?"

Asbjorn stood. "I wasn't aware of an alliance before the expedition to Dumbarton, but it's possible that one exists now. My father told me many stories about Amlaíb, and from what I remember, Amlaíb will want to crush Alba with one massive invasion to avenge his kinsman, Ívarr. As a Lochlannach, he also believes that his gods demand he prove his worth against an enemy that has already shown itself to be a difficult opponent. There have always been the occasional exchange between Áth Cliath and the Lochlannach who control the islands around Alba. If Amlaíb wants to invade Alba within the next five years, he'll need allies, and the island Lochlannach would be the perfect choice."

"I heard that you believe Amlaíb will be back in less than two years," Raibeart commented.

Asbjorn nodded. "He knows he needs to rebuild his fleet and replace the warriors that were lost when Ívarr attacked us last year. It takes time to build longships and prepare that many warriors for battle. He also needs to elevate hundreds of warriors into the ranks of the berserkers, and that's not an easy thing to do. Unlike Ívarr, Amlaíb's patient, and he's not going to repeat the mistakes of his kinsman. He'll spend every bit of gold and silver he has to make sure Alba cannot possibly survive the next invasion, and sending tribute to the island Lochlannach to secure their support is something he'd consider a smart way to use his treasure."

"How do we defend against this?" Raibeart asked.

Asbjorn shook his head. "I don't know, Sir. He'll send a huge fleet against us, hoping that the size of the fleet will terrify us into surrendering peacefully, but after what happened on the river to Ívarr's fleet last year, I don't think he'll have all of his forces with him. I think we can assume that he'll have the island Lochlannach also attack from the north and east to spread us too thin to defend ourselves from the main invasion force."

Asbjorn sat down and the room was silent as the assembled chiefs and retainers thought about what he had said. Then Raibeart stood up.

"Thank you for sharing your thoughts, Asbjorn," he said. "The King has asked us to help identify how we can defend ourselves against the Lochlannach, and from what you have shared, it seems that defending ourselves will be much more difficult than anyone believed."

The group discussed the matter for the next two days, but was no closer to identifying a solution to the problem than they had been when the meetings started. Shortly after lunch, a messenger from the King arrived with a summons for Raibeart and his chiefs to join the King for a war council meeting at Scone. Raibeart sent messengers to the villages to let them know their chiefs wouldn't be returning as quickly as planned, and then he, along with the chiefs and their retainers, left Dunadd and rode northeast with the King's messenger in the lead.

The council had been going on for two days when King Causantín slammed his fist on the table in frustration at their lack of progress. "Can we at least agree that Amlaíb and his forces will make for Scone by the most direct route when they invade?" he asked the council members.

"Yes, My King," Raibeart answered for the assembled earls, chiefs, and retainers.

"And if you were Amlaíb, and you didn't want to sail all the way around Alba to attack us from the east, where would you land your forces?"

"I would land them just upriver from Dumbarton," the earl from the lands east of Airer Goídel stated. "It's an area that he already controls, so there'd by less risk to his fleet, and it's the narrowest part of Britain for an overland expedition to Scone. It's also one of the few places large enough for a fleet the size of the one we're speculating he's going to send."

"King Rhun is our ally!" one of the northern earls protested. "He'd never allow a Lochlannach fleet to land in Alt Clut and invade us."

"Would King Rhun help Amlaíb by protecting his ships and giving his warriors safe passage across our southern border?" Raibeart asked the King.

"He'd have no choice," the King replied. "He may be married to my sister, but his kingdom is under Amlaíb's control and Amlaíb would kill Rhun like he killed Arthgal if Rhun offered any resistance. Rhun would even have to provide soldiers to march with the Lochlannach invaders if Amlaíb insisted. We have no friends in Alt Clut when it comes to defending ourselves from the Lochlannach."

Raibeart shook his head in disbelief. It seemed impossible that King Rhun would turn his back on Alba. After all, Alba had come to his aid when Dumbarton was besieged. For the first time,

Raibeart felt concerned about Alba's chances against Amlaíb's invasion.

"But there are other rivers that Amlaíb's fleet might take along our western shores, are there not?" the King asked, returning to the more pressing issue.

"Yes, My King," the earl from the lands east of Airer Goídel replied. "But he'd have to leave his fleet beached in enemy territory for an overland march through the middle of Alba. He'd have to leave a large force behind to guard the ships, and the way to Scone would be difficult. If Amlaíb's smart, he'll land near Dumbarton and approach Scone from the southwest while the Lochlannach from the islands attack our northern and western shores at the same time to cover his movements. Our forces would be spread thin fighting the island Lochlannach, and he'd be able to take Scone almost unopposed."

There were nods around the room, and King Causantín agreed with the earl. "Which brings us back to the two questions we still need to answer," the King said. "How do we know when they're coming, and how do we stop them from reaching Scone?"

"Are we certain that Amlaíb's fleet won't be ready to sail for another two years?" the earl from the lands east of Airer Goídel asked.

"No, that's just an estimate of how long we think it'll take to rebuild his fleet and train new warriors," the King replied. "I think we have to assume that Amlaíb will sail for Alba any time after the rivers thaw two springs from now."

"Then I suggest we begin preparing immediately," the earl continued. "We need to train more soldiers, and we need to prepare a rapid method of signaling the clans when the army is needed to defend Scone."

"I don't think signaling the clans to raise the army will work this time," Raibeart said.

"Why not?"

"Because it's a shorter distance for Amlaíb to get from Dumbarton to Scone than it is for most of the clans to get to Scone," Raibeart replied. "By the time the fleet's sighted and messengers are sent out to the clans to raise the army, Amlaíb will have landed his warriors and be crossing our southern border.

Unless the army is already at Scone, there's no way we can stop Amlaíb from taking the capital."

"But if the army is at Scone, we'll be defenseless when the Lochlannach from the islands attack," one of the northern earls stated.

Raibeart thought about this for a moment, and then said, "Then each clan will need to split its forces. Half will be sent to Scone and half will remain behind to defend our villages from raiders."

"If we split our forces, we won't have enough soldiers to defeat Amlaíb, and there won't be enough soldiers left to defend any village that's raided," the King pointed out.

"Once Amlaíb is sighted, the soldiers from villages that aren't being raided can be summoned to help defeat Amlaíb's forces," Raibeart suggested. "The army at Scone just needs to be able to slow down the Lochlannach advance until the rest of the army can arrive."

"Then I think we need to increase the number of horsemen we can put in the field as quickly as possible," the King stated. "If we keep a large force of horsemen at Scone, we can harass Amlaíb once he crosses the border. If the horsemen can slow down his march to Scone, it'll give us the time we need to summon the rest of the army and prepare for battle on ground of our own choosing."

"I agree," Raibeart said. The other earls echoed their agreement.

"Good," the King said, happy that they were finally making progress. Then he asked, "So what's the fastest way to signal the clans when Amlaíb's forces have been sighted?"

"Beacons," Ciaran said, speaking up for the first time that day. "We could build signal towers like the Romans used. We can have watchers near Dumbarton keep an eye out for the Lochlannach fleet and light beacons to alert Scone when the fleet's been sighted. Then Scone can light beacons to alert the clans. It'll take a lot of towers and a lot of men to be constantly ready to light their beacons, but it will get the news across Alba quickly."

The King thought about this for several minutes. Then he said, "And what if the fleet approaches from somewhere else?"

"The beacons can still be used," Ciaran replied. "Whoever first spots the fleet will light their beacon and the message will reach Scone. As long as the clans are to send their soldiers to Scone when the beacons are sighted, the plan will still work. If the army has to leave Scone before the rest of the army arrives, messengers can be sent out to alert the clans where the army has gone."

The King nodded. "It's a good plan. It solves the problems of knowing when the invasion has started and where the army needs to be. Now we just need to make sure we're strong enough to defeat Amlaíb's warriors when he comes."

"What about training women to defend the villages?" Ciaran asked. "I know the Bishop would probably object, but our women are capable of fighting as well as our men, and since they'd be the ones taken prisoner and sold as slaves, they should be allowed to defend themselves and their families."

"We might lose the backing of the church if we do that," one of the northern earls remarked.

"And we might lose the kingdom, our freedom, and our lives if we don't," Ciaran stated.

"I agree," the King said. "The church may frown on women fighting, but this isn't a religious debate. We need soldiers to defeat Amlaíb's invasion force. Women need to defend their villages so the men can be with the army. There's no other choice."

For the rest of the afternoon, the meeting focused on selecting where to build the beacon towers so each tower would have a clear view of the next tower. It was well after dark when the King called for a break in the discussions until morning.

"I'm sure Caitlin will approve of your suggestion about women fighting," Asbjorn said to Ciaran later that night after everyone had eaten.

"I'm hoping she can help teach the women of our village to fight and ride," Ciaran said. "Many know already, but the rest need to be trained. A fighter can do more damage on horseback than on foot, so I want as many as possible to be trained as horsemen. It will also allow them to retreat faster if it looks like the village will be overrun."

"I'm glad we kept the swords and knives of the raiders we've killed. At least everyone in the village can be armed. How do you think Iain will react to the idea of training the women of the village to fight?"

"The King said he'd discuss the plan with the Bishop. I'm hoping the Bishop will write a note to his priests telling them to support the King. Otherwise, I'll have to take a different approach to make sure Iain doesn't object."

Amlaíb walked down to the harbor to check on Thorleik's progress. Rebuilding the fleet was critical before any invasion was attempted, and Amlaíb felt that it was taking too long to get the new ships finished.

He saw fifteen longships at various stages of completion on the shore near the harbor, but there seemed to be little progress made since the last time he checked. Looking around, he finally saw Thorleik and walked quickly toward him.

Before Amlaíb said anything, Thorleik held up his hand. "I know what you're going to say, Amlaíb, and you're right. We're not making much progress on the new ships."

"Why is that?" Amlaíb asked.

"Because we're running out of wood," Thorleik replied. "We've clear-cut the forests around the harbor, and now we have to get wood from farther inland and from north of the river. It has to be cut and either dragged here or floated down river. Then it has to be dried, cured, and cut before we can build the ships. It's a slow and tedious process. I have search parties out trying to get us the wood we need as quickly as possible, but the more we cut, the farther we have to go to find more wood for the ships."

"Do you need more help?" Amlaíb asked.

"I'll take all you can give me. I have all the builders I need, but I'd be building twenty ships at a time if I had the wood."

"I'll send more men to you starting tomorrow," Amlaíb said. "We need these ships finished."

"I understand. We can be training new warriors on the ships already completed, so this won't delay getting the men prepared."

"But it will delay when we can sail for Alba," Amlaíb pointed out.

"I know. At the rate we're going now, we won't be able to sail the fleet for at least another two summers."

"And if you have the wood you need?"

"I can shorten that by a fourth," Thorleik stated confidently.

"Then I'll get you your wood," Amlaíb promised. Amlaíb turned and left the harbor. Launching the invasion in a year and a half fit his timeframe perfectly, and he was determined to prevent any delays.

The council meeting at Scone ended with a long list of assignments for the earls and chiefs. Ciaran hoped there'd be enough time to get the assignments completed, but he knew that there was no choice if they were going to survive the anticipated invasion.

Ciaran, Ringean, Dùghall, and Asbjorn made camp next to a stream on the first night after they left Scone. As they ate, Ciaran told everyone what he wanted them to do when they returned home. Dùghall was given the assignment to build the beacon towers in the clan's territory, which would require coordinating with the other clans in Airer Goídel. Ringean was given the assignment to begin training everyone in the clan to be a better fighter and horseman. Caitlin and Asbjorn would be responsible for training the women in the village to ride and fight, but there was also a special assignment Ciaran gave to Asbjorn that none of the others knew anything about.

"Asbjorn, if something goes wrong and the army is overrun by Amlaíb's forces," Ciaran said after Ringean and Dùghall had fallen asleep, "I want you to promise me something. I want you to return to the village and lead the clan to safety – to a place where the Lochlannach raiders won't look or can't reach."

"Where would that be?" Asbjorn asked.

"I don't know," Ciaran admitted. "You need to find a place."

"Why wouldn't you be leading them?"

"Because if the army is overrun, then I'll probably be dead and so will Ringean and Maol-Chaluim. It'll fall to you to lead the clan and keep them safe."

Asbjorn was about to protest, but he saw the seriousness in Ciaran's face and realized that this was very important to him. "I promise," Asbjorn said.

Ciaran nodded. "Thank you, Asbjorn. If things start looking bad during the battle, I'll come to you and tell you to go. No matter what's happening on the field or what happens to me, you will stop fighting and run for the village as fast as you can. If you see me and my sons fall in battle, you will stop fighting and run for the village as fast as you can. Do you understand?"

"Yes, Ciaran. I understand, but I hope it won't be necessary."

"So do I, but as chief, I have to put the needs of the clan before anything else. If Maol-Chaluim, Ringean, and I fall in battle, you'll need to act as chief of the clan until the oldest of my grandsons is mature enough to take on those duties. I'm entrusting you with their lives."

"I'll do what you ask. I swore an oath to you when you spared my life, and I'll never break that oath."

Ciaran smiled and put his hand on Asbjorn's shoulder. Then the two men joined the others to rest before they had to continue their journey back to the village.

Ciaran, Ringean, Dùghall, and Asbjorn arrived on the farm just as the sun was setting two days later. Maol-Chaluim came out to greet them, followed by Caitlin, the other women, and the children.

Ciaran gave his family the details of the meetings with Raibeart and the King while they ate supper, and then he told Maol-Chaluim to send messengers out the next morning to summon everyone to a gathering of the clan. "I need to tell everyone what will be happening over the next several months," he said. "We have much work to do and little time to get it all finished."

Later that night, after Alasdair was asleep, Caitlin and Asbjorn talked quietly in their bed. "So you and I are going to train the women to ride and fight?" she asked.

Asbjorn nodded. "With our forces split, the King thinks speed will be the key to pushing the raiders away from the villages and keeping Amlaíb's warriors away from Scone until the rest of the army can be summoned."

"I'll bet Iain will have a fit when he hears about this," Caitlin said, trying not to laugh and wake the baby.

"Not this time. The King had the Bishop write a letter to all of his priests supporting the plan. Ciaran has the letter, and he'll give it to Iain tomorrow. I'm sure Iain will do whatever the Bishop tells him to do without argument."

"Do you think it'll be as bad as father thinks?" Caitlin asked seriously.

It was only because of how much Asbjorn loved her that he answered honestly. "Yes, I do. Amlaíb will make Alba pay for the defeat at Dunadd. Between his warriors and the raiders from the islands, he'll outnumber us. And his warriors are well-trained fighters. They'll hit us like a flood, and we'll lose a lot of men before it's all over."

"What will happen to us here if the army is defeated?" Caitlin asked.

"Your father gave me instructions that no one else knows about. I'll tell you, but you have to promise to never mention it to anyone, agreed?"

"Agreed," Caitlin replied.

"He told me that, should things be going badly, he'll find me and tell me to leave the battle and come back here. He wants me to lead the clan to safety until the raiders are gone. He also told me that if he and your brothers fall in battle, I'm to leave the battle right then and act as chief until his oldest grandson is ready to be chief."

"He really asked you to do that?" Caitlin asked in disbelief. *Father must be expecting the worst to happen if he's making plans like this.*

Asbjorn nodded. "The problem is that I don't know where to take everyone where the raiders either can't reach us or wouldn't look for us."

"We have time to work it out," Caitlin said. "I'm sure you'll find the right place."

CHAPTER 18

Asbjorn had never seen a gathering of the entire clan before. Men, women, and children from the outlying settlements and farms started arriving the day after Maol-Chaluim sent out the messages. By the end of the second day, every member of the clan had arrived.

At the beginning of the gathering, Iain stood and delivered a blessing. Ciaran had given Iain the letter from the Bishop earlier that day. As expected, Iain kept to himself any objections he had regarding women riding and fighting.

Ciaran then told the gathered members of the clan about the Lochlannach raids in the north and about the invasion that the King believed would happen sometime in the next two years. When Ciaran talked about the need to split the army and train women to ride and fight to defend the clan's territory, he heard murmuring coming all around.

Ciaran looked over at Iain and nodded. Iain stood and said, "I have a letter here from the Bishop in Scone endorsing the King's plan to train women to defend our territory. Regardless of what the Church in Rome may say about the role of women in Christendom, the safety of our lands isn't something that can be left to just the men this time."

Ciaran smiled at Iain and then continued letting everyone know what would be required over the coming months. "We need to be ready for the unexpected," he said at the end of the meeting. "That means we need to train like the invasion is coming this spring, rather than the spring after that. Everyone will need to devote several hours a day to training with the sword, spear, bow, and horse. Once the harvest is over, training and preparing for the invasion should take up most of your days until the spring planting. The members of the clan who live in the outlying settlements need to move closer to each other or to the village, as do those who live on the farms between the settlements. I don't want anyone caught alone when the raiders come."

Ciaran then allowed the members of the clan to speak their minds or ask questions. The meeting lasted until after midnight. By the time it ended, everyone knew what to do. Ciaran then spent the rest of the night walking around and talking with people individually. The sun was low in the morning sky when Ciaran finished speaking with everyone who wanted to talk.

He watched as the members of the clan from the outlying settlements and farms left for their homes. Instead of returning to the farm to get some rest, he walked north toward the stone circle. He needed time to be alone and think.

He walked along the path through the ancient forest to the south of the stone circle, listening to the sounds coming from deep inside the woods. As he entered the clearing where the stone circle was located, though, he saw someone already there, sitting near the large stone in the center and looking toward the east. As he got closer, he recognized Asbjorn.

"What brings you here this morning?" Ciaran asked as he entered the circle.

"I needed time to think, and I wanted to watch the ravens."

"Where are they?" Ciaran asked, looking around.

Asbjorn pointed to the northeast. "They're flying over the forest on this side of the rocky peaks." Ciaran looked and saw three ravens flying in circles above the trees of the ancient forest in the distance. Ciaran sat down next to Asbjorn and watched with him.

"Tell me again about your relationship with the ravens," he asked.

"You remember that I told you the ravens were the symbol of Odin, one of the chief gods of the Lochlannach?" Asbjorn asked. When Ciaran nodded, Asbjorn continued. "Ravens are supposed to be messengers from Odin."

"But you renounced Odin when you were baptized, didn't you?" Ciaran asked.

Asbjorn nodded. "I did, but the ravens keep coming, and I don't think it's a coincidence. The first time the ravens led me somewhere was the day I asked my father to be part of the

169

expedition to Alt Clut. A raven landed on the longphort wall right in front of me and then flew off and circled my father.

"The second time I saw them was on the day I let Caitlin escape. Two were flying overhead and then one flew off to the north. I thought they were telling me to let Caitlin escape, so I did. The third time I saw them was on the day you saved my life. They were perched on the holding pen while I was waiting to be executed, and they were flying overhead while I was waiting for the swordsman to strike. They flew between the swordsman and me and then flew north. I took that to mean I should accept your offer to live and go north with you."

"What about after you came here?" Ciaran asked.

"I followed one here the first time I found you in the circle. Another one was perched on one of the stones when you asked if I wanted to marry Caitlin, and then it flew south toward the farm, which told me it approved of the marriage. Several were flying over us on the day of the wedding, and one was perched on my roof the day Alasdair was born."

"Did they lead you here today?"

"Not exactly," Asbjorn replied. "I was thinking about what you asked me to do and struggling with where there were places the Lochlannach wouldn't go or couldn't reach. I came here to think since it's quiet, and I remembered seeing those rocky peaks when the raven led me here the first time. When I got here, the ravens were flying in circles like they are now, and I was wondering if they were trying to show me something. I was about to follow them when you arrived."

"You think they may be showing you a hiding place where you can take the clan?"

"It's possible," Asbjorn admitted.

"Then let's go find out," Ciaran suggested.

They both stood up and started walking northeast toward the ravens, which were still circling the rocky peaks in the distance. When they reached the edge of the forest on the far side of the stone circle, the foliage and undergrowth was so dense that it formed what seemed to be an impenetrable barrier. Neither Asbjorn nor Ciaran saw a way inside the forest, but they kept looking.

After almost an hour, Ciaran found a small opening in the barrier. He turned around and faced the circle. Several of the wooden posts and one of the great stones were in a straight line between the opening and the center of the circle.

"I found an opening," Ciaran called to Asbjorn. Asbjorn came over to where Ciaran was standing and looked at the opening in the barrier. Ciaran then showed Asbjorn the part of the circle pointing to the opening.

"That'll help us find it again," Asbjorn commented as he pushed through the opening and entered the forest with Ciaran behind him.

In the low light of the forest, the men made out the remnants of a path leading straight toward the rocky peaks where the ravens had been circling. "Do you think the circle was built to point people in this direction?" Asbjorn asked as they made their way through the forest.

"It makes sense," Ciaran replied. "If so, then I wonder what the other posts and stones point toward."

The deeper into the forest they went, the easier it was to walk. The trees were less dense and there was less undergrowth obscuring the path. After a while, they reached a huge clearing at the base of several large hills. Looking up, they saw the rocky peaks above and the ravens still circling.

"You could almost fit the entire village in here," Asbjorn commented.

Ciaran nodded, looking around. Then he walked toward the hills and started climbing. It only took a few minutes to reach the summit. From the top of the hill, he saw that the rocky peaks were actually part of a much larger set of hills behind the outer hills. In the valley between the outer hills and the inner hills was a large lake.

Turning around, Ciaran couldn't see over the tops of the trees from where he was standing. He walked around the lake and started climbing up the inner hills. Asbjorn followed him, and in less than an hour they were standing at the base of the rocky peaks, looking over the top of the forest for miles. They saw the stone circle in its clearing, and they saw the smoke from the cooking fires in their village rising to the south.

"We could easily hide the clan inside the forest," Ciaran commented. "There's water, plenty of wood, and lots of places to hide if raiders ever tried to find this place. This is good ground to defend from attack, too."

"What about the cooking fires?" Asbjorn asked. "Wouldn't the Lochlannach see the smoke?"

Ciaran felt the wind blowing past his face and said, "If the wind around these hills blows like this all the time, most of the smoke will be carried off to the northeast. And if we have lookouts posted up here, they can signal the rest of us to put out the fires so the Lochlannach won't know that the clan is here."

Asbjorn looked up and saw that the ravens had flown away. "I guess this is what the ravens wanted us to find," he commented, pointing upwards.

Ciaran nodded. Seeing from the sun that it was past midday already, he motioned for Asbjorn to follow him as he started climbing back down. They passed the lake and found the path to lead them back to the stone circle. Once in the clearing, they looked back and barely saw the opening to the path.

"It should be easy to close that opening so no one can find it once we're safely hidden inside," Asbjorn commented.

"I think we need to keep this just between us," Ciaran said as they walked through the stone circle and headed toward the village. "If the Lochlannach take prisoners and interrogate them, they might find out where everyone else is hiding. Nobody should know about this place until they're led here by you."

"Is there anything we should do to prepare the clearing to be the new village?" Asbjorn asked. "We'll need tools, lumber for shelters, pens for the livestock, containers to hold grains and other foods, and weapons. If we have to make a run for the clearing during a raid, most of those things will be left behind, and we won't survive long in there without provisions of some sort."

Ciaran thought about this for a moment as they approached the outer edge of the village. "That's a good point, Asbjorn. Perhaps we need to let a few people know so they can help make the necessary preparations. But is there a way to lead them there without them knowing where the entrance in the forest is?"

"I don't think so," Asbjorn answered.

Ciaran nodded. "Then we'll need to choose people we can trust not to betray the location if they're captured."

Thorleik smiled with satisfaction as he looked around and saw the progress being made on the new longships. The new lumber had started arriving shortly after his conversation with Amlaíb, and now that it had been cured and cut, the construction on the longships resumed.

"I see things are back on track," Amlaíb said as he stood next to Thorleik.

Thorleik nodded. "Your men cut down an entire forest northwest of here and floated the logs downriver. We should have enough lumber to build at least seventy longships. If you want more ships, we'll need more lumber."

"I'll get you the lumber," Amlaíb stated confidently. "I want at least a hundred and thirty new ships built for the expedition."

"Is there that much lumber left on the island?" Thorleik asked. "It's starting to look a bit bare right now."

"If we have to get lumber from Britain, then we'll send over the cargo ships to get it," Amlaíb assured Thorleik. "I'll do whatever it takes to get the ships finished."

"You might want to do that soon," Thorleik said. "The weather's been getting nasty and you don't want the cargo ships trapped on the other side of the channel."

"Why not wait until spring?" Amlaíb asked. "You have enough lumber to last through the winter, don't you?"

"Yes, but the lumber takes time to cure and cut. If you send the cargo ships in the spring, it'll stop construction until the lumber is ready."

"Very well," Amlaíb conceded. "I'll alert the captains to sail as soon as possible."

"Have them bring back several flocks of sheep as well," Thorleik added. "We'll need the wool for the new sails."

Amlaíb nodded. He watched the construction for a while longer, and then he left to find the cargo ships' captains and give them their orders.

Thorleik continued overseeing the construction, grateful to Amlaíb for helping find the materials needed to build the new ships. *If we get the lumber before winter, I'll have Amlaíb's fleet finished by next winter. We'll be able to launch the expedition as soon as the spring thaws arrive, and Alba will be ours!*

Asbjorn took Caitlin to the hiding place northeast of the stone circle the day after he and Ciaran had discovered it. She was shocked to find that the clearing had been there for years without anyone knowing about it.

"I can't believe no one has been here before," she said as she stood on top of the inner hill for the first time.

"I guess people were too scared of the stone circle to really start looking around," Asbjorn speculated. "Since there are no settlements around here, the forest was allowed to grow and hide all evidence of the place."

"Do you think's it's a sacred place to whoever built the circle?" Caitlin asked.

"It's possible. The stone circle did point to it, so that may be why there's no sign of anyone else ever being here."

"Do you think we can hide the entire clan in here safely?" she asked as they started walking back to the clearing.

"I hope so. If we have to come here, it's because the battle was lost and the Lochlannach are in control. You know they'll take all the young women and children with them to sell at the slave markets. Our only chance is to hide here and hope we're not discovered."

"I'm surprised to hear you talk about your people as the enemy, Asbjorn," Caitlin commented.

"You're my people now," Asbjorn replied. "You, Alasdair, Ciaran, your brothers, the clan, all of you are my family. You gave me a home and a purpose that doesn't involve trying to take what belongs to others for glory or to prove myself to gods who value conflict more than anything else. The Lochlannach are responsible for my birth, but my life is in Alba, and I'll defend this place to my dying breath."

Caitlin took his hand and smiled. "And that's one of the reasons why I love you, my husband."

Once the harvest was finished, Asbjorn and Caitlin spent most of their days either training the women and young people of the village to fight and ride, or working with the small group of people who had been trusted to know the location of the hiding place northeast of the stone circle. By the time the winter snows arrived, Asbjorn and Caitlin were pleased with the progress the women and young people had made in learning to fight and ride. They were also pleased with the progress being made in the clearing beyond the stone circle. Lumber, tools, and weapons had already been placed there, and work would begin in the spring to build shelters for the food and pens for the livestock.

Asbjorn selected a small group of people to relocate quietly to the clearing in the spring and begin tending to the flocks, cutting down trees, and planting crops to sustain the members of the clan while they were in hiding. Asbjorn knew this would be the only way for the clan to survive for an extended period of time while the Lochlannach raiders roamed the countryside looking for tribute and prisoners.

Ciaran wished fewer people knew the location of the clearing, but he finally admitted that Asbjorn was right. The clearing could serve as a short-term hiding place the way it was, but to protect the clan for a longer timeframe would require much more work to prepare the land. He agreed to allow members of the clan to relocate to the clearing.

The winter turned out to be a mild one, allowing the women and young people to continue their training through most of the coldest months. Preparations in the clearing were also able to continue, and by early in the new year, the people who'd spend the next year preparing the clearing had already relocated and were building shelters and preparing the ground for planting.

Asbjorn and Caitlin visited the clearing at least once a week while they were supposedly riding on patrol. Flocks were brought to the clearing, as were horses and seeds for planting. By late spring, the clearing looked like a miniature of the village and was well on its way to being ready to sustain the clan until the Lochlannach left Alba with the spoils of their invasion.

During the summer months, Asbjorn and Caitlin created a series of scenarios where the men would pretend to attack the village and the women and young people would try to defend themselves against them. Asbjorn explained to the villagers that no training could ever fully prepare someone for battle, but having the men and women skirmish against each other would come close. Asbjorn also had the horsemen practice attacking the foot soldiers so the new horsemen would understand better how horses were used to allow a small force to defeat a much larger force.

Ciaran and Raibeart were both pleased with the results of the training. "I wish the other clans were training this hard and well," Raibeart commented late in the summer as he watched one of the skirmishes.

"Do you still think the invasion will come in the spring?" Ciaran asked.

"The King does, and I agree. They should have rebuilt their fleet by now. The raids from the islands have all but stopped, which tells me the Lochlannach are preparing for something big."

"When does the King want us to send half of our forces to Scone?"

"Before the first snow," Raibeart replied. "He doesn't want to wait until the spring thaws and find the Lochlannach knocking on his door before the army arrives."

"I can send the horsemen to Scone to act as scouts in a month, and send the foot soldiers a month later," Ciaran said.

"I think the King will appreciate that," Raibeart said. "Who will you leave in charge of the village?"

"Caitlin. I'll have my sons and Asbjorn with me at Scone."

"Do you think she's ready to lead the defense of the village?" Raibeart asked.

"See for yourself," Ciaran said as he pointed to his daughter leading a force of female horsemen in a practice skirmish against foot soldiers from the village.

Raibeart watched as Caitlin led a charge against the left side of the foot soldiers, smashing their lines. The seasoned soldiers scattered, scrambling in all directions to get away from her. Then she whirled around and led her horsemen to attack the rear of the foot soldiers, forcing them to break and run for safety.

Caitlin and the women she had been training fought with a ferocity that took Raibeart by surprise. Their attacks seemed almost vicious, as Caitlin had instilled in them a sense of rage at their enemy. Raibeart had always heard that, to be effective in battle, a soldier must be calm. But he had to admit that Caitlin had helped the women turn their anger into a fighting style that few could defend against.

"I guess she's ready after all," Raibeart commented with a smile.

Like Ciaran, Raibeart was grateful that women were being allowed to fight against the anticipated invasion. He remembered hearing the stories of the great women warriors who had fought the Romans and the Saxons, and he felt the women being trained to fight were carrying on the proud tradition of their ancestors. *Everyone has the right to defend our land. Regardless of what the church says, our women aren't inferior creatures who only exist to serve and make babies. They're Albans. And they're just as capable of fighting off invaders as the men are.*

Five weeks later, early in the morning as the autumn winds started blowing harder, Asbjorn held Caitlin in his arms and said good-bye. "When will I see you again?" Caitlin asked.

"It might be as long as six months," Asbjorn replied. "We'll be serving as scouts all winter, and we expect Amlaíb's fleet to arrive in the early spring. I'm guessing the raiders will hit the villages about the same time as Amlaíb lands with his fleet."

"I'll miss you, my husband."

"I'll miss you, too, my love. Take care of Alasdair and the others. And make sure that the signal towers are manned all the time and that things are ready in the clearing. When you see me again, we may have little time to get everyone left to safety."

"Why do you and my father think the battle will go badly?" Caitlin asked. "I've never seen soldiers more prepared for a fight."

"Because we'll be outnumbered by warriors who are better fighters in almost every way. Our sole advantage is our horsemen and the fact that we're fighting on our own land. It's a question of whether those advantages will be enough to overcome their numbers. We're preparing for the worst, but hoping for the best."

"I wish you could stay," she said, pulling him closer.

"So do I, but you know I can't."

He bent down to kiss her. Then he heard Ciaran shouting, "Asbjorn, get moving!"

Asbjorn pulled away and smiled at Caitlin. "I have to go."

"I know. Be safe, Asbjorn."

"You, too, Caitlin."

Asbjorn mounted his horse and waved. Then he turned around and followed Ciaran to the place where the rest of the horsemen had gathered. Caitlin watched her husband, her father, her uncle, and her brothers ride toward the village, and then she heard the sound of a great host of horsemen riding away as the first rays of the sunrise appeared on the horizon.

"Just come back home to me, Asbjorn," Caitlin whispered before going inside to check on Alasdair.

Chapter 19

The river and most of the harbor of Áth Cliath froze hard as the winter winds and snows came in from the north like a hungry wolf pack. Thorleik had just finished testing the last ten longships on the open waters when the first snows moved in to blanket the longphort with white ice. Amlaíb was with him as the last of the new longships beached and its crew jumped down and secured the ship.

"How did the ship fare?" Thorleik called to the longship's captain.

"She handles well, Thorleik," the captain replied, jumping down from the longship to the beach. "Your builders did another outstanding job."

Thorleik nodded as the captain and crew walked past him toward the longphort. Turning to Amlaíb, he said, "Your fleet is ready, Amlaíb. We can sail for Alba as soon as the spring thaws arrive."

"Excellent," Amlaíb said with a smile. "Now we just need to finish gathering supplies and then alert our allies on the islands that everything is ready."

"I'm not completely comfortable emptying the longphort of every warrior we have for this expedition," Thorleik said as they walked back to the longphort. "Our families will be defenseless while we're gone, and we might be gone a long time."

"Defenseless from what?" Amlaíb asked. "Who do we have to fear here?"

"The Irish, the Dalriadan Scots, the Norse kings from the continent…" Thorleik listed.

"I'm not worried about the Scots or the Irish here," Amlaíb said dismissively. "They'll never attack the longphort and risk the reprisals."

"And what about the Norse from the mainland?" Thorleik asked.

Amlaíb thought about this as the two men walked through the main gates of the longphort. "There have been no reports of them planning anything," he said finally.

"They've told our island allies that we're all behind paying tribute to them, Amlaíb. They've heard that you're about to conquer all of Britain, and they want their share of the spoils. You know we can't defeat their fleets and their warriors if they decide to attack, and we can't defend Britain either if they decide they want it for themselves. We're vulnerable right now, and I'm worried."

"Do you think we should call off the invasion?" Amlaíb asked.

"No, I just wanted to voice my concern about what's happening on the mainland right now. Our kinsmen have finally stopped fighting among themselves and are unified for the first time in many years. They have their eyes on the west, and we'll find this a very small island if they decide to move on us."

"Britain's a much bigger island," Amlaíb reminded him.

"Yes, but it's too big to defend. We've killed or sold most of the Briton soldiers that we might have enlisted to help us fight off an invasion, and the rest might welcome new masters just to get back at us for what we've done to them."

Amlaíb was troubled as he and Thorleik made their way to the center of the longphort. *I never considered that before. When our forefathers first sailed to settle in Ireland and Britain, it was with the understanding that tribute would be paid to the Norse kings on the mainland. When the various Norse kingdoms started fighting among themselves, we saw this as an opportunity to keep all of our wealth. Now that the fighting is over, the Norse High King has once again turned his attention to the west and wants what he feels is rightfully his.*

Amlaíb knew he could never defeat the Norse from the mainland if they decided to attack Ireland or invade Britain. *Would they use the Alba expedition as an opportunity to take the Alban islands and Ireland back under their control? Would the lands we've conquered welcome invaders from the mainland just to spite us for having conquered them?*

"What are you thinking, Amlaíb?" Thorleik asked.

"That there's risk no matter what we do," he replied. "If we don't invade Alba, there's a part of Britain that still defies us, and we don't have enough men to prevent our mainland kinsmen from taking everything we have. If we do invade Alba, we might lose most of our strength, and then we'll have even fewer men to stand up to our mainland kinsmen."

"So what do we do?" Thorleik asked.

"We go forward with the plan," Amlaíb stated. "We don't know if our mainland kinsmen will come for their share this year, but we do know that the Albans still defy us and refuse to pay tribute. Once we have Alba under our control, we'll turn our attention to fortifying Britain in case our kinsmen decide they want the west for themselves."

"You mean relocating all of our people to Britain?"

"Yes. I'll be the High King of all of Britain once Alba is defeated, so I need to be there. And I'll need all my warriors with me to hold Britain and prepare for any attempts to take it from us."

Thorleik nodded. He still had grave concerns, but he knew there was little choice in the matter. *We need to focus on what we know is happening, rather than what we think might happen. The Albans are there and we need to defeat them. The rest will take care of itself.*

The two men continued walking in silence. There was nothing else that needed to be said aloud, but both men looked troubled.

Christmas came and went with little celebration in Airer Goídel since most of the men had left for the army encampment near Scone. The winter snows blanketed the ground, making the daily patrols difficult but also making any invasion equally difficult. The surface of the rivers and streams were frozen, causing it to be impossible for any longships and longboats to sail inland.

Caitlin missed her father and her brother, but she missed Asbjorn most of all. Their house seemed empty, even with Alasdair there to keep her company. Caitlin kept herself busy by training with the women soldiers, and Ringean's wife looked after Alasdair during the day so Caitlin and the other defenders of the village could continue their patrols.

Once a week, Caitlin rode to the clearing in the forest beyond the standing stones to check on the villagers who were preparing the area. She was pleased that they were still making progress on building the shelters in spite of the weather, and the livestock seemed to be thriving. Some of the men had made a trench up the hill to the lake so water would flow to the clearing. At first, Caitlin wondered why they had gone to the trouble, but one of the men explained it to her.

"It'll keep us from having to go up and down the hill to get water for drinking, for the crops, and for the livestock. We don't want the animals wandering free up in the hills and getting lost."

Caitlin thought that the plan made sense. There were too few men living and working in the clearing to be spending most of their days fetching water when there were so many other tasks to complete before spring.

Caitlin also made a point of riding to the three watchtowers that her uncle Dùghall had built to warn the countryside of any approaching Lochlannachs. There were four men posted on each of the watchtowers at all times – two watching the coast and the waterways, and two watching the other watchtowers in the area. Hundreds of watchtowers had been built across Alba on the King's orders, and Caitlin was determined that the ones near the village would stay in a constant state of readiness should the enemy suddenly appear.

The Alban army that was encamped southwest of Scone spent their days preparing for the anticipated Lochlannach invasion. Asbjorn rode out of the encampment daily with the rest of the horsemen to patrol the southern and western approaches to Alban capital. Because of the winter snows, the horsemen couldn't patrol far, but Asbjorn knew that, once the weather began to clear in the spring, the patrols would ride as far south as the Alt Clut border to watch for and harass any Lochlannach making their way overland from Dumbarton.

Asbjorn watched Ciaran closely during the patrols. A melancholy had settled on his father-in-law, and Asbjorn worried that Ciaran had resigned himself to his own death in the coming conflict with Amlaíb's forces. Ciaran never gave any indication of this while the men were around, but Asbjorn saw it when the two of them were alone – especially when they were discussing the need for Asbjorn to return to the village should the battle go badly for the Albans.

King Causantín sent emissaries to several of the Lochlannach settlements on the islands surrounding Alba. The winter ice was so thick that the emissaries could walk across the sea from Alba to the islands to deliver Causantín's messages of friendship and proposals to end the continual conflict. As expected, the proposals were rejected. The emissaries saw a great deal of activity taking place around the Lochlannach settlements, giving Causantín a strong indication that the island Lochlannach would be participating in Amlaíb's invasion.

King Causantín met with his earls and chiefs frequently to review the preparations for the coming invasion, looking for anything that they might have missed. As the skies cleared and the air grew warmer, the King and his council concluded that there were no additional steps to take to defend the country from Amlaíb's forces.

The patrols began riding further across the countryside as the snows melted. Ciaran led the horsemen from Airer Goídel down to the border of Alt Clut and deployed the horsemen across a wide front to watch for any sign of the Lochlannach. If the invaders were found approaching overland from that direction, Ciaran's horsemen would harass and attack Amlaíb's forces, pushing the invaders toward a series of hills and valleys that would slow their advance and give the army time to create a defensive position well away from Scone.

Ciaran rode out of his camp near the Alt Clut border each morning and checked on his horsemen. He watched the border intently, willing the Lochlannach to appear. He had been preparing for invasion for two years, and he was anxious for the battle to start. Each evening, though, he returned to his camp, disappointed that there was no activity along the border.

Thorleik climbed up to the walkway that ran along the upper wall of the longphort overlooking the harbor of Áth Cliath. Amlaíb was there already, staring intently to the northeast.

"You summoned me?" Thorleik asked.

"Yes," Amlaíb replied, continue to stare into the distance. "Can you smell it?" he asked, turning to look at his old friend.

"Smell what?" Thorleik replied.

"Spring," Amlaíb said with a hungry look in his eyes. "I've been smelling the scents of spring all day. It's all around us, and you know what that means, don't you?"

Thorleik nodded.

"It's almost time to light the torches, old friend, and get the men to their ships." Amlaíb turned back to stare toward the channel. "I've already sent the messengers to our allies on the islands around Alba. We sail in two weeks."

"I'll take care of it, Amlaíb," Thorleik promised. As he left the wall to notify each of the longship captains, Amlaíb remained where he was, staring toward Alba and breathing in the smells of spring.

There were two watchtowers built near the northern bank of the river that led from the channel to Dumbarton in Alt Clut. King Causantín had ordered the watchtowers built far enough away from the river so the Lochlannach wouldn't see them lit, but close enough so that horsemen on patrol along the river could ride to the watchtowers quickly to raise the alarm that Amlaíb's forces had been sighted.

It was a beautiful spring morning when two horsemen on patrol along the river first spotted a strange sight moving northward on the channel.

"What do you make of that?" one of the horsemen asked.

"Looks like longships to me," the other horseman answered.

"How many do you think there are?" the first one asked.

The second horsemen looked for a while, and then replied, "I reckon close to three hundred."

"Do we alert the watchtowers?" the first one asked.

"Wait until we see if they turn or keep heading north," the second horseman answered.

The two horsemen watched the approaching fleet for several minutes. At first, it looked like the ships would continue north, but then the lead ship turned east and lowered its sail. The horsemen were concealed in a small grove of trees, and from their hiding place they saw the other longships turning and lowering their sails as well.

"Looks like they're heading toward Dumbarton like the King thought," the second horseman said as he mounted his horse. "We'd better alert the watchtower."

The first horseman mounted his horse and followed the second horseman to the north away from the river, which was now filled with longships rowing inland.

Caitlin was patrolling along the western edge of the farms surrounding the village when she heard one of her companions shout out a warning. Turning, she saw where the other horsemen were looking and pointing. The beacon on the watchtower to the south of the village was lit. She watched as its fire climbed high into the morning sky and realized that her hands were shaking.

She felt her heart racing as she looked toward the other nearby watchtower and saw its beacon catch fire. *They're coming from the southwest, based on which of the two beacons were lit first.*

She shouted for her patrol to ride to all of the outlying settlements and alert everyone that the beacons had been lit. Then she rode toward the standing stones north of the village to alert the villagers living in the forest clearing. If the invasion fleet had been sighted, it wouldn't be long before the island Lochlannach would begin raiding the coastal villages and cities of Alba. Caitlin needed to make sure that the clearing was ready since the entire village might have to hide there from the Lochlannach raiders looking for tribute and slaves.

Ciaran was riding along the Alt Clut border with Asbjorn and a company of thirty horsemen when something caught his eye to the west of their position. He ordered his men to stop while he tried to identify what he was seeing.

Asbjorn looked in the direction where Ciaran was staring, and saw a strange orange spot in the distance. A minute later, another orange spot appeared to the northwest, and then another one appeared just north of their position. Asbjorn turned his horse to the north and saw two more orange spots appear close to where the army encampment was located.

"Are those…" Asbjorn started to ask.

"The watchtower beacons? Yes," Ciaran stated. "Amlaíb's fleet has been sighted."

Ciaran turned his horse to the west and took off at the gallop to alert the rest of his horsemen along the border.

King Causantín was just finishing breakfast when one of his guards burst into his chambers.

"What is the meaning of this?" Causantín demanded to the guard, who seemed out of breath.

"I'm sorry, My King, but the watchtowers are lit. The Lochlannach have been sighted in the west."

"Are they heading for Dumbarton?" the King asked, getting to his feet.

"I don't know, My King. Riders have been sent to find out."

The King nodded and dismissed the guard. Then he shouted for his valet and began dressing. By the time he was ready to ride to the army encampment to join his soldiers, he saw all of the watchtowers in the distance burning to alert his people that the invaders had finally arrived.

CHAPTER 20

Rhun mac Arthgal, King of Alt Clut, sat at a large table in the makeshift house at the base of Dumbarton Rock that served as his palace. As he stared at the two documents on the table, a servant slipped in quietly and added several logs to the fire across the room to help take away the early-spring chill in the air. Rhun barely noticed the intrusion. He just stared at the two documents. *What choice do I have?*

He heard a soft knock at the door and looked up. "Enter!" he said with little enthusiasm. *Can't I get any peace around here?*

His wife, sister to King Causantín mac Cináeda of Alba, opened the door and stepped inside. "Good morning, My King," she said, bowing her head to her husband.

"Good morning," Rhun responded, sounding distant. "And don't call me 'king'. I'm not really a king, and you know it."

His wife started to speak, but then closed her mouth. It was an old argument.

"According to our Lochlannach overlords," Rhun continued, "I'm allowed to retain the title of 'king,' but I'm not allowed to do anything that a king is allowed to do. I can't rebuild the fortress on Dumbarton Rock to protect my people because it could be seen as an act of defiance. I can't raise troops to protect my people because it could also be seen as an act of defiance. I can't even attend council meetings with other rulers in the region because it could be seen as an attempt to organize an act of defiance! So what do I get to do as king? I get to dispense justice on minor offences. I get to settle petty squabbles between my subjects. I get to watch Amlaíb's men cut down half of our forest and sail off with the lumber and several flocks of sheep that don't count against our annual tribute. And I get to bleed my country dry every year to pay the tribute our Lochlannach overlords require from us. That's what I get to do as king! And if I fail to pay the tribute, Amlaíb and his warriors will sail here, kill anyone who objects, and sail away with everyone else to the slave markets. Does that sound like a king to you?"

His wife crossed the room and sat down in a chair facing him. "You care about what happens to your people, my husband. So much so that you agonize over how to keep them free from Amlaíb's threats. You spend your days making sure that the tribute taxes are collected and protected until they have to be paid – just so your people won't have to endure another and more terrible invasion of our lands. That sounds like the acts of a true king to me."

Rhun glared at his wife, but then his gaze softened as he realized that she was right. *I do spend every waking moment trying to keep my people from being sold in the slave markets in distant lands. I can't do it with an army, so I do it in the only ways left open to me.* He nodded and smiled at his wife.

His wife smiled. "So, tell me, my husband, what kept you in here all night and away from my bedchamber."

Rhun gestured to the one of the documents on the table. "Your brother sent another petition requesting my assistance in the defense of Alba from the invasion that he anticipates will happen any day now."

"Are you going to honor his request? After all, he did send his army here when the Lochlannach invaded."

I've made up my mind, but do I tell her the truth? Rhun shook his head sadly and picked up the other document on the table. "I can't. Amlaíb, the Norse King of Britain, has sent a message reminding me that Alt Clut is part of his kingdom and subject to his will. He doesn't specifically say anything about an invasion of Alba or the consequences of helping your brother, but the implications are clear."

"What are you going to do?" she asked after a moment.

"What can I do?" Rhun replied. "I'm going to do my duty and keep my people safe, and I'm going to pray for your brother. If there were ever a time when Alba needed divine intervention, I think this is it."

Rhun slammed the document back onto the table. His wife lowered her head and nodded.

188

A moment later, there was a loud knocking on the door.

"Enter!" Rhun called.

The door opened, and one of the sentries posted in the ruins of the fortress entered the room.

"What is it?" Rhun demanded.

"My King, longships have been sighted on the river!" the sentry reported, out of breath.

"Heading in what direction?" Rhun asked with concern.

"Here, My King!"

"How many longships?"

"Hundreds, My King!"

Rhun jumped to his feet and shouted for a servant. "Saddle my horse and prepare an escort!"

He paused to kiss his wife and then started for the door. He stopped suddenly. Turning back toward his desk, he grabbed the petition from King Causantín, crumpled it, and threw it in the fire. *I can't risk anyone finding out what the real plan is – not even my wife.* He left the room with the sentry following close behind.

Rhun and his escort were waiting on the riverbank when Amlaíb's longship beached. Rhun bowed deeply to his Lochlannach overlord as Amlaíb approached. "I can assure you that the tribute was paid on time and in the correct amount, Great King," Rhun said when Amlaíb gestured for him to straighten up.

Amlaíb grunted. "I'm not here about the tribute, Rhun," he said, turning back to watch the other longships begin unloading their warriors and supplies. "And I'm not here for your people."

Rhun looked at Amlaíb. Then he said, "You're invading Alba."

Amlaíb nodded. "You haven't received any messages from King Causantín asking for help, have you?"

Rhun look directly into Amlaíb's eyes. "Not a word, Great King," he lied. *I may not be able to send help to my brother-in-law, but I'm not going to let Amlaíb know that the Albans are expecting him.*

"Good," Amlaíb said. "We should reach Scone before he even knows we're here!"

Amlaíb started walking away from the village and motioned for Rhun to follow him. "An overland expedition, Great

King?" Rhun asked as they walked. "Aren't there places closer to Scone where you could land your warriors? Why land your fleet here?"

"There are," Amlaíb replied. "My kinsmen from the islands around Alba will be landing there. I don't want the Alban King to know where to send his army until it's too late."

"So you're not just planning an invasion, are you? You're planning to crush the Albans!"

"Crush them and grind them into dust," Amlaíb replied coldly. "They have much to answer for, including the death of my kinsman, Ívarr."

Rhun looked back at the Lochlannach warriors on the riverbank and the longships that were still on the river waiting to unload. "Now I see why you needed so much lumber. What else do you require of me, Great King?"

"Guard my fleet," Amlaíb replied. "I don't want anything to happen to a single one of my ships. For every ship I lose, one hundred of your people will be taken to the slave markets as restitution – starting with you and your family. Do you understand?"

"I understand, Great King. Is that all?"

"No, I also need guides who know the way to the Alban capital."

Rhun kept his face expressionless, but inside he was smiling. "I can supply you with at least a dozen good men who know the way, Great King. When do you need them?"

"At first light," Amlaíb replied. "It'll take most of the day to unload the fleet, and I don't want to start the overland part of the expedition in the dark."

"Yes, Great King," Rhun replied. *Oh, I'll give you guides, my dear Lochlannach overlord, but don't expect them to lead you on the most direct route to Scone. I can't send help to Causantín, but I can still help him. If I can slow your approach, it will give the Alban army time to assemble.*

The scouts returning from Alt Clut found Ciaran shortly before mid-day. "What did you find?" he asked as they approached.

"It's a massive invasion fleet," one of the scouts answered. "They're landing just north of Dumbarton."

"How many ships?" Ciaran asked.

"Hundreds – filled with warriors."

Ciaran nodded. Turning to one of his other men, he said, "Ride back to the encampment and inform Raibeart that Amlaíb's fleet is at Dumbarton."

"Yes, Ciaran," the scout said as he turned his horse and rode north.

King Causantín arrived at the Alban army encampment after midday. There was no word yet about where the Lochlannach invasion fleet had landed, and Causantín was frustrated. It was nightfall before Raibeart mac Stiùbhart came to find him.

"Amlaíb's fleet landed at Dumbarton, My King," Raibeart reported.

Causantín nodded and smiled. "That means Amlaíb's forces are heading for Dolair."

"How do you know that?" Raibeart asked.

"Because in my last letter to Rhun, I asked him to offer guides to Amlaíb to show them the way to Scone, but to have the guides lead Amlaíb easterly toward Dolair so the hills in that region will slow them down."

"I'm surprised that's all you asked of King Rhun," Raibeart commented. "He's married to your sister, and you did come and help him when the Lochlannach invaded Alt Clut."

"It's all he can do for us," the King replied. "He has his own problems. To help us openly puts his entire kingdom at risk. Besides, he doesn't even have an army anymore. No, this was the best way for him to help us – the only way he can help and keep Amlaíb from knowing what he's doing."

"Yes, My King," Raibeart said.

"Send out messengers and tell the army to start moving southeast toward Dolair."

"And if Amlaíb takes a more direct approach to Scone?" Raibeart asked.

"Then we attack him from the rear and make sure he never makes it back to Dumbarton and his fleet."

Raibeart nodded and left to carry out his orders.

Causantín watched Raibeart leave. *I hope Rhun sends guides with Amlaíb and sticks to the plan. If Amlaíb reaches Scone, we'll never be able to pry him out of Alba.*

The Lochlannach encampment was set up north of Dumbarton. Even though the Alt Cluts could offer little in the way of resistance, heavily armed Lochlannach sentries patrolled the edges of the encampment.

Two hours before dawn, Rhun met with the men selected to guide Amlaíb's invasion force to Scone. A map of Alba and northern Britain was on the table that they stood around.

Pointing to the map, Rhun said, "Do not lead the Lochlannach on a direct route to Scone. Lead them easterly toward Dolair. The hills in that region will slow the Lochlannach down and give the Alban's time to assemble their army, assuming it isn't assembled already. Once the Alban's attack with the bulk of their forces, slip away from the battle and make your way back here. Understood?"

The men nodded. "Good. Come with me, then. I'll lead you to the encampment and present you to Amlaíb. He wants to leave at first light."

Rhun led the men out of the palace. *Dawn can't come soon enough for me. I don't care what Amlaíb says. This many Lochlannach warriors inside my borders makes me nervous. With any luck, most of them won't be returning from Alba. I just hope my brother-in-law is ready to defend his kingdom from Amlaíb's forces.*

Caitlin and some of her newly-trained horsemen were patrolling to the southwest of the village when she saw a rider approaching.

"Longboats are on the river!" the rider shouted excitedly when he reached Caitlin.

"You're sure it's longboats and not longships?" Caitlin asked.

"Yes. They're using the smaller boats – probably twenty to twenty-five warriors in each."

"How many?" Caitlin asked.

"About a dozen," the rider replied.

Caitlin nodded. *If they're using longboats then they aren't part of the main invasion fleet. They must be raiders from the islands that are supposed to attack the undefended villages and keep the army from knowing where the main invasion force is landing.*

"We need to warn the others," she said.

"I'll go back to the river and keep watch on the longboats," the rider said.

"Good," Caitlin said. Turning her horse around, she motioned for the other horsemen to follow her and raced back to the village.

CHAPTER 21

Caitlin and the rest of the defenders were in position, waiting for the island Lochlannach to attack the village. She allowed their longboats to land unchallenged, not wanting them to know that the villagers were prepared to fight. The Lochlannach took their time unloading the longboats. *They're not acting like a normal raiding party that attacks and leaves quickly. I guess they're planning on staying for a while. They must think that they're going to claim our lands for their own and use our village as their base to raid the countryside. Not while I'm alive!*

Her horsemen were hiding behind the eastern houses in the village and just inside the woods to the north of the village. The foot soldiers she trained were hiding inside the eastern houses. Ringean's wife took the children, including Alasdair, to the stone circle, and Caitlin told her to wait there. Caitlin didn't want the children anywhere near the village when the fighting started, but she wasn't ready to reveal the existence of the hiding place that she and Asbjorn had built.

Shortly after Caitlin sent the children away, she instructed a dozen archers to make their way to the river. Once the fighting started, they were to burn the longboats and the supplies that had been unloaded. Caitlin didn't want any of the Lochlannach to escape and bring back reinforcements.

Caitlin was impatient. *When are they going to attack?* She was about to send a scout to the river to see what was going on when she saw the Lochlannachs approaching the village. *There must be over two hundred of them!* She drew her sword and gripped the horse's reins tightly.

As the Lochlannachs made their way north from the river to the clearing in the center of the village, the first squad of foot soldiers ran out of the houses and formed ranks facing the invaders. The Lochlannachs stopped their advance, but when they saw who the defenders were, Caitlin heard laughter coming from the Lochlannach ranks. *I guess they don't think women can offer much resistance.*

The leader of the Lochlannachs made a gesture, and two dozen warriors ran forward to deal with the defenders. Caitlin watched as the Lochlannach ranks laughed and shouted insults at the women standing bravely in front of the houses.

The warriors reached the defenders and tried to disarm them. The defenders attacked, and within moments only one of the warriors remained standing. The wounded warriors cried out for help, and the sight of the slashed bodies of the dead caused the Lochlannach ranks to fall silent.

The Lochlannach leader raised his axe and shouted something that Caitlin didn't need translated. The Lochlannachs surged forward, determined to kill the defenders.

Caitlin whistled loudly. The remaining foot soldiers ran out of the houses and joined the first squad. Then Caitlin raised her sword and led her horsemen north, using the houses on the eastern side of the village to mask their movement. When she reached the north end of the village, she led her horsemen west until she reached the northernmost edge of the clearing. At first, the Lochlannachs didn't notice the horsemen; their attention was on the additional foot soldiers facing them. They shouted and charged the foot soldiers, but right before they reached the defenders, Caitlin and her horsemen slammed into them from the north.

Caitlin and her horsemen hacked at the Lochlannach invaders. The horsemen waiting in the woods to the north left their hiding place and rode around the western edge of the village to attack the Lochlannach from the rear.

The foot soldiers ran forward and attacked. The Lochlannachs weren't prepared for the village to be so well-defended, and they never expected women to be such good fighters. The leader of the invaders fell quickly, as did many of his warriors.

Caitlin wheeled around, and her horsemen broke off their attack as the other horsemen attacked the Lochlannach from behind. She led her horsemen around the warriors to attack them from the south and cut off their escape back to the river. Just before she crashed into the southern edge of the warriors' ranks, she noticed thick plumes of smoke coming from the river. *I think they've lost some of their longboats.*

As Caitlin attacked, she felt something grab her wrist. Someone pulled her off her horse, and she landed hard on the ground next to a Lochlannach warrior. She saw the glint of metal as the warrior lifted his axe, but a moment later he crumpled to the ground as his head went flying into the midst of the warriors. "Thanks!" she shouted to the horseman who had come to her rescue. She ran for her horse to rejoin the fight.

The Lochlannachs were leaderless and unprepared for the fighting skills of the defenders. They outnumbered the villagers, but they were never able to press their advantage. One of the warriors shouted something, and the surviving Lochlannach broke off the attack and ran for the river. Caitlin and her horsemen followed while the foot solders remained behind to kill the wounded warriors and tend to the fallen villagers.

As the warriors approached the river, they stopped in horror at what they saw. Their longboats and supplies were burning out of control. Before they could do anything, several of the warriors suddenly fell – arrows protruding from their bodies. The archers who had destroyed their encampment fired wave after wave of arrows from every direction, thinning the ranks of the surviving warriors with every volley.

Caitlin caught up to the confused warriors and attacked them from the rear. Unable to escape, the warriors fought for their lives, but the shock of the loss of their fleet and the ferocity of the Alban defenders had demoralized them. Soon, none of the warriors were left standing, and the archers moved in to kill the wounded Lochlannach. Caitlin checked on her horsemen before riding back to the village to check on the foot soldiers.

The villagers spent the rest of the day tending to the wounded villagers and dragging the bodies of the fallen warriors to their encampment to burn. Less than thirty villagers had been killed, but almost everyone had some sort of injury from the fighting. Two hundred and fifty warriors had been killed, and their longboats and supplies had been completely destroyed. The swords, helmets, and other weapons of the warriors were cleaned and stored where the weapons from other raiding parties were kept.

Each of the defenders kept their own arms with them in case the scouts sighted another raiding party.

Caitlin sent word to Ringean's wife to bring the children back. When she saw Alasdair, she hugged him tightly. She ordered sentries to keep a watch on the river and on the roads leading to the nearby villages, and then she walked back to her house with Alasdair in her arms.

You'd be proud of us today, Asbjorn. We defeated the invaders just like you taught us. I just hope there aren't more raiders coming.

Ciaran's horsemen were deployed in three squads to observe the Lochlannach when they crossed the border into Alba. His orders were to wait at least two days before harassing the enemy. Until then, he and his horsemen were to watch and report on the enemy movements.

Dùghall, Ciaran's brother, led the squad to the east. Ringean led the squad to the west. Ciaran led the squad in the center, and Asbjorn rode alongside him. Asbjorn watched his father-in-law carefully. Confirmation that the Lochlannach were approaching seemed to lift Ciaran's melancholy, but Asbjorn was still worried. *A man who thinks he's going to die usually does something to make it happen.*

Asbjorn and Ciaran watched from a safe distance as Amlaíb's forces moved northeast. "Aren't there more direct routes to Scone?" he asked.

"Yes, but Raibeart sent me a message stating that King Rhun loaned Amlaíb some scouts that are leading the Lochlannachs toward Dolair," Ciaran replied.

"That's hilly country," Asbjorn noted.

"That's the plan. While the hills hamper the progress of Amlaíb's forces, we have more time to assemble the army and set a trap for him. Besides, there are few villages between Dolair and the border, so there's little for Amlaíb's men to pillage on their way. He shouldn't find it strange that he's meeting no resistance since there's no one around to resist him."

Asbjorn nodded. It was a good strategy. Then he thought about Caitlin. *I wonder what's going on at home. Have the raiders from the island started their attacks?*

"It's time to let the Lochlannach know we're here," Ciaran told his horsemen the next morning. Ringean and Dùghall were there, having brought their horsemen to Ciaran's camp the night before.

"How do we do that?" Dùghall asked.

"The King doesn't want us to fight a pitched battle here, but he needs more time to prepared the trap he setting near Dolair. We need to harass Amlaíb's forces and slow them down. That means night raids and ambushes. We also need to keep Amlaíb from changing direction or he could get past the rest of the army, reach Scone, and wait for us there behind the safety of the city walls. We can't let that happen."

"When do we attack?" Ringean asked.

"Just before nightfall," Ciaran replied. "Right as they're making camp for the night. We'll attack from the rear and then break off before it gets too dark to see. Then we'll hit them again just before first light. Once they reach the hills, our archers will start ambushing them to thin out their ranks. We'll keep this up until we get orders to ride for Dolair."

Thorleik was walking along the perimeter of the encampment just as the sun began to set behind the hills to the west. *We made good time today. The ground is firm, and there's no sign of resistance from the Albans. If our island allies are doing what they promised, the Albans might not even know that we're here. Amlaíb's plan might just work. I hope so. There's too much at stake on this expedition.*

He was about to find Amlaíb and get something to eat when he heard a loud commotion coming from the southern perimeter of the encampment. He ran in the direction of the sound, grateful that there was still enough light to see where he was going.

Up ahead, he saw what was causing the commotion. *Horsemen! The Albans are attacking! They know we're here and where we're heading.* He ran forward, shouting orders to the warriors who were trying to get away from the attackers.

Hundreds of horsemen were attacking along the perimeter. Thorleik saw their dark hair protruding from beneath their helmets, confirming that they were Albans. As he got closer the attacking horsemen, he saw that one of them had thick blond hair sticking out from beneath his helmet. Curious, Thorleik ran toward the horseman to get a closer look at him.

The setting sun shone in the horseman's face, and Thorleik stopped in his tracks. He knew that rider instantly, even though he hadn't seen him in over three years. *Asbjorn! My son is alive, and fighting with the Albans!* Thorleik felt both joy that his son was alive and betrayal that his son would be fighting against his own people. He ran forward, hoping to catch Asbjorn's attention, but the horsemen wheeled around and rode off just as the sun disappeared.

"Are you sure it was him?" Amlaíb asked later as the two men surveyed the damage caused by the attack.

"I know my own son, Amlaíb," Thorleik answered. "It was Asbjorn. He's joined with the Albans."

"That explains what happened at Dunadd," Amlaíb commented.

"I know. I was hoping it wasn't Asbjorn who talked, but it seems obvious that is was."

"What are you going to do?"

"What we came here to do, Amlaíb," Thorleik said bitterly. "And I'll kill any Alban or traitor who tries to stop us."

The longphort in Áth Cliath was nearly deserted after Amlaíb and his fleet sailed for Alba. Only the women, children, and the aged remained behind, waiting for the men to return with tribute and tales of glorious battle. The longphort walls were manned by youngsters not yet old enough to be part of a major expedition and a few older warriors who could still hold a spear.

None of the inhabitants of the longphort believed that they had anything to fear while the men were gone. No one had ever attacked the longphort. The Britons were under control from the burden of their annual tribute and couldn't afford to raise a force to send against the longphort. The mainland Norsemen weren't likely to attack so early in the spring. And the local Irish population knew to keep clear of the longphort or face dire reprisals. It never occurred to anyone in Áth Cliath that someone might take advantage of the men being gone – even though the preparations for the expedition had been going on for a long time.

A week after Amlaíb and his fleet sailed for Alba, there were only eleven sentries along the upper walls of the longphort. Most of them were gambling with other sentries, looking out over the walls every now and then to make sure that no one approached unchallenged.

The main gates were just about to be shut for the night when a small delegation of the local Irish arrived and asked to be given entry. They had several wooden carts with them, and the smell of freshly roasted meats filled the night air. The sentries at the gate allowed the Irish to enter, looking forward to feasting that night.

Once the Irish had passed through the gates, the sentries came down off the walls to inspect the carts. A sentry pulled back the covering off one of the carts, but instead of seeing roasted meat, he saw a flash of metal before feeling a sharp pain in his chest. As he staggered back, he realized he was bleeding. He sank to his knees. As his vision blurred, he saw several figures jump out from the back of the carts. He saw the torchlight reflecting off metal and watched as his fellow sentries fell. His mind could barely register the shadows of a large number of people running through the gates into the longphort. He felt cold, and everything went black as his last breath escaped him.

The Irish raced toward Amlaíb's palace, killing anyone they encountered. Once inside the palace, they located the treasury and took everything they could carry. Then they set the palace on fire. The Irish proceeded to loot the remaining houses of the longphort, leaving only fire as payment. By the time the Irish left the longphort, most of the gold and silver had been taken, and every building was on fire. The Irish then moved on to the nearby Norse settlements along the river, liberating their wealth and burning everything.

As the first light appeared on the horizon the next morning, the longphort and settlements of Áth Cliath were completely destroyed. The few Norse survivors, cold, hungry, and poorly clothed, began the long trek to the northern tip of the island where there was another Norse settlement.

The Irish watched the survivors leave and made no attempt to stop them. The longphort, the symbol of their oppression by the Norse invaders, had been destroyed. It was a time for celebration.

CHAPTER 22

"We're not moving fast enough," King Causantín said to the earls who were with him just outside the village of Dolair. "We're not strong enough to face Amlaíb's forces yet, and the defenses are nowhere near finished."

"The rest of the army is on its way, My King," Raibeart said. "It's just taking longer for them to join us since we moved south. And the island Lochlannach have engaged many of the soldiers that were to join us here."

"How is that possible?" the king asked. "Didn't we prepare for more than a year to keep that from happening?"

"It was unexpected, My King," Raibeart replied. "The soldiers left their villages to come here and ran into the raiding parties. It's taking a while for the soldiers to deal with the raiders and finish making their way here. We never anticipated the number of Lochlannachs from the islands that would be helping Amlaíb."

"If Amlaíb's forces get here before the rest of the army arrives, we'll be outnumbered!" the King reminded his earls. "It won't matter that we have the advantage of position in the coming battle. His warriors will wash over us and drown us in our own blood!"

"The horsemen and archers are doing everything they can, My King," Raibeart said. "But Amlaíb has so many warriors with him that the losses we're causing aren't enough to slow his advance. If anything, he's moving his forces faster."

"Then order the horsemen and archers to break off and join us here," King Causantín commanded. "I want all of our forces consolidated as quickly as possible."

"Yes, My King."

Caitlin was exhausted. So were the other defenders of their village. In the five days since the first Lochlannach raiding party had been defeated, two more raiding parties had attacked the village overland from the territories of nearby clans.

Caitlin sat on the ground, wiping blood off her sword and shield. Her face and clothes were covered in Lochlannach blood. Her horse had been killed in the first minutes of the battle, and she had several cuts on her arms and her left hip. It had been a difficult fight, and Caitlin ached all over. *If only ten Lochlannach raiders appeared right now, they could defeat the entire village. I wonder how many we lost today. I wonder if it's time to abandon the village and take everyone to the hiding place before we lose too many.*

Ringean's wife approached Caitlin. It was clear that she had been crying.

"What's wrong?" Caitlin asked.

"Beathag and Maol-Chaluim's wife were killed," Ringean's wife sobbed. "They were helping me get the children to safety. A Lochlannach followed us and attacked Beathag. Maol-Chaluim's wife killed the Lochlannach, but their injuries were too serious. They both died before we reached the standing stones."

Caitlin tried to hold back her tears. *I need to stay strong and be an example for the village.* But the tears couldn't be stopped, and soon Caitlin was sobbing, causing the blood on her face to run down her cheeks like red rain.

"Look at them!" Raibeart said when he saw the Lochlannach army approaching.

King Causantín stood next to his earls on one of the hills to the southwest of Dolair. Less than two-thirds of the army had arrived, and there was no more time. The Lochlannach would be ready to attack within the hour, and even with the archers and horsemen hiding on either side of Amlaíb's forces, waiting for the signal to attack, the King knew that this was a battle he might not win.

Reports continued coming in about the losses caused by the island Lochlannach. Skirmishes and battles raged all around Alba, tying up the soldiers that the King needed with him to defeat the main invasion force approaching from the southwest.

"No one else is coming," the King said bitterly.

"It doesn't appear so, My King," Raibeart said.

Causantín took in a deep breath and grabbed his sword. "Then it's time to see what Albans are truly made of. Signal the men. We attack immediately!"

Asbjorn watched Amlaíb's forces move past the horsemen's hiding place. Ciaran had deployed the horsemen just behind a ridge to the west of the Lochlannach's position. The berserkers led the Lochlannach invasion force, and Asbjorn saw that their elixir bags were hidden. *I guess they figured out that someone told the Albans about the elixir and they're keeping the bags better protected.* Asbjorn clearly saw Bjornkarl shouting orders to the berserkers. *He must have been elevated in rank since I last saw him. It looks like he's in command of the berserkers!*

Asbjorn continued scanning the Lochlannach ranks until he sighted Amlaíb's banner. *He likes to stay closer to the front than Ívarr did. And wherever he is, my father will be close by.* Asbjorn looked at the banners near Amlaíb's until he finally saw Thorleik's banner just ahead and to the right of the Norse King's. *Hello, Father. Forgive me for what I must do today.*

"Do you see them?" Ciaran whispered.

Asbjorn nodded and pointed out Bjornkarl and Thorleik. "It looks like Bjornkarl's commanding the berserkers. I can't see their elixir bags anywhere."

"You know they have the bags with them," Ciaran commented.

"I know, but they're keeping them hidden. I guess they learned their lesson at Dunadd."

"Too bad," Ciaran said. "We need some kind of advantage today."

A horn sounded to the north, and Ciaran and Asbjorn looked to see what was happening. The Alban army was taking the field with King Causantín in the lead. Maol-Chaluim and the rest of the foot soldiers from Airer Goídel were on the far western edge of the Alban army.

The Lochlannach invaders stopped. Two unarmed Lochlannachs continued moving forward, and King Causantín and his earls rode out to meet them halfway between the opposing forces. Asbjorn watched what was happening. Then he saw King Causantín raise his arm and point at the Lochlannach forces. The two unarmed Lochlannachs turned and walked back toward the invasion force. A moment later, King Causantín and his earls rode back to the Alban army.

No one moved. Then Asbjorn saw the berserkers kneel. *They must be using their bodies to shield the elixir bags.* When the berserkers stood up, Asbjorn could tell that the fighting frenzy was building. *Whatever Amlaíb's men demanded, the King must have rejected. Now we fight.*

Another horn blew and the Alban army advanced. Asbjorn heard Bjornkarl's voice shouting, and the berserkers started running forward. A moment later, the berserkers reached the Albans. The Battle of Dolair had begun.

Ciaran led the horsemen into the battle within an hour of the battle starting. He had been ordered to wait as long as possible, but it was clear that the battle was going against the Albans as soon as it started. Amlaíb's forces were too large and too well-prepared. The Alban archers killed hundreds of Lochlannachs, but the invaders continued moving forward.

Asbjorn and Ringean were pulled off their horses in the first moments of their attack. Asbjorn stood back-to-back with his brother-in-law, and together they fought off the invaders, hoping that Ciaran would come to their aid quickly. They fought for several minutes before Asbjorn realized that he couldn't feel Ringean at his back anymore. Glancing down, he saw Ringean face down on the ground.

Rage built up in Asbjorn as he saw his brother-in-law lying dead. He turned toward the three invaders who were approaching him. Before they knew what was happening, he unleashed a vicious attack.

Asbjorn didn't feel injury. He didn't feel pain. He felt rage. He shouted at his attackers in the tongues of the Lochlannach and the Albans. He hacked at anything within his reach until he saw a squad of horsemen coming to his aid.

Ciaran tossed him the reins of a riderless horse and turned to attack a Lochlannach trying to pull him off his own horse.

Asbjorn pulled himself onto the horse's back and charged at the invaders who were attacking his father-in-law.

It was well after mid-day when Ciaran's horsemen reached Maol-Chaluim and the foot soldiers from Airer Goídel. The men were fighting in clusters as Maol-Chaluim tried to get them back into some sort of formation. Asbjorn saw Iain fall from the blow of a Lochlannach axe and disappear beneath a wave of blond-haired invaders. Maol-Chaluim fought off one Lochlannach, but another came from behind and killed Ciaran's other son with a mighty blow to his back. Asbjorn charged the two Lochlannachs, and soon they were both dead on the ground.

Asbjorn looked around and saw Thorleik's banner approaching. Before he could move, Dùghall and a squad of horsemen raced forward to attack. Asbjorn saw Thorleik pull Dùghall off his horse, and the two men began circling each other.

Asbjorn fought his way toward his father and Caitlin's uncle. Dùghall cut a deep gash on Thorleik's forearm, but Thorleik's axe hit Dùghall in the shoulder, knocking the Alban to his knees. Thorleik raised his axe to finish off Ciaran's brother.

"Father, don't!" Asbjorn shouted in the tongue of the Lochlannachs.

Thorleik hesitated, looking around. When he saw Asbjorn approaching, he stepped back. Dùghall, seeing an opening, pulled a dagger from his belt and stabbed Thorleik in the stomach. Thorleik brought his axe down on Dùghall's head, and both men fell to the ground.

Asbjorn dismounted and ran to his father. Thorleik was bleeding from his wound, and Asbjorn saw the color leaving his father's face.

"Is it really you, Asbjorn," Thorleik said, trying to get the words out. "I thought you were dead."

"No, Father. I was spared." Tears formed in Asbjorn's eyes.

"And you chose to live as an Alban?" Thorleik's voice was becoming raspy.

"I took a wife. You have a grandson, Father. His name is Alasdair."

"Was it that girl you captured?" Thorleik whispered.

"Yes, Father."

Thorleik nodded. Blood was coming out of his mouth. "I'm sorry for the way things happened, my son."

"So am I, Father."

Thorleik noticed the cross that Asbjorn was wearing on a chain around his neck. "So, you've abandoned our people *and* our gods?" He coughed blood, making a choking sound.

"I live as a Christian, Father, but Odin still watches over me. Everything I have done, everything I am, I was led to do by Odin's ravens."

Thorleik smiled. "Then may whatever god protects you lead you to find peace, my son. I'm going to join your mother now, Asbjorn. Perhaps we shall meet again in Valhalla."

Thorleik's stare became distant, and Asbjorn realized his father was no longer breathing. Asbjorn's hands shook as he held onto his father. *Goodbye, Father. Tell Mother I'm sorry I didn't get to say goodbye to her.*

"Asbjorn, come on!" Ciaran shouted as he rode up. "It's not safe here."

Asbjorn let go of his father and stood up. Seeing several of Thorleik's men approaching, he turned and ran back to his horse. Then he followed Ciaran and the other horsemen as Thorleik's men reached their fallen leader.

The battle raged all day. Losses were high on both sides, but the Albans suffered the highest losses. With no reinforcements coming, the King was worried that Amlaíb might win the day. *We must keep fighting. If we lose today, Alba is lost.*

The sun was sinking lower in the sky, but the battle showed no signs of stopping. A full moon rose in the east, allowing the soldiers and the warriors to keep fighting throughout the night.

An hour after sunset, Asbjorn was helping his clan's foot soldiers retain control of a hill near where King Causantín and his guards were fighting. A low mist was rising off the battlefield, giving the approaching Lochlannach a ghostly appearance. Ciaran was on foot, rallying his men, and Asbjorn and the horsemen were massed on the west side of the hill, preparing to charge the invaders.

Asbjorn heard the Lochlannach leaders giving orders, and he recognized one of the voices. *That's Bjornkarl! Berserkers are heading for us!*

The berserkers were using the mist to hide their approach. When Bjornkarl shouted, they rose up – right in front of Ciaran – and attacked. Ciaran wasn't prepared for the sudden and savage attack of the berserkers.

Asbjorn shouted for the horsemen to follow him. He charged at the berserkers closest to him, aiming his sword for where he believed the elixir bags should be. *I have to get to Ciaran before Bjornkarl kills him. I can't go back and tell Caitlin that her entire family is dead.*

Asbjorn saw an opening and wheeled his horse around. He rode straight for Ciaran and Bjornkarl. Ciaran tried to keep Bjornkarl from getting too close, but Asbjorn's father-in-law was exhausted, and the berserker, high on elixir, fought like he felt no fatigue at all. Ciaran swung his sword wide, and Bjornkarl rushed forward, stabbing Ciaran several times with a long knife.

Asbjorn, seeing Ciaran fall, leaned forward on his horse. When he was almost on top of Bjornkarl, he leapt off the horse and slammed into his brother just as Bjornkarl was about to plunge his axe into Ciaran's chest. The axe went flying, and Asbjorn and Bjornkarl fell to the ground.

Asbjorn was the first to get to his feet, and he stood between his father-in-law and his brother. "Hello, Brother," Asbjorn said in the tongue of the Lochlannach as Bjornkarl got to his feet.

Bjornkarl looked confused – partly because of the stupor caused by the elixir and partly because of how hard Asbjorn had knocked him to the ground. He shook his head. "Asbjorn?" he sneered. "Is that little Asbjorn back from the dead?"

"It is. And if you want to kill this man, you'll have to get past me first."

Bjornkarl roared with laughter. "Don't play brave with me, little brother. I could get past a hundred of you. Does Father know you're alive and fighting for the Albans?"

"Father's dead. You're next."

"Did you kill our father, little Asbjorn? Did you do it to impress your new people?"

"No, but I was there when it happened. He mentioned that Mother was dead, but he didn't say anything about you."

Bjornkarl bent down and retrieved his axe. "Well I guess I won't have any relatives after today, will I? I'll claim all of Father's titles and property. I'll be Amlaíb's second-in-command!"

Asbjorn reached for his belt, making sure his dagger was still there. Then he pointed his sword at his brother. "You're not going to survive this day, Bjornkarl. And no Valkyrie will choose a warrior like you for Valhalla."

"What do you mean by that?" Bjornkarl snapped.

"You've dishonored your house. What good is a warrior without honor to the gods?"

If I can get him angry enough, the elixir will begin wearing off and he'll have to drink more. If I can cut open his bag and keep him from drinking, I might just be able to beat him.

Bjornkarl swung his axe at Asbjorn, but the axe missed. Asbjorn thrust with his sword, and when Bjornkarl stepped back to avoid the thrust, his heel caught on a fallen soldier and he fell backwards.

Asbjorn roared with laughter to make Bjornkarl angrier. "Some berserker you are, Brother. You can't even stand on your own feet."

Bjornkarl leapt up and ran at Asbjorn, snarling like a wounded bear. Asbjorn waited until the last moment before jumping to the right and swinging his sword upwards. He caught the underside of Bjornkarl's wrist, cutting through the leather wrist guard and causing Bjornkarl's axe to spin away into the darkness.

Bjornkarl shouted in pain and reached for his bag of elixir. When Asbjorn saw the bag, he ran forward and thrust at it with his sword. The blade caught the bag and spilled the elixir on the ground.

"No!" Bjornkarl shouted.

"What's the matter, Bjornkarl?" Asbjorn taunted. "Can't fight your little brother without the elixir? Are you that afraid of me? Is that the real reason you've bullied me my whole life?"

Bjornkarl threw the bag aside and ran at Asbjorn. Asbjorn tried to block the blow, but Bjornkarl wrestled the sword out of Asbjorn's hands and threw him to the ground.

"Now, Brother," Bjornkarl said triumphantly. "You will die, and I will win."

As Bjornkarl raised the sword over his head, Asbjorn drew the dagger his father had given him and slashed Bjornkarl's leg. Bjornkarl screamed from the pain and staggered backward. Asbjorn got to his knees and thrust the dagger into Bjornkarl's stomach. Bjornkarl went rigid and then fell onto his back.

Asbjorn put the dagger against his brother's throat. "You win *nothing*, Bjornkarl."

"I'm not afraid of *you*, Asbjorn," Bjornkarl spat out. "You can't kill me. I'm always the stronger one, and the strongest always wins. Just like I'd have taken that girl you captured in Dumbarton, there's nothing you have that I can't take."

"You're right, Bjornkarl. There's nothing I have that you can't take. In fact, remember that dagger that Father gave me?"

Bjornkarl nodded.

"Well here it is. Take it."

Asbjorn thrust the knife upward, burying the blade deep into his brother's chest. Bjornkarl's eyes went wide and his body shook. Then his body relaxed, but his eyes remained open wide and fixed.

"Goodbye, Brother," Asbjorn said, retrieving his sword. "Enjoy hell."

Asbjorn looked around and saw where Ciaran had fallen. He rushed over to his father-in-law, who was bleeding from several wounds.

"Ciaran!" Asbjorn said, shaking Caitlin's father to see if the man were still alive.

"Asbjorn," Ciaran said weakly, opening his eyes. "Are you all right?"

"Yes."

Ciaran grabbed Asbjorn by the shoulder. "I'm not. You promised to do something for me if I fell."

"I know," Asbjorn said with a choked voice. *Please don't die, Ciaran.*

"It's time, Asbjorn. Find the men from our clan and lead them to the clearing past the stone circle. Keep our people safe. You promised."

"I know Ciaran, but how can we leave before the battle is finished? What will the King say? What will Raibeart say?"

"Raibeart is dead, Asbjorn," Ciaran said weakly. "He fell hours ago when he attacked Amlaíb's guards. The battle is already lost – the King just can't bring himself to stop fighting. But that doesn't mean we have to die with him. You must leave now."

"I can't leave you," Asbjorn said.

"I'm gone already," Ciaran said, coughing blood. Then he looked at Asbjorn. "No father could be more proud of a son than I am of you, Asbjorn. Take care of my daughter and my grandson. Tell our people that I did the best I could, and now it's your turn to lead them."

"Please, Ciaran..." Asbjorn whispered, wiping the tears from his face.

"Asbjorn..." Ciaran began, but he never finished his sentence.

Asbjorn knelt next to his father-in-law, ignoring the sounds of battle all around him. He wanted to say a prayer for Ciaran, but words failed him.

How can I leave the battle? How can I just run away in the night and ignore the oath I swore to the King? How can I ask the rest of my clansmen to do that? I know what I promised Ciaran, but what about what I promised Causantín? Is my oath to the King who rules Alba of less importance than my promise to the man who saved my life?

Asbjorn closed his eyes. *Oh, God in heaven, please tell me what to do.*

A familiar sound caught his attention. He opened his eyes and saw something on the ground. When he turned his head, he saw a raven staring up at him.

"Are you here to tell me what to do?" Asbjorn asked the raven.

The raven cocked its head but never stopped staring.

"Do I keep my promise to my father-in-law, or do I fulfill my oath to the King?"

The raven stared at Asbjorn silently.

Asbjorn shook his head. "No. I can't leave the battle. The King needs every man who can still fight. I won't abandon him."

211

Asbjorn looked around at the fighting nearby, but he was still wrestling with his decision. He felt a sharp pain on his hand and turned back to the raven. The raven pecked his hand again with its beak.

"What? I've made up my mind."

The raven pecked at his hand again, and Asbjorn pulled it away. "What do you want me to do?" he demanded.

The raven cocked its head and spread its wings.

"I don't understand."

The raven spread its wings again.

"What are you telling me?" Asbjorn suspected that the raven was trying to get him to change his mind.

The raven hopped onto Asbjorn's hands and spread its wings one more time. Then it flew off to the west.

Asbjorn watched the raven disappear into the distance. *It wants me to go west – to go home. I've followed the ravens my entire life, and they've always led me to where I needed to be. Do I refuse to follow one now? God – whichever god watches over me – has shown me what to do. I will obey and keep my promise to Ciaran.*

He stood up. Seeing some of his horsemen nearby, he shouted to them. They rode up to him, and he told them what he had promised Ciaran to do. "We need to find the men of our clan and lead them away from here before sunrise. Our women and children need us at home."

"What will the King say?" one of the horsemen protested.

"Assuming he's still alive, he'll think we were killed like all of the others here today," Asbjorn replied. "I don't want to leave before the battle's finished, but if the island Lochlannach are raiding along the coast, what will we have to come home to if we don't leave now to protect what's ours? This is what Ciaran wanted, and I'm going to honor my word to him."

The men nodded reluctantly. Asbjorn mounted his horse, and he and the horsemen began looking for their clansmen in the mist and darkness.

CHAPTER 23

Leaving the battlefield before dawn proved difficult. The fighting between the Alban soldiers and the Lochlannach warriors continued until well after midnight. It took hours for both sides to withdraw to new positions so that those still able to fight could rest and the healers could treat the wounded. Hundreds of Alban soldiers and horsemen were captured by the Lochlannachs, including many of the wounded Albans.

The carrion-birds began their work on the dead and dying, creating an eerie sight in the mist and moonlight. The sound of tearing flesh and the cries of the wounded unable to chase off the birds was terrifying. The smells of the battlefield assaulted Asbjorn's nose until he finally had to tie a piece of cloth around his nose and mouth so he could keep looking for his clansmen.

Asbjorn and his horsemen searched for the remnants of their clan for several hours. By the time the moon passed its zenith, Asbjorn knew that they couldn't spend any more time looking if they wanted to be clear of the battlefield before sunrise. *We need to leave now. I hate leaving any of our clansmen behind, but it'll be dawn soon, and we need to be far away from here by then.*

Asbjorn led his clansmen west. They had to move slowly at first to avoid the Alban and Lochlannach patrols. Once they were past the hills where they had hidden before the battle, they were able to move much faster.

Many of the wounded clansmen were unable to walk, so Asbjorn had some of his horsemen carry the wounded on the backs of their horses. He sent scouts to look for Lochlannach raiders, but he kept most of the horsemen and the foot soldiers together for the trek home.

By sunrise, they were miles away from the battlefield. At one point, Asbjorn looked back and saw what looked like smoke rising over the battlefield. *That must be the carrion-birds. If they're in the air, then the battle must have started again.* He said a prayer for the King and his surviving soldiers, and then he turned his back on Dolair.

The clansmen had to stop frequently to rest on the first day. The hours of fighting, followed by hours of traveling west, had brought many of the clansmen to the point of exhaustion. By late afternoon, the scouts reported a large wooded area ahead, and Asbjorn decided to camp there for the night.

Sentries were posted around the camp once they arrived. There was a stream running through the woods that wasn't contaminated by blood and battle. Asbjorn and the horsemen watered their horses first and then sent some of the men to look for food.

"What happens when we get home?" one of the men asked after the clansmen had eaten. "Won't we still have raiders to deal with? I don't think we're strong enough to face fresh warriors from the islands, and if we can't fight, we'll either be killed or taken prisoner."

"Ciaran had a plan to keep us all safe," Asbjorn replied. "He told me to find a place where the clan can hide until the raiders are no longer a threat. Caitlin and I have been getting it ready for almost a year. We'll all go there as soon as we get home."

"Where is this hiding place?" one of the foot soldiers asked.

"It's well-hidden," Asbjorn stated. "But I'll show you how to get there when we return to our village. It has plenty of water, lumber to build houses, room to plant crops and raise livestock... it has everything we need. The Lochlannach can burn the village and pillage our farms, but we'll be safe from them for as long as we need to be."

The next day, Asbjorn and his clansmen spotted a Lochlannach patrol ahead and had to run for cover to keep from being seen. The patrol passed by without noticing the clansmen. *They're patrolling openly this deep into Alba! They must think that we can no longer resist them.*

Two of the wounded clansmen died that night from their injuries. *We don't have time to dig proper graves for them. I'll have the men cover the bodies with branches and dirt so the Lochlannach won't desecrate them.*

The next morning, the clansmen stumbled onto another Lochlannach patrol, but they weren't able to hide before they were seen. It was a bloody skirmish, but the thirty Lochlannach warriors were soon dead. Asbjorn only lost one more clansman during the fighting, but several were wounded.

The clansmen stripped the Lochlannach of their weapons and supplies. The patrol was carrying enough food for three days, so Asbjorn let the men eat and rest before starting for home again.

"How are the men doing?" Asbjorn asked one of the horsemen after he returned to the camp from checking on the sentries.

"In good shape, now that they've eaten, My Chief."

"What did you call me?" Asbjorn asked.

"My Chief," the horseman repeated.

"Why did you call me that?"

"You're the last surviving man in Ciaran's family. He asked you to lead us home, he asked you to prepare a place for us to hide from the raiders. It's clear to us that he wanted you to be our chief."

"*Us?*" Asbjorn asked. "Do the others feel the same way?"

The horseman nodded. "As far as we're concerned, you're our chief, and we pledge to you our allegiance for as long as you live."

Asbjorn didn't expect this. He looked around and saw his clansmen nodding in agreement. *I promised Ciaran that I'd lead the clan until his oldest grandson was ready to be chief. I can't break my promise, but if the clan wants me to be the chief, there's little I can do about that.*

Finally, he held up his hand. "I appreciate your confidence in me, but let's not make any decisions right now. Wait until we get home, and then we'll figure out who will be chief of the clan."

"Yes, My Chief," the men said.

Two days later, Asbjorn recognized where he was. After avoiding two more Lochlannach patrols, he had led the clansmen to the edge of Dùghall's farm. Asbjorn couldn't see anyone nearby. He drew his sword and motioned for the clansmen to do the same.

Dùghall's house was a pile of ashes. In the distance, Asbjorn saw that Ciaran's house had also been destroyed. Asbjorn rode to the house he shared with Caitlin. There was nothing left but scorched timbers.

Asbjorn feared the worst. "Spread out. Look for bodies," he ordered the men.

The clansmen searched through what used to be Dùghall's and Ciaran's houses while Asbjorn searched his own house. There was no evidence that anyone had been in the houses when they burned.

Where's Caitlin? Where are Beathag and the rest of the women? Where's my son?

Asbjorn led the clansmen to the village. Not a single building was left standing, but there were no bodies anywhere.

"Were they all captured?" one of the clansmen asked.

Asbjorn shook his head. "Caitlin and the women trained to fight wouldn't have allowed themselves to be captured easily. They would have fought, and we'd see the bodies of the fallen around here somewhere."

Asbjorn and the men continued looking around the village for some sign of what had happened. *Did the Lochlannach surprise them in the night? Was everyone captured and carried away as prisoners? Where are they?!*

Asbjorn grew more concerned. The men stood around him, waiting for him to tell them what to do, but he couldn't think of anything apart from his wife and son. Then he heard something. Looking up, he saw a flock of ravens flying overhead in the direction of the standing stones. They were flying fast and soon disappeared in the distance.

Maybe they're at the hiding place. "We need to go to the standing stones and see if they're already in hiding."

Asbjorn led the men through the forest to the stone circle where he and Ciaran used to sit and think. Some of the horses didn't want to enter the circle at first, but the men dismounted and led them through the poles to the stones standing in the center.

216

Asbjorn showed the men which stones and poles pointed the way to the hiding place. When he reached the entrance to the path, he found there was a barrier covering the entrance. He poked at it with his sword and realized it was made of wood and ropes designed to look like part of the forest's undergrowth. *This will keep the Lochlannach from accidently finding the entrance.*

Asbjorn moved the barrier aside and motioned for his men to follow him. "Let everyone else enter and then put the barrier back in place before you follow us," Asbjorn said to one of his horsemen.

"Yes, My Chief."

As Asbjorn led the men through the forest, he heard the sounds of people ahead. When he stepped into the clearing, he immediately felt relieved.

They're all here. They must have abandoned the village.

Asbjorn looked around as his men entered the clearing behind him. There were several new houses since he last visited, and new crops had been planted. Livestock drank from the water flowing down from the lake in the hills, and children played in the grass.

Looking up toward the hills, Asbjorn saw some of the women that he and Caitlin had trained standing watch over the clearing. Then he saw a familiar face coming down the hill.

"Caitlin!" he shouted.

Caitlin saw her husband and started running. Many of the other women heard Asbjorn shouting and saw that the men had returned. They ran forward to see if their loved ones were among the survivors.

Asbjorn grabbed Caitlin around the waist and picked her up. "I've missed you, Caitlin!" he said, kissing her.

"I've missed you, too, Asbjorn," Caitlin said, crying from joy. "I knew you were coming home today. I just knew it."

"How did you know that?" Asbjorn asked.

"Didn't you see the flock of ravens flying overhead?" she responded. "Even *I* know that a flock of ravens flying overhead has something to do with you."

Asbjorn smiled. "I saw them. It's why I decided to come looking for you here."

Caitlin looked around at the other clansmen. "There are so few of you. Where are the others? Where's my family?"

Asbjorn looked at her, but said nothing. Caitlin's eyes grew wide. "Father?"

Asbjorn shook his head.

"Maol-Chaluim? Ringean?"

Asbjorn shook his head again.

Caitlin buried her face in Asbjorn's shoulder, sobbing uncontrollably.

"So that's what happened," Asbjorn concluded later that afternoon when everyone was gathered together to share stories about the battle and the defense of the village. "We lost two-thirds of the men we sent into battle against Amlaíb's forces. None of the men in Ciaran's family survived the first day except for me. Iain was killed early in the battle. Raibeart mac Stiùbhart was also killed. I don't know about King Causantín or about Amlaíb. Ciaran ordered me to lead our clansmen back home and bring everyone here to the clearing. I guess the village had to be abandoned before we got back."

"We had no choice," Caitlin said, watching Asbjorn holding Alasdair. "We fought off three raids, but I didn't think we could survive another one. We've been here for almost two weeks."

"There's a matter that needs to be settled, Asbjorn," one of the clansmen said, standing up. "Ciaran is dead, along with his sons. He asked you to lead the men home, and he asked you to find us a place to hide and survive until the raiders leave our shores. For most of us, that means Ciaran wanted you to be our chief."

"Ciaran asked me to lead the clan until his oldest grandson was ready to be chief," Asbjorn replied. "I'm not ready to go against Ciaran's wishes."

Caitlin stood. "Alasdair is the only one of my father's grandsons who survives, Asbjorn," she said. "We lost one during the winter. The others were killed during the second raid."

Asbjorn looked at the tears building in Caitlin's eyes as she sat down. *Alasdair will be our chief when he comes of age.*

"Asbjorn, that leaves you as the only person who can be our chief," the clansman stated.

"Do you really want a former Lochlannach as your chief?" Asbjorn asked. "Look at what the Lochlannach have done to our country."

"I'm looking at what you've done for our clan. You taught us how to defeat the Lochlannach. Do you remember Dunadd? Do you remember the raiders we've defeated since you came here? Look around! What you've done by leading us home and giving us a safe home to return to is what a chief is supposed to do."

"Do you all feel the same way?" Asbjorn asked.

"We do," the members of the clan replied.

Asbjorn nodded. "Very well, then. I'll be your chief. But I'm not Ciaran. He was a great leader. All I can do is try to live up to his example."

A few hours later, Asbjorn and Caitlin finally had a chance to be alone. They sat next to each other on the hill overlooking the village. Alasdair was asleep on Caitlin's lap.

"I'm sorry about your family, Asbjorn," Caitlin said softly as they watched the sunset.

"And I'm sorry about your family, too," Asbjorn replied. "I'm sad that Thorleik's dead, but at least I got to say goodbye to him. I think he understands why I did what I did, and he forgave me for it."

"And your brother?" Caitlin asked.

"I don't mourn his death," Asbjorn said. "He was never a brother to me. It's funny. His last words were words of defiance. He could never accept defeat, not even in death. I think the world is a better place without him in it."

"I guess we're both all alone in the world now," Caitlin said as she put her head on his shoulder.

"No we're not," Asbjorn stated. "We have each other. We have Alasdair. As long as we have that, we have everything we need."

Caitlin leaned over and kissed Asbjorn. "You're right, my husband. God brought you back to me. I have everything I need right here."

EPILOGUE

History records the Battle of Dolair as a Lochlannach victory. The battle raged all day, into the night, and again the next morning. King Causantín mac Cináeda killed Amlaíb on the second day of fighting, but he lost two thirds of his army during the battle. He withdrew his surviving solders back behind the protective walls of Scone and prepared for a siege. Between Raibeart's death, the confusion caused by the defeat of the Albans, and King Causantín's hasty retreat to Scone, no one noticed that Ciaran's clansmen had disappeared before the second day of battle began.

Leaderless, the Lochlannach forces from Ireland withdrew with their prisoners and returned to their fleet at Dumbarton. When the fleet returned to Áth Cliath, they discovered that the longphort and settlements were destroyed and the people gone. All Norse settlements in southern Ireland had also been destroyed. The Lochlannach found their people and, with no home to return to, they sailed east and resettled in Britain.

The Norse kings on the mainland regained control of the island Lochlannach, trapping Alba in the middle between the Mainland Lochlannachs and the Lochlannachs in Britain, who continued to defy the mainland Norse kings.

King Causantín was captured and executed two years after the Battle of Dolair during another attempted Lochlannach invasion. Alba suffered many raids and invasions over the years, but the Kingdom of Alba never fell to the Lochlannachs. They lost many men and much territory, but in the end, they regained all that they had lost – a testament to the fighting skills and the determination of the Albans.

Asbjorn and his clan remained in hiding for a year until the last of the Lochlannach raiders left Alba. Rather than rebuild their old village, they cut roads through the forest that connected the new village in the clearing to the villages of the neighboring clans. In time, they built a thriving community.

Asbjorn led the clan well for many years. Upon his death, Alasdair became the clan chief. He buried his father near the center of the stone circle that Asbjorn loved so much. On the day of the funeral, a huge flock of ravens flew in circles over the standing stones. When the ceremony was over, the ravens flew off in all directions. No ravens were ever seen in that part of Alba again.

The End

Historical Context
of the Novel

The Picts were a Celtic people who migrated to what is now Scotland sometime during the 6th Century BC, but some scholars place them there as early as the Bronze Age. They referred to themselves as the "Kaldis" or "Kaltis," depending on which scholar you read, and didn't start referring to themselves as Picts until their conversion to Christianity. They were great equestrians, and lived in hill forts of timber, earthworks, and stone. The Picts recorded genealogy by the female lines, and maintained a system of succession whereby the crown was passed down to a brother or a nephew through the mother's line. They had a refined agricultural culture, language, and artistic tradition. They were fierce warriors.

When the Romans invaded Britain, they called the Picts the "Caledonii," or Caledonians. They were also called the "Picti," meaning "tattooed or painted ones," because of their habit of painting their bodies blue before battle. Women fought in their armies and were just as feared as the men were.

When the Romans left Britain in the 453 AD, the Picts had adopted many aspects of the Roman society, just as the Romans had adopted many of the Pictish aspects, including their equestrian skills.

The Irish, who were Celts that migrated to Ireland during roughly the same time period that the Picts migrated to Scotland, had never been Romanized, and therefore maintained almost the same culture they had since before the Romans invaded Britain.

Irish culture was divided between the early Celtic settlers: the "Cruithne" who were Celtic Picts who migrated from Scotland around 200 AD, and the "Goidels" who were Celtic Gaels that migrated to Ireland later. The Scots, or "Scoti," were a branch of the Celtic Gaels. Irish raiders plundered the Roman provinces in England and what is now Wales. Once the Romans left Britain, England became easy targets for the Scotic raiders.

In the 5th Century AD, the Scoti landed in what is now Argyll, Scotland and established a permanent settlement called "Dalriada" (or Dál Riata). The Picts didn't care for these new neighbors, and for the next 400 years, they fought each other off and on. The Scottish kings of Dalriada were tolerated, but never acknowledged by the Picts as rulers over Pictland, as the rest of Scotland was known.

Once the "Lochlannach" (what the Picts and Scots called the Norsemen or Vikings) raids along the Scottish coast began, the Picts and Scots would put aside their differences and fight together against these invaders. The Picts had a better-organized and larger army, but the Scots were cunning and were fierce fighters. The Picts took heavy casualties from the Lochlannach raids, allowing the Scots to begin infiltrating Pictish lands by intermarrying with the Picts.

The Picts were under constant threat of invasions from the Lochlannach, the Welsh Britons, the German Saxons, and the Scots. They lost many battles, but always managed to regain their lands eventually, extracting a terrible retribution from their enemies.

In 837 AD, however, the Picts suffered their worst loss up to that point. The Lochlannach killed their king and most of their leaders, resulting in the loss of most of their northern and western territories, including the Hebridies, Orkneys, Shetland, and Faroes islands. Their society fell into constant infighting and anarchy at this point.

Cináed mac Ailpín, later referred to as "Kenneth MacAlpin" or Kenneth I of Alba, was heir to the Scottish throne of Dalriada. His father was Alpin MacEochaid, and his mother was either a Pictish princess or the daughter of Achalas, the King of Argyllshire, which gave him a claim to both the throne of Dalriada, as well as the throne of Pictland.

In 839, the Scots were battling the Picts, when Lochlannach raiders approached. The Lochlannach watched the battle and planned to attack the winners, who would be too tired to defend themselves. The Scots withdrew and the Lochlannach attacked the

Picts, which proved disastrous for the Picts. So many of the remaining Pictish leaders were lost that the Picts were never able to defend their country again.

Cináed mac Ailpín used the situation to petition for the throne of Pictland, but his petition was rejected several times. The Picts didn't want a unified crown between the Scots and the Picts. However, through an incident known as "MacAlpin's Treason," he finally succeeded in being proclaimed King of the Picts.

In 847 AD, Cináed mac Ailpín invited the remaining Pictish nobles to a banquet to discuss his claim to the throne. During the meal, he had the nobles killed, clearing his way to the throne. He named his unified kingdom Alba, which included all of Scotland north of the Forth and Clyde rivers that wasn't controlled by the Lochlannach who had settled in the north and on the north and western islands. He moved his capital inland to Scone (near modern day Perth), and the area once known as Dalriada was renamed to "Airer Goídel." Alba met with many defeats at the hands of the Lochlannach, but the kingdom endured.

Cináed mac Ailpín died in 858 AD and was succeeded by his brother, Domnall mac Ailpín, or Donald I of Alba. When Domnall mac Ailpín died in 862 AD, Causantín mac Cináeda, the son of Cináed mac Ailpín, became Constantine I of Alba. In 877 AD, he was captured and executed, or killed in battle depending on which scholar you read, while defending his kingdom from a Lochlannach invasion.

Lochlannach raids on Scotland increased during Causantín mac Cináeda's reign. Lochlannach leaders Ívarr (Ímar in Irish sources), Halfdán (Albdann in Irish, Healfdene in Old English), and Amlaíb (or Óláfr) were the most notable raiders who appear in the surviving historical records from the time. Amlaíb's base of operations was a "longphort" (an Irish Viking ship enclosure or shore fortress) at "Áth Cliath" (modern day Dublin, Ireland) where he launched his raids to Scotland and northern England.

While Lochlannach were attacking East Anglia, Northumbria (York), and Mercia, Amlaíb brought an army from Ireland to Alba in 866 AD and took tribute (plunder) and many prisoners.

In 870 AD, Amlaíb and Ívarr launched another raid from Ireland to the kingdom of "Alt Clut" (later the kingdom of

Strathclyde), which was southwest of Alba. They laid siege to the fortress at Dumbarton Rock on the River Clyde. Causantín mac Cináeda's brought his army down to help his neighbors defeat the invaders (his sister was married to the son of the King of Alt Clut), but after a four month siege, the fortress fell and the Lochlannach returned home to Ireland with many prisoners, including the King of Alt Clut.

According to Irish sources, Amlaíb was killed by Causantín mac Cináeda's in 871 or 872 AD when his Lochlannach raiders returned to Alba to seek plunder and prisoners. Ívarr died in 873 AD during another such raid.

According to Pictish sources, a large Lochlannach army under Amlaíb Conung, the first Norse King of Dublin, raided Alba in 874 or 875 AD, reaching the central territories near "Dolair" (modern day Dollar near Stirling). The battle was a victory for the Lochlannach, and may Picts and Scots were killed.

About The Author:

Award-winning author William Speir was born in Birmingham, Alabama in 1962, attended the University of Alabama, and graduated from the University of Alabama at Birmingham in 1984. He spent over 25 years in corporate America, serving as a management consultant, consulting practice leader, IT executive, and HR/Payroll executive for top tier consulting firms and Fortune 100 companies.

During William's corporate career, he published several articles on leadership and the human impact of organizational/technology change. His first experience with book publishing was with a series of ten textbooks he authored about field artillery in the 19th century. These textbooks were later consolidated into a single volume and re-published in 2015 as *Muzzle-Loading Artillery for Reenactors*.

In addition to his artillery manual, William has published 14 novels, including an 8-book action-adventure series (*The Knights of the Saltire Series*), four historical novels (*King's Ransom, The Saga of Asbjorn Thorleikson, Nicaea – The Rise of the Imperial Church*, and *Arthur, King*), one fantasy novel (*The Kingstone of Airmid*), and one science fiction novel (*The Olympium of Bacchus 12*).

William is a 5-time Royal Palm Literary Award winner: 2014 Second Place Unpublished Historical Fiction for *King's Ransom*, 2015 Second Place Unpublished Historical Fiction for *The Saga of Asbjorn Thorleikson*, 2017 Second Place Published Historical Fiction for *Arthur, King*, 2017 First Place Published Historical Fiction for *Nicaea – The Rise of the Imperial Church*, and 2017 First Place Published Science Fiction for *The Olympium of Bacchus 12*.

For more information about William Speir, please visit his website at WilliamSpeir.com.

Progressive Rising Phoenix Press is an independent publisher. We offer wholesale discounts and multiple binding options with no minimum purchases for schools, libraries, book clubs, and retail vendors. We also offer rewards for libraries, schools, independent book stores, and book clubs. Please visit our website and wholesale discount page at:

www.ProgressiveRisingPhoenix.com

Progressive Rising Phoenix Press is adding new titles from our award-winning authors on a regular basis and has books in the following genres: children's chapter books and picture books, middle grade, young adult, action adventure, mystery and suspense, contemporary fiction, romance, historical fiction, fantasy, science fiction, and non-fiction covering a variety of topics from military to inspirational to biographical. Visit our website to see our updated catalogue of titles.

9 781940 834719